# My Lost Prize

# My Lost Prize

Steven Payne

Caspar David Friedrich (1774-1840): *Man and Woman Contemplating the Moon* (c. 1830-1835); oil on canvas, 13.39 × 17.32 in. / 34 × 44 cm, Alte Nationalgalerie, Berlin.

This book was printed in the United States of America.

**To order additional copies of this book, contact:**
Xlibris Corporation
0-800-644-6988
www.Xlibrispublishing.co.uk
Orders@Xlibrispublishing.co.uk
302002

for B.J.T., always

*Como para acercarla mi mirada la busca.*
*Mi corazón la busca, y ella no está conmigo.*
— Pablo Neruda

# Contents

# Introduction

> There are disappointments which wring us, and there are those which inflict a wound whose mark we bear to our graves. Such are so keen that no future gratification of the same desire can ever obliterate them: they become registered as a permanent loss of happiness.—Thomas Hardy, *A Pair of Blue Eyes*.

Writers are no more or less likely to fall in love than anybody else, but because of their profession they are arguably more likely to try to capture the experience and encapsulate it in words—and, if they know their craft at all, are likely to be better at doing so than the rest of us.

Possibly the definitive text of first love in Western fiction is the 1860 novella of that name by Ivan Turgenev (1818-1883), briefly summarised in my previous book *Carrying the Torch* (2011). Vladimir Petrovich is a callow sixteen year old staying at a country estate with his family who meets and falls in love with the beautiful but fickle and rather distant Zinaida Alexandrovna Zasyekina, five years his senior, who already has a retinue of devoted and lovelorn suitors whom she treats with light-hearted, even flippant disdain. Vladimir Petrovich discovers that Zinaida is having a clandestine affair with a mysterious man who turns out to be none other than Pyotr Vasileyevich—his own father. Although naturally deeply hurt by this revelation, Vladimir Petrovich is able to take a surprisingly sanguine view of the whole experience, believing that it conferred an early maturity and an understanding of the tortuous byways of human emotion, romantic emotion especially.

Also mentioned in *Carrying the Torch* was the Northamptonshire-born 'peasant poet' John Clare (1793-1864) whose lifelong unrequited love for his muse Mary Joyce, the local girl who inspired so much of his most tender love poetry. Covertly or overtly Mary was behind many if not most of his numerous romantic poems, including 'First Love':

> I ne'er was struck before that hour
> With love so sudden and so sweet,
> Her face it bloomed like a sweet flower
> And stole my heart away complete.
> My face turned pale as deadly pale.
> My legs refused to walk away,
> And when she looked, what could I ail?
> My life and all seemed turned to clay.
>
> And then my blood rushed to my face
> And took my eyesight quite away,
> The trees and bushes round the place
> Seemed midnight at noonday.
> I could not see a single thing,
> Words from my eyes did start—
> They spoke as chords do from the string,
> And blood burnt round my heart.
>
> Are flowers the winter's choice?
> Is love's bed always snow?
> She seemed to hear my silent voice,
> Not love's appeals to know.
> I never saw so sweet a face
> As that I stood before.
> My heart has left its dwelling-place
> And can return no more.

Like unrequited love, first love has become one of the most perennially popular, the title of at least half-a-dozen motion pictures and television series and countless poems and songs.

For the majority of people first love is but a memory: that is to say, very few people (in today's world especially) remain with their first loves for the rest of their days. The experience of losing a first love is therefore very close to universal. In an essay on the sometimes bitter personal and literary friendship-rivalry between F. Scott Fitzgerald and Ernest Hemingway, Scott Donaldson has written:

> Being jilted is a rite of passage that few people, in a dating culture, are lucky enough to avoid. There is something terribly banal about rejection by a loved one, particularly by a first love. We are inclined to smile about the indignity of it, as we might smile at *Reader's Digest* accounts of 'Life's Most Embarrassing Moments.' But the smile only emerges retrospectively, or when it is someone else who has been jilted. At the time, rejections hurt, for they strike directly at one's sense of self-worth.
>   One indication of the emotional cost of a jilting is that the word itself has almost vanished. College students talk of being 'dumped,' and social scientists reject even that term, with its visually comic overtones. "I haven't heard anyone use *jilted* in twenty years," one of them said recently. "Nowadays we talk about 'failed relationships' instead." This psychobabbling phrase nicely skirts the issue, for if it is the *relationships* that fail and not the people in them, there need be no question of assigning blame, or of acknowledging one's own shortcomings and another's fickleness and cruelty. Alternatively, one can say that 'things didn't work out,' as if euphemism could make the pain go away.[1]

This latter interpretation—that relationships fail, not people—is as Donaldson points out a modern development. Eighty years ago W. Somerset Maugham was more brutally blunt; into the mouth of Kitty Fane in his 1925 novel *The Painted Veil* he put the following harsh words: "If a man hasn't what's necessary to make a woman love him, it's his fault, not hers."

Because for the vast majority of people it occurs early in life—usually in adolescence or in the first years of adulthood—first love has often been casually dismissed by some older heads as a fleeting part of growing up not to be taken seriously: the terms used to refer to such feelings, terms such as 'calf love' and 'puppy love' (or sometimes 'kitten love') point toward an experience which may be all but universal yet is considered to be ultimately shallow and transient and without deep roots and durable sincerity of emotion, something to be written off as the expected, even normal but in the end immature, facile and inchoate feelings of adolescents drunk on their own half-formed feelings. Calves, puppies and kittens are immature animals: therefore calf/puppy/kitten love is immature love—mere 'crushes' and decidedly not 'the real thing'.

We can now surely consider such an offhand dismissal of genuine human emotion to be definitively disproven. In *Carrying the Torch* mention was made of some of the findings of contemporary science (principally evolutionary psychology and neurology) which, it is claimed, can help to shed some light on

why people form unrequited romantic attachments. It will probably not come as a great surprise to anyone that the same sorts
of statements—undeniably tentative and provisional as they also
are—are now being made about first love. In the American bi-
monthly publication *Psychology Today* Dr Nancy Kalish, Emeritus
Professor of Psychology at the California State University, Sacra-
mento, observes:

> Adults who underestimate the strength of the bond—or the
> impact of the loss—of a first love may have forgotten what a blow
> it was when they lost their own first loves. They may even try to
> comfort teenagers with lighthearted lessons: a surprising number
> of men and women wrote to me to bitterly complain about parents
> who joked years ago, 'Don't worry! Boyfriends/girlfriends are like
> buses . . . a new one comes along every ten minutes!' This was
> not helpful, and it was not funny. The loss of a first love can be so
> crushing to some teenagers that they become suicidal.
>
> *The pain of the breakup will subside with time, but the love may
> stay buried and dormant for decades. While most men and women
> find satisfying partners after first love breakups, there are adults who
> spend their married years aware that 'something is missing.' They
> continue to think about their lost first loves. Perhaps if they had
> married their first loves when they were younger, they tell me, they
> could have formed lasting and fulfilling marriages, but they will never
> know . . .*
>
> In my recent survey of 1600 people (who had never tried a
> reunion with a lost love), ages 18 to 92, 56% of the participants
> said they would not want to go back to their first loves, 19% were
> not sure—but 25% said they would!
>
> Even the adults who had no current interest in their first loves,
> including those who had only bitter memories, revealed that these
> early romances influenced their life-long attitudes about love, and
> even about themselves.
>
> *The longer I study lost loves and lost love reunions, the clearer it
> becomes to me how important young love really is. First love, young
> love, is indeed real love. This intense love does not come along every ten
> minutes. For some people, it may come only once in a lifetime.*[2] (My
> emphasis).

The same point is made by Dr Frank Tallis, a London-based clinical psychologist who has written perceptively and at length on the infinite varieties of human romantic love. In his 2004 book *Love Sick* he observes:

> Most people experience falling in love at first sight between the ages of sixteen and twenty. Therefore, it might be the case that sexual maturity coincides with a critical period during which individuals—particularly young men—are prone to form strong emotional attachments . . . The 'crushes' and infatuations of adolescence almost invariably lead to heartache, particularly when the individual (unaware of his or her place in the beauty hierarchy) falls in love with one who is unattainable…It is certainly true that during the course of normal sexual development, most people's first experience of love tends to be imbued with manic qualities. Indeed, intensity, insecurity and ambivalence are typical of adolescent romance. *Terms such as 'puppy love'—evoking comfortable images of innocent, loyal attachment—fail almost entirely to capture the confused, anxious and frankly miserable state that the majority of adolescents pass through on their journey to adulthood.* (My emphasis).[3]

In 2001 Jennifer Beer, a graduate student at the University of California at Berkeley (later earning her doctorate in anthropology) published the results of a survey which revealed that the emotional impact of first love can be such that it affects the subject for a very long time indeed, possible even for the rest of life. Beer's findings were based on the first-love stories of 303 Berkeley undergraduates collected in 1997. "Some of the problems you have in the romantic domain may have more to do with your first love than with your parents," she explained. "First love":

doesn't mean a childhood crush on a teacher or movie star, but the first real relationship of a romantic nature between two individuals, often experienced in adolescence or early adult years. Those who remember the experience positively are more likely to consider themselves securely attached to their current romantic partners . . . and to perceive their romantic partners as securely attached to them . . . In the case of first love, such memories often range from bittersweet but fond—perhaps recollections of a poignant puppy love tinged with regard or regret for a long-ago sweetheart—to deeply painful, soul-crushing experiences" . . . As an example of a good experience, Beer cited one respondent who suffered greatly because her former boyfriend dated other women immediately after their relationship ended. But, prior to that, the experience had been a positive taste of what love could be, and the woman learned what made her happy in a relationship. Alternatively, Beer described a stormier experience that left the respondent years later with the unshakeable suspicion that all men were untrustworthy. "This is wrong, but I cannot help myself," the respondent commented. "One negative experience has been enough to change my entire outlook on men."[4]

Whatever happens, whether the outcome is positive or painful, "it can set you up as thinking, 'This is what I am like as a relationship partner'," Beer said.

Subsequent research has served to bolster Beer's conclusions. In January 2009 under the headline WHY WE CAN NEVER RECOVER FROM FIRST LOVE *The Guardian* reported the publication of *Changing Relationships*, a collection of sociological research papers edited by Dr Malcolm Brynin, the principal research officer at the Institute for Social and Economic Research at the University of Essex. (As an aside it is a curious and notable fact how different newspapers can spin the same story in two entirely different direction: while the *Guardian* contented itself with the WHY WE CAN NEVER RECOVER FROM FIRST LOVE, the *Daily Mail*, in its take, offered the somewhat more prescriptive headline WHY YOU *SHOULD* FORGET YOUR FIRST LOVE). According to Dr Brynin: "Remarkably, it seems that the secret to long-term happiness in a relationship is to skip a first relationship. In an ideal world, you would wake up already in your second relationship." This is so because for some people their first romantic attachment, being by definition new and often more intense than any subsequent relationship can ever be again, can lead to them using it as the sole yardstick for any relationships which come after and which are almost invariably found wanting when compared to the unrealistically high standard of first love. "If you had a very passionate first relationship and allow that feeling to become your benchmark for a relationship dynamic, then it becomes inevitable that future, more adult partnerships will seem boring and a disappointment":

> The problems start if you try not only to get everything you need for an adult relationship, but also strive for the heights of excitement and intensity you had in your first experience of love. The solution is clear: if you can protect yourself from intense passion in your first relationship, you will be happier in your later relationships.[5]

This stance is supported by Dr Gayle Brewer, a lecturer in social psychology at the University of Central Lancashire. "If you judge adult relationships against your first relationship," she says, "you are using a single benchmark: that of an intense and unrealistic passion. Adult relationships need all sorts of other virtues to survive, many of which are not compatible with that level of intensity":

> For example, you might have felt passionate about your first love because their spontaneity was breathtakingly exciting. Adult relationships, however, require people to be committed and reliable. Someone who excels in spontaneity is unlikely to also have those characteristics. So you're caught in a bind: the characteristics that excite you are the ones that lead to the failure of an adult relationship. If you emotionally fixate on having the excitement, while knowing you need the reliability, you're making demands that no relationship can satisfy.[6]

Professor Helen Fisher, a biological anthropologist at New Jersey's Rutgers University and the author of numerous academic and popular articles and books on the biological basis of romantic love, takes precisely the opposite view however: actively trying to recapture the once-in-a-lifetime excitement and intensity of first love, she suggests, can be the very thing that keeps a long-established relationship alive. Professor Fisher used MRI scans and observed similar brain activity among those who had been happily married for well over twenty years to those who had been in a relationship for less than six months. There was almost no significant difference between the two. "I found incontrovertible, physiological evidence that romantic love can last," she said.[7]

Both sides of the issue however are agreed however that the first experience or episode of love—usually in adolescence or early adulthood—cannot be casually dismissed as 'puppy love' but is a quite literally life-changing event, an emotional upheaval so intense and far-reaching that it can establish a template or a script that a person follows for a very long time thereafter, possibly even for the rest of their lives—"No love, no friendship," wrote Francois Mauriac, "can cross the path of our destiny without leaving some mark on it forever"—and that the end of a first love relationship can be so devastating that it can lead to severe and serious depression, even attempted or completed suicide, and that some people never truly recover from such a loss. Because first love usually (though by no means always) happens early in life, most commonly in the teenage years, this has been used as an excuse by older people to dismiss first love as childish. Nothing, as should now be obvious, could be further from the truth. The loss of a first love can be of a devastating magnitude, a tragedy as exemplified by the great poem *Thoughts of Phena at News of Her Death* written by Thomas Hardy about his cousin Tryphena Sparks, more than ten years his junior—not Hardy's first love but a great and never-to-be-forgotten love nevertheless whose loss hurt Hardy deeply and bitterly when, whatever the exact nature of their relationship (something which continues to exercise Hardy biographers and scholars to this day), she ultimately married another man and who died very shortly thereafter:

> Not a line of her writing have I
>    Not a thread of her hair,
> No mark of her late time as dame in her dwelling, whereby
>       I may picture her there;
>    And in vain do I urge my unsight
>       To conceive my lost prize
> At her close, whom I knew when her dreams were upbrimming
>       with light
>       And with laughter her eyes.
>
>    What scenes spread around her last days,
>       Sad, shining, or dim?
> Did her gifts and compassions enray and enarch her sweet ways
>       With an aureate nimb?
>    Or did life-light decline from her years,
>       And mischances control
> Her full day-star; unease, or regret, or forebodings, or fears
>       Disennoble her soul?
>
>    Thus I do but the phantom retain
>       Of the maiden of yore
> As my relic; yet haply the best of her—fined in my brain
>       It may be the more
>    That no line of her writing have I,
>       Nor a thread of her hair,
> No mark of her late time as dame in her dwelling, whereby
>       I may picture her there.

The theme of a lost prize and perpetual regret haunts the poem as it haunted the poet. Each of the three writers examined in this book similarly had their own 'lost prize' which informed their work and in two cases—Dickens and Fitzgerald, the latter especially—for many years afterwards.

In his long poem *The Tower* of 1928 W.B. Yeats famously asked: "Does the imagination dwell the most / Upon a woman won or woman lost?" For Yeats himself the answer to that question was never in any doubt whatever: in his lifetime (as detailed in chapter five of *Carrying the Torch*) it was his own woman lost, Maud Gonne, who became the theme, subject and inspiration of so many of his greatest poems. The three individuals examined in the present work—all men, all writers—played out essentially the same drama of first love in their lives also: love found, requited, lost and unrequited. This is not coincidental, for the story is of course timeless and universal. All three were the same age—eighteen—when they met their first loves; all were rejected for different reasons after a comparatively short time (three years for Dickens; two years for Fitzgerald; just nine months for Hemingway); all three in their fundamentally strikingly similar ways were consumed by the 'saddest words of tongue or pen'— what might have been; none of them can be said to have 'got over it' for each of them not only used the experience more or less thinly disguised in their fiction but returned to it, in some cases repeatedly if not almost obsessively—Fitzgerald especially in this regard—for many years afterwards. *Dolor verba aspera dictat* wrote Silius Italicus in his epic first-century poem *Punica*: grief dictates the words that I write.[8] Without this ability to turn excruciatingly painful and humiliating real-life experience into a believable human story to which others may respond we would never have had Dickensian characters such as Dora Spenlow in *David Copperfield* and Flora Finching in *Little Dorrit* and, according to some biographers at least, the glacial Estella in *Great Expectations*; Daisy Buchanan in Scott Fitzgerald's *The Great Gatsby*; the doomed Catherine Barkley in Ernest Hemingway's *A Farewell to Arms.* Hemingway and Agnes von Kurowsky corresponded desultorily for a time after the end of their very short story in early 1919 but never met again in person; Hemingway ignored Agnes's overtures of friendship. Charles Dickens and Maria Beadnell and F. Scott Fitzgerald and Ginevra King did however meet up with each other again, in both cases over twenty years after their initial youthful romances ended. In neither case did any further relationship, romantic or purely platonic, persist. In all three cases however the love that each of these three men bore for these three women was unforgettable. Dickens married (unhappily, at the end) and had no fewer than ten children: Fitzgerald married rather more happily and fathered a beloved daughter; Hemingway married four times and had several children: but although each man went on to find love and domestic comfort and security elsewhere, each of them carried the unfinished business of their first loves with them throughout the rest of their lives. "A man does not recover from such a devotion of the heart to such a woman," remarks Captain Frederick Wentworth in Jane Austen's *Persuasion*. "He ought not; he does not."

In each of the three examples examined in this book we have just half of the story. Dickens, Fitzgerald and Hemingway were indefatigable letter writers but there are yawning gaps in their epistolary communication with the women they loved in youth. From 1860 onward Dickens periodically burnt nearly all of his vast incoming correspondence and he almost certainly destroyed Maria's letters himself, both the early ones and also the later ones after they renewed contact in 1855. After the end of their love affair Scott Fitzgerald, for reasons known only to himself, asked Ginevra King to destroy his voluminous correspondence to her, a request with which she complied. (She asked him to burn her letters to him in return but he didn't do so). After the end of their brief romance in a Milan hospital Agnes von Kurowsky met and fell in love with an Italian soldier who jealously demanded that Hemingway's letters be destroyed, which he either did himself or induced Agnes to do. These are grievous losses but we are fortunate that as much survives as actually does: Dickens's initially long and heartfelt letters to Maria after she wrote to him out of the blue in 1855 and the letters and diaries of Ginevra King and Agnes von Kurowsky.

And then there are the books. All three men were highly autobiographical writers who drew deeply and directly upon their own real-life experiences as inspiration for their fiction and basing characters on their first loves. As already noted Dickens turned Maria Beadnell into the touching, rather childlike Dora Spenlow in *David Copperfield* and the faintly ridiculous if endearing Flora Finching in *Little Dorrit*, possibly even Estella in *Great Expectations*. Scott Fitzgerald used Ginevra King repeatedly as the template for many of his female characters from the beginning almost to the end of his writing career, most notably Daisy Buchanan in what is arguably his masterpiece, *The Great Gatsby*. Agnes von Kurowsky was the model for Catherine Barkley in *A Farewell to Arms* and for other female characters in his fiction. For these three writers drawing upon real people and real situations from their own early lives—often with the thinnest of disguises—was doubtless a means of coping with the heartbreak of separation and the loss of a precious first love, a way of salving the persistence of what can be excruciatingly and permanently painful memories.

To be in love is always a life-changing experience; to be in love for the first time most of all. For the vast majority of people first love happens early in life—in the teenage years, early adulthood—and is thus a formative, life-altering, character-moulding experience. However it may turn out, few if any of us ever forget it and its unique, unparalleled magic. *On revient toujours à ses premieres amours,* as the French have it: we always go back to our first loves. But for many of us that indefinable and unforgettable magic is, in the words of Benjamin Disraeli, enshrined in our ignorance that it can ever end. "I thought that love would last for ever," wrote W.H. Auden in *Funeral Blues.* "I was wrong."

# One:
## Enough Love to Drown In

If I may so express it, I was steeped in Dora. I was not merely over head and ears in love with her, but I was saturated through and through. Enough love might have been wrung out of me, metaphorically speaking, to drown anybody in; and yet there would have remained enough within me, and all over me, to pervade my entire existence . . . To be allowed to call her 'Dora', to write to her, to dote upon and worship her, to have reason to think that when she was with other people she was yet mindful of me, seemed to me the summit of human ambition—I am sure it was the summit of mine.—Charles Dickens, *David Copperfield*.

### I

Some first loves, when lost, are lost for ever. It is given to a very few exceptionally fortunate individuals to remain with their first love happily for the rest of their lives. It is given to even fewer to be reunited and to rekindle a former romance. It is given to fewer still—in this case fortunately—to meet again and find things changed utterly and for the worse by time and the vagaries of fortune. It is hard to know which is the worst course in life: to lose someone for ever or to see them again after a lengthy interval and to find them altered, to find that love has died on either one side or the other or on both.

Charles John Huffam Dickens was born in Landport, Portsmouth on the 7th of February 1812, the second child and first son of John Dickens, a clerk in the Navy Pay Office, and his twenty-three year-old wife Elizabeth. (Charles's sister Fanny was two years his senior: a brother came along a year after Charles but died in infancy, followed by another five siblings, all but one of whom survived into adulthood). Charles's childhood was poor but by and large happy: he was a bright, lively little boy, an avid reader with as one might expect a vivid imagination, and in later life the memories of the first few years of his upbringing would be described by him as almost idyllic even though his family circumstances were those of fairly extreme poverty. In January 1815 the Dickens family decamped to London for two years before moving to Sheerness in Kent and then yet again to the naval town of Chatham. That John Dickens was the model for Wilkins Micawber in *David Copperfield* has always been known: loving but improvident; kindly but feckless, always hoping that 'something would turn up'. Yet nothing did turn up: the family's indigence went from bad to worse—notwithstanding a move back to London in mid-1822—and it became clear that in order to bring a little desperately needed money into the house young Charles would have to be sent out to work. Thus it was that on the 9th of February 1824, just two days after his twelfth birthday, he went to Warren's blacking factory at Hungerford Stairs, immediately next to the Thames and close to the site of the present-day Charing Cross station. Years later Dickens recalled that the factory was:

> A crazy, tumbledown old house, abutting of course on the river, and literally overrun with rats. Its wainscotted rooms and its rotten floors and staircase, and the old grey rats swarming down in the cellars, and the sound of their squeaking and scuffling coming up the stairs at all times, and the dirt and decay of the place, rise visibly up before me, as if I were there again.

The twelve year old boy was expected to prepare pots of boot-blacking—that is, boot polish—by covering them with paper, tying the pot round with string, snipping the paper neatly and then pasting on a label from a pot of glue. This he did for ten hours a day, five days a week, with a break for lunch and tea, for the princely sum of six shillings a week. Just twelve years old, Dickens worked in conditions of meanness and squalor to which he would later lend his name—Dickensian. It is scarcely overstating the case to say that this experience scarred Dickens for ever. "It is not too much to say," writes Peter Ackroyd, "that his childhood came suddenly to an end, together that that world of reading and of imagination in which the years of his childhood had been passed . . . it had ended so suddenly that it did not gradually fade and disappear as most childhoods do. Instead it was preserved entire in the amber of Dickens's rich memory."[1] The time at Warren's—somewhere between six months and a year;

even now the exact duration is uncertain—weighed so heavily upon him for ever after that he never told his children about it and it is uncertain if he ever even told his wife. Only to his closest friend and later biographer John Forster did he confide the painful secret: otherwise he kept the specifics to himself, although it clearly appears and reappears again and again throughout much of his fiction.

Worse was to come. No more than a few days after Charles started at Warren's blacking factory John Dickens was arrested for debt under the Insolvent Debtors' Act 1813. He had been arrested for a debt of £40 10s. (equivalent to about £3,000 at 2011 prices) owed to a baker named James Karr and sent to the Marshalsea prison for fourteen weeks. The Marshalsea was a notoriously gloomy and brutal gaol dating back to the fourteenth century in Southwark on the south bank of the Thames. Imprisonment for debt (and the concomitant existence of debtor's prisons) was rife in this era. "It was a common offence in this period and for some years after," writes Ackroyd. "It has been estimated, for example, that in 1837 there were between thirty thousand and forty thousand arrests for debt—but nevertheless the insolvent debtor was classed as a quasi-criminal and kept in prison until he could pay or could claim release under the Insolvent

Debtors' Act. It often happened that such a prisoner remained indefinitely within the prison."[2] For a few weeks after her husband's imprisonment Elizabeth and the children remained in their sparsely-furnished lodgings, much of their property having already been sold off, but in April she and three of the children went to the Marshalsea to live with John Dickens—not an unusual practice at the time. Charles was not among them: he was sent to stay for a time with a Mrs Roylance, a friend of the family, in Camden Town, visiting the rest of his family in the Marshalsea every Sunday.

John Dickens's paternal grandmother (also called Elizabeth) died and left her grandson the princely sum of £450. The expectation of the legacy meant that he was able to pay off his debts—in effect buying his way out of prison—and in May 1824 he was released and the family were reunited. Nevertheless Elizabeth Dickens was extremely reluctant to see her son give up his job at Warren's and the badly-needed money that it brought in. This was a point of serious resentment for Dickens for the rest of his life. "I never afterwards forgot, I never shall forget, I never can forget, that my mother was warm for my being sent back," he wrote years later. Nevertheless Charles's formal education began when he was enrolled at the Wellington House Academy where he spent two years. But Dickens was growing up to what was in those days seen to be responsible manhood and feeling the burden of having to make his own way in the adult world. He needed to find a steady career.

It came, probably not entirely unexpectedly, through the ministrations of his mother. Her aunt, a Mrs Charlton, kept a boarding house in Berners Street: one of the lodgers was a young lawyer called Edward Blackmore. Elizabeth used this tenuous connection to persuade Blackmore to take on her son in his business. Blackmore readily agreed so in May 1827, aged fifteen, Charles Dickens became a junior legal clerk at the firm of Ellis and Blackmore (earning not much more than he had at Warren's—thirteen shillings a week to the blacking factory's ten). Dickens was fairly content and was certainly popular here but it was a short-lived venture, lasting only about eighteen months. His abiding interests were elsewhere, principally the theatre at this early stage of his life: he would be a dedicated theatregoer all his life and may even (this is the most poorly recorded stage of Dickens's life and the details are sketchy) have trod the boards himself as an actor on occasion. And of course, behind everything else, was writing. While still a legal clerk in about three months he had arduously taught himself the Gurney system of shorthand with a view to becoming a journalist of some kind.

## II

In the year 1830 John Beadnell was the manager at the banking firm of Smith, Payne and Smith at no. 1 Lombard Street. Beadnell lived very close by at no. 2, sharing the property with his brother George (who also worked at the bank and later replaced his brother as the manager), his wife Anne and their three daughters Margaret, Anne and Maria Sarah.

When they met in May 1830 Dickens was eighteen; Maria was nineteen-and-a-half, born on the 17th of November 1810. They met a dinner party thrown by Mr and Mrs Beadnell. How Dickens met the Beadnells originally is not known with any certainty: it is possible that they were introduced by his friend Henry Kolle who at that time was a bank clerk (possibly with Smith, Payne and Smith) and was courting Maria's sister Anne: their mutual friend David Lloyd was courting the eldest sister Margaret and now Dickens fell head over heels in love with Maria. She was fairly short (her nickname was 'the pocket Venus') but she was dark-eyed, dark-haired and beautiful. The scant images of her that survive from this time, a decade or so before the invention of recognisably modern photography, are conventional and somewhat stylised artistic representations which, if surviving accounts are true, in no way do justice to her attractiveness. Dickens was more or less instantly smitten: at the age of eighteen he was in love for the first time in his adult life. Maria's feelings

on the other hand are very much less easy to discern. She left no

record and all we have to go on are oblique references from a few

scattered letters and the reminiscences of well over twenty years

later. Nevertheless Dickens was head over heels in love. It was,

according his biographer Fred Kaplan, a maladroit choice:

> With an obsessiveness unprepared for by any other experience,
> he fell in love. His notion of an appropriate object reflected his
> lower-middle-class Anglican upbringing, his image of feminine
> sexuality the blond, curly-haired ideal, embodying both the pure
> sister and the innocent wife, on the golden wings of whose spirit,
> education, and social position he would ascend to bliss. His need
> was for a woman who, unlike his mother, would nurture and
> support him, who be the good, beautiful, and morally elevated
> genius of his aspirations. In the case of Maria, his judgment was
> significantly off-target. She was too much like his mother, self-
> involved and emotionally frivolous. That he fell in love at the age
> of eighteen, with a seriousness so deep that he desired to marry,
> dramatizes the extent of his unfulfilled need and the emotional
> poverty of his experiences as a son.[3]

As well as a mismatch in emotional investment there was a dif-

ference of social class—not nearly as pronounced as that between

Scott Fitzgerald and Ginevra King but a difference nonetheless,

one that made no difference to a young and aspirational Dickens

but may well have been a consideration for Maria, or at least for

her parents later on.

Dickens was writing more than his parliamentary reports.

Probably in the autumn of 1831—the high point of Dickens's

relationship with Maria according to his biographer Michael Slater—he wrote a 360-line poem (inspired by Goldsmith's long poem 'Retaliation', one of several such parodies that he wrote around this time) which he called 'The Bill of Fare'. In the poem he penned humorous if rather leaden portraits of his friends and others around him (Mr Beadnell is referred to as a "good fine sirloin of beef", Mrs Beadnell as "an excellent *Rib* of the same"). Dickens says of himself that he is "A young Summer Cabbage without any heart;—/ Not that he's *heartless* but because, as folks say / He lost his a twelvemonth ago, from last May"—a clear reference to, and directed at, his sweetheart Maria: "My bright hopes and fond wishes were all centred here." This was part and parcel of the way that Dickens acted like any lovelorn young swain at the height of his relationship with Maria: he affected to be jealous, for instance, of the love and attention that she lavished on her lapdog Daphne, renamed Jip when Dickens used Maria as the basis for Dora Spenlow in *David Copperfield* years later.

The youthful romance of Charles and Maria was a classic example of in some sense star-crossed lovers whose relationship is effectively killed off by parents (in this case, hers) though ostensibly without any deliberate malice. Mr and Mrs Beadnell felt that Charles, a pleasant young man though he may have been, was simply not a good enough prospect for their daughter and there are indications that he was made unwelcome at 2 Lombard Street—or at least Dickens felt himself to be so: all such indications come from him. Dickens therefore relied on Henry Kolle as a go-between to convey letters and messages to Maria. Maria's friend Mary Anne (or Marianne) Leigh was another confidant and intermediary. Dickens may have been handsome and obviously intelligent and he was living an independent life too: toward the end of 1831 he started to share rooms with a young law student in Buckingham Street off the Strand. Yet he came from a lower-class family, he was but a lowly parliamentary reporter, he was not well-off and seemed to be without any discernible future prospects. According to the 'official' version of events, in the autumn of 1831 Mr and Mrs Beadnell sent Maria away to the finishing school of a Madame Martinez in Paris, perhaps hoping that separation would extinguish Dickens's ardour and induce Maria to forget about him, though in *Dickens and Women* Michael Slater points out that there is no firm evidence that Maria was at Madame Martinez's establishment at that time. She was certainly there earlier, in April 1830 to be precise: it is far more likely that Maria would have been sent there at the earlier date, when she was nineteen, rather than the later one after she had come of age. That there cannot have been any open enmity between Dickens and Mr Beadnell is attested to by the fact that for many years after the end of his romance Dickens and Mr Beadnell carried on an occasional correspondence so it was clearly nothing personal: the Beadnells simply hoped for a suitor for their daughter with a better start in life and better prospects. Michael Slater makes the point that Mr and Mrs Beadnell would not have explicitly discouraged a romance between their daughter and the young parliamentary reporter for the simple reason that they did not take him and his feelings seriously enough to do so. Fred Kaplan agrees: "Her parents did not need to disapprove"—did not need to because there presumably cannot have been any point at which he was seriously thought of by them as a realistic choice of suitor. "Young women who thought of themselves as witty, well educated, and beautiful, with the security of a substantial middle-class home, rarely married economically insecure younger men who were less experienced, less well educated, and socially inferior."[4] Dickens was in short a likeable enough young man, nice to have around at gatherings occasionally but scarcely anything more than that and certainly not a likely candidate for marriage into the family, either in the eyes of Mr Beadnell or his wife (who could not even get Dickens's name right, consistently referring to him as 'Mr Dickin') and likely not of Maria herself, perhaps indeed in the eyes of anyone but Dickens himself. "*You can do no wrong,*" Dickens told Henry Kolle with ill-disguised bitterness; "*I* am not so sure of coming off well." Slater suggests

that we can get a fair idea of how Dickens was thought of by

the elder Beadnells by looking at 'The New Year' from 1836's

*Sketches by Boz* (his first substantial work, appearing just ahead of

*The Pickwick Papers*) where Dickens himself becomes young Mr

Tupple:

> Charming person Mr. Tupple—perfect ladies' man—such a
> delightful companion, too! Laugh!—nobody ever understood
> papa's jokes half so well as Mr. Tupple, who laughs himself into
> convulsions at every fresh burst of facetiousness. Most delightful
> partner! talks through the whole set! and although he does seem
> at first rather gay and frivolous, so romantic and with so MUCH
> feeling! Quite a love. No great favourite with the young men,
> certainly, who sneer at, and affect to despise him; but everybody
> knows that's only envy, and they needn't give themselves the
> trouble to depreciate his merits at any rate, for Ma says he shall
> be asked to every future dinner-party, if it's only to talk to people
> between the courses, and distract their attention when there's any
> unexpected delay in the kitchen.

"He was more desirable," as Fred Kaplan puts it, ". . . as a friend

and a guest than as a member of the family . . . The Beadnells

were hospitable to the boyish entertainer, not to the serious

suitor."[5] There are a few intriguing, tantalising half-hints that

Dickens's own family may not have been particularly happy

about Maria either. It need hardly be said that none of this—the

indifference of the Beadnells, the (possible) disapproval of his

own family—made the slightest bit of difference to the young

Dickens himself. Familial disapproval of a choice of love object, parental disapproval especially, almost inevitably tends to harden and entrench romantic ardour.

Over a period of nine years between 1860 and 1869 years Dickens sporadically wrote a series of thirty-seven fairly short pieces and recollections which were grouped under the title of *The Uncommercial Traveller*. (A complete set of these essays was published posthumously in 1875). The twentieth of these, 'Birthday Celebrations', harks back to Dickens's coming-of-age party in February 1833. We don't know for sure that Maria Beadnell was a guest and we must always bear in mind that in Michael Slater's words "his ostensibly autobiographical essays [are] slippery guides to the actual biographical truth"; but it is highly likely that she was there:

I gave a party on the occasion. She was there. It is unnecessary to name Her, more particularly; She was older than I, and had pervaded every chink and crevice of my mind for three or four years. I had held volumes of Imaginary Conversations with her mother on the subject of our union, and I had written letters more in number than Horace Walpole's, to that discreet woman, soliciting her daughter's hand in marriage. I had never had the remotest intention of sending any of those letters; but to write them, and after a few days tear them up, had been a sublime occupation. Sometimes, I had begun 'Honoured Madam, I think that a lady gifted with those powers of observation which I know you to possess, and endowed with those womanly sympathies with the young and ardent which it were more than heresy to doubt, can scarcely have failed to discover that I love your adorable daughter, deeply, devotedly.' In less buoyant states of mind I had begun, 'Bear with me, Dear Madam, bear with a daring wretch who is about to make a surprising confession to you, wholly unanticipated by yourself, and which he beseeches you to commit to the flames as soon as you have become aware to what a towering height his mad ambition soars.' At other times periods of profound mental depression, when She had gone out to balls where I was not the draft took the affecting form of a paper to be left on my table after my departure to the confines of the globe. As thus: 'For Mrs. Onowenever, these lines when the hand that traces them shall be far away. I could not bear the daily torture of hopelessly loving the dear one whom I will not name. Broiling on the coast of Africa, or congealing on the shores of Greenland, I am far far better there than here.' (In this sentiment my cooler judgment perceives that the family of the beloved object would have most completely concurred). 'If I ever emerge from obscurity, and my name is ever heralded by Fame, it will be for her dear sake. If I ever amass Gold, it will be to pour it at her feet. Should I on the other hand become the prey of Ravens' I doubt if I ever quite made up my mind what was to be done in that affecting case; I tried 'then it is better so'; but not feeling convinced that it would be better so, I vacillated between leaving all else blank, which looked expressive and bleak, or winding up with 'Farewell!'

How directly autobiographical all this may have been—whether Dickens ever really did write so many unsent letters—is hard to judge; but it has the ring of truth about it, not least in the statement that a certain young lady had penetrated every chink and crevice of his mind for several years previously. This much was absolutely true. In any case 'Birthday Celebrations' seems to imply that not only was Maria present at Dickens's party but that she slighted her beau and mortally wounded him by referring to him as a boy:

. . . on my twenty-first birthday I gave a party, and She was there. It was a beautiful party. There was not a single animate or inanimate object connected with it (except the company and myself) that I had ever seen before. Everything was hired, and the mercenaries in attendance were profound strangers to me. Behind a door, in the crumby part of the night when wine-glasses were to be found in unexpected spots, I spoke to Her—spoke out to Her. What passed, I cannot as a man of honour reveal. She was all angelical gentleness, but a word was mentioned—a short and dreadful word of three letters, beginning with a B- which, as I remarked at the moment, 'scorched my brain.' She went away soon afterwards, and when the hollow throng (though to be sure it was no fault of theirs) dispersed, I issued forth, with a dissipated scorner, and, as I mentioned expressly to him, 'sought oblivion.' It was found, with a dreadful headache in it, but it didn't last; for, in the shaming light of next day's noon, I raised my heavy head in bed, looking back to the birthdays behind me, and tracking the circle by which I had got round, after all, to the bitter powder and the wretchedness again.

It may have been this event at Dickens's birthday party which became the straw that broke the camel's back and led Dickens to write, on the 18th of March, a long, heartfelt letter, partly of self-justification, breaking off their romance in spite of the fact that to Henry Kolle, Dickens described this missive as "a very conciliatory note sans pride, sans reserve sans anything but an evident wish to be reconciled." This letter was clearly of such importance to them both for their different reasons that although Dickens asked her to return it to him, she first made a copy in her own hand:

Dear Miss Beadnell,—
          Your own feelings will enable you to im-
agine far better than any attempt of mine to describe the painful
struggle it has cost me to make up my mind to adopt the course
which I now take—a course than which nothing can be so directly
opposed to my wishes and feelings, but the necessity of which
becomes daily more apparent to me. Our meetings of late have

been little more than so many displays of heartless indifference on the one hand, while on the other they have never failed to prove a fertile source of wretchedness and misery; and seeing, as I cannot fail to do, that I have engaged in a pursuit which has long since been worse than hopeless and a further perseverance in which can only expose me to deserved ridicule, I have made up my mind to return the little present I received from you sometime since (which I have always prized, as I still do, far beyond anything I ever possessed) and the other enclosed mementos of our past correspondence which I am sure it must be gratifying to you to receive, as after our recent relative situations they are certainly better adapted for your custody than mine.

Need I say that I have not the most remote idea of hurting your feelings by the few lines which I think it necessary to write with the accompanying little parcel? I must be the last person in the world who could entertain such an intention, but I feel that this is neither a matter nor a time for cold, deliberate, calculating trifling. My feelings upon any subject, more especially upon this, must be to you a matter of very little moment; still *I* have feelings in common with other people,—perhaps as far as they relate to you they have been as strong and as good as ever warmed the human heart,—and I do feel that it is mean and contemptible of me to keep by me one gift of yours or to preserve one single line or word of remembrance or affection from you, I therefore return them, and I can only wish that I could as easily forget that I ever received them.

I have but one more word to say and I say it in my own vindication. The result of our past acquaintance is indeed a melancholy one to me. I have felt too long ever to lose the feeling of utter desolation and wretchedness which has succeeded our former correspondence. Thank God I can claim for myself and feel that I deserve the merit of having ever throughout our intercourse acted fairly, intelligibly and honourably. Under kindness and encouragement one day and a total change of conduct the next I have ever been the same. I have ever acted without reserve. I have never held out encouragement which I knew I never meant; I have never indirectly sanctioned hopes which I well knew I did not intend to fulfil. I have never made a mock confidante to whom to entrust a garbled story for my own purposes, and I think I never should (though God knows I am not likely to have the opportunity) encourage one dangler as a useful shield for—an excellent set off against—others more fortunate and doubtless more deserving. I have done nothing that I could say would be very likely to hurt you. If (I can hardly believe it possible) I have said any thing which can have that effect I can only ask you to place yourself for a moment in my situation, and you will find a much better excuse than I can possibly devise. A wish for your happiness al-tho' it comes from me may not be the worse for being sincere and heartfelt. Accept it as it is meant, and believe that nothing will ever afford me more real delight than to hear that you, the object of my first and my last love are happy. If you are as happy as I hope you may be, you will indeed possess every blessing that this world can afford.

CD.

All contact was not quite brought to a complete end, however. Their relationship, such as it was, limped along for another couple of months, a period of time in which Dickens returned to his great love of the theatre by taking a small part in an 1823 musical drama called *Clari, the Maid of Milan* (now forgotten and probably not undeservedly save for the fact that it included the subsequently famous sentimental song *Home, Sweet Home*). Dickens's role was very minor and confined to a few lines in the last act: but given that it so happened that Maria was present in the audience Dickens did not pass up the chance to direct a few lines in her direction whilst pointedly looking directly at her. His efforts were to no avail: Maria could not be moved. He wrote again:

I do feel, Miss Beadnell, after my former note to you that common delicacy and a proper feeling of consideration alike require that I should without a moment's delay inform you (as I did verbally yesterday) that I never, by word or deed, in the slightest manner, directly or by implication, made in any way a confidante of Mary Anne Leigh, and never was I more surprised, never did I endure more heartfelt annoyance and vexation than to hear yesterday by chance that days even weeks ago she had made this observation—

not having the slightest idea that she had done so of course it was
out of my power to contradict it before. Situated as we have been
once I have—laying out of consideration every idea of common
honour not to say common honesty—too often thought of our
earlier correspondence, and too often looked back to happy hopes
the loss of which have made me the miserable reckless wretch I
am, to breathe the slightest hint to any creature living of one single
circumstance that ever passed between us—much less to her.

In replying to your last note I denied Mary Anne Leigh's
interference, and I did so hoping to spare you the pain of any
recrimination with her. Her duplicity and disgusting falsehood,
however, renders it quite unnecessary to conceal the part she
has acted, and I therefore have no hesitation in saying that she,
quite unasked, volunteered the information that *you* had made
her a confidante of all that had ever passed between us without
reserve. In proof of which assertion she not only detailed facts
which I undoubtedly thought she could have heard from none but
yourself, but she also communicated many things which certainly
never occurred at all, equally calculated to excite something even
more than ordinary angry feelings.

On hearing this yesterday (and no consideration on earth shall
induce me ever to forget or forgive Fanny's [Dickens's sister] not
telling me of it before) my first impulse was to go to Clapton: my
next to prevent misrepresentation, to write immediately. I thought
on reflection however that the most considerate and proper course
would be to state to you exactly what I wish to do. I ask your
consent previously for this reason—because it is possible that you
may think that my writing a violent note would have the effect of
exciting ill nature which had better be avoided. I candidly own
that I am most anxious to write. I care as little for her malice as I
do for her, but as you are a party who would perhaps be mixed up
with her story I think it is proper to ask you whether you object to
my sending the note which I have already written. I need hardly
say that if it be sent at all it should be at once, and I therefore hope
to receive your decision tomorrow, assuring you that I will abide
by it whatever it be.

I will not detain you or intrude upon your attention by any more
observations. I fear I could say little calculated to interest or please
you. I have no hopes to express, no wishes to communicate. I am
past the one and must not think of the other. Though surprised
at such inconceivable duplicity I can express no pleasure at the
discovery, for I have been so long used to inward wretchedness
and real, real misery, that it matters little, very little to me what
others may think of or what becomes of me—I have to apologize
for troubling you at all but I hope you will believe that a sense of

respect for and deference to your feelings has elicited this note to which I have once again to beg your immediate answer.

Charles Dickens

## Two days later he wrote:

I cannot forbear replying to your note this moment received, Miss Beadnell, because you really seem to have made two mistakes. In the first place you do not exactly understand the nature of my feelings with regard to your alleged communications to M[ary] A[nne] L[eigh], and in the next you certainly totally and entirely misunderstand my feeling with regard to her—that you could suppose, as you clearly do (that is to say if the subject is worth a thought to you), that I have ever really thought of M. A. L. in any other than my old way you are mistaken. That she has for some reason and to suit her own purposes, of late thrown herself in my way, I could plainly see, and I know it was noticed by others. For instance on the night of the play, after we went up stairs—I could not get rid of her. God knows that I have no pleasure in speaking to her or any girl living, and never had. May I say that you have ever been the sole exception? 'Kind words and winning looks' have done much, much with me—but not from her—unkind words and cold looks, however, have done much, much more. That I have been the subject of both from you as your will altered and your pleasure changed, *I* know well—and so I think must you. I have often said before, and I say again, I have borne more from you than I do believe any creature breathing ever bore from a woman before. The slightest hint, however, even now of change or transfer of feeling I cannot bear and do not deserve.

Again, I never supposed nor did this girl give me to understand that you ever breathed a syllable against me. It is quite a mistake on your part, but knowing (and there cannot be a stronger proof of my disliking her) what she was; knowing her admirable qualifications for a confidante and recollecting what had passed between ourselves, I was more than hurt, more than annoyed at the bare idea of your confiding the tale to her of all people living. I reflected upon it. I coupled her communication with what I saw (with a jaundiced eye perhaps) of your own conduct; on the very last occasion of seeing you before writing that note [i.e. the letter of the 18th of March] I heard even among your own friends (and there was no Mary Ann present), I heard even among them remarks on your own conduct and pity—pity, Good God!—for my situation, and I did think (you will pardon my saying it for I am describing my then feelings and not my present) that the same light butterfly feeling which prompted the one action could influence the other. Wretched, aye almost brokenhearted, I wrote to you—(I have the note for you returned it,' and even now I do think it was written 'more in sorrow than in anger,' and to my mind—I had almost said to your better judgment—it must appear to breathe anything but an unkind or bitter feeling),—you replied to the note. I wrote another and that at least was expressive of the same sentiments as I ever had felt and ever should feel towards you to my dying day. That note you sent me back by hand wrapped in a small loose piece of paper without even the formality of an envelope and that note I wrote after receiving yours. It is poor sport to trifle on a subject like this: I knew what your feelings must have been and by them I regulated my conduct.

To return to the question of what is best to be done. I go to Kolle's at 10 o'clock tomorrow evening and I will inclose to you and give to him then a copy of the note which if I send any I will send to Marianne Leigh. I do not ask your advice; all I ask is whether you see any reason to object. You will perhaps inclose it after reading it, and say whether you object to its going or not.

With regard to Fanny if she owed a duty to you she owed a greater one to me—and for this reason because she knew what Marianne Leigh had said to you; she heard from you what she had said of me and yet she had not the fairness the candour the feeling to let me know it—and if 1 were to live a hundred years I never would forgive it.

As to sending my last note back, pray do not consult my feelings but your own. Look at the note itself. Do you think it is unkind, cold, hasty, or conciliatory and deliberate? I shall— indeed I need—express no wish upon the subject. You will act as you think best. It is too late for me to attempt to influence your decision. I have said doubtless both in this and my former note much more than perhaps I ought or should have said had I attempted disguise or concealment to you and I have no doubt more than is agreeable to yourself. Towards you I never had and never can have an angry feeling. If you had ever felt for me one hundredth part of my feeling for you there would have been little cause of regret, little coldness little unkindness between us. My feeling on one subject was early roused; it has been strong, and it will be lasting. I am in no mood to quarrel with any one for not entertaining similar sentiments, and least of all, Miss Beadnell, with you. You will think of what I have said and act accordingly—destitute as I am of hope or comfort, I have borne much and I dare say can bear more.

Yours,
                    Charles Dickens


## And yet again:


Dear Miss Beadnell—
                    I am anxious to take the earliest opportunity
of writing to you again, knowing that the opportunity of addressing
you through Kolle—now my only means of communicating with
you—will shortly be lost [because Kolle was due to marry Anne
Beadnell, which he did on the 21st of May 1833], and having your
own permission to write to you—I am most desirous of forwarding
a note which had I received such permission earlier, I can assure
you you would have received ere this. Before proceeding to say
a word upon the subject of my present note let me beg you to
believe that your request to see Marianne Leigh's answer is
rendered quite unnecessary by my previous determination to
shew it you, which I shall do immediately on receiving it—that
is to say, if I receive any at all. If I know anything of her art or
disposition however you are mistaken in supposing that her
remarks will be directed against yourself. / shall be the mark at
which all the anger and spleen will be directed—and I shall take
it very quietly for whatever she may say I shall positively decline
to enter into any further controversy with her. I shall have no
objection to break a lance, paper or otherwise, with any champion
to whom she may please to entrust her cause but I will have no
further correspondence or communication with her personally or
in writing. I have copied the note and done up the parcel which
will go off by the first Clapton Coach to-morrow morning.
   And now to the object of my present note. I have considered
and reconsidered the matter, and I have come to the unqualified
determination that I will allow no feeling of pride, no haughty
dislike to making a conciliation to prevent my expressing it
without reserve. I will advert to nothing that has passed; I will not
again seek to excuse any part I have acted or to justify it by any
course you have ever pursued; I will revert to nothing that has
ever passed between us,—I will only openly and at once say that
there is nothing I have more at heart, nothing I more sincerely
and earnestly desire, than to be reconciled to you.—It would be
useless for me to repeat here what I have so often said before; it
would be equally useless to look forward and state my hopes for
the future—all that any one can do to raise himself by his own
exertions and unceasing assiduity I have done, and will do. I

have no guide by which to ascertain your present feelings and I have, God knows, no means of influencing them in my favour. I never have loved and I never can love any human creature breathing but yourself. We have had many differences, and we have lately been entirely separated. Absence, however, has not altered my feelings in the slightest degree, and the Love I now tender you is as pure and as lasting as at any period of our former correspondence, I have now done all I can to remove our most unfortunate and to me most unhappy misunderstanding. The matter now of course rests solely with you, and you will decide as your own feelings and wishes direct you. I could say much for myself and I could entreat a favourable consideration on my own behalf but I purposely abstain from doing so because it would be only a repetition of an oft told tale and because I am sure that nothing I could say would have the effect of influencing your decision in any degree whatever. Need I say that to me it is a matter of vital import and the most intense anxiety? — I fear that the numerous claims which must necessarily be made on your time and attention next week will prevent your answering this note within anything like the time which my impatience would name. Let me entreat you to consider your determination well whatever it be and let me implore you to communicate it to me as early as possible. — As I am anxious to convey this note into the City in time to get it delivered today I will at once conclude by begging you to believe me,

Yours sincerely,<br>Charles Dickens

It would be the last time that Dickens wrote to Maria for over twenty years. No further letters of this first set are known to exist.

What of Maria's feelings in all this? In his biography of Dickens, Fred Kaplan states: "Despite her claim to the contrary twenty-five years later, there is no reason to believe that she ever took him seriously."[6] However it is also true that there is no evidence to the contrary either. We simply cannot know for certain either way. Although Dickens himself felt that Maria had treated him with callous disdain or sheer indifference this is only his side of the story, the way that Dickens himself saw it. Maria left no contemporaneous record of her feelings for the young Dickens and her surviving comments on their youthful romance all stem from the mid-1850s, nearly a quarter of a century after the events to which they relate, by which time both parties were married and had had children.

It was in May 1833, not long after the previously quoted letter, that their relationship finally came to an end. Dickens was, quite predictably, shattered. We have to imagine his heartbreak because his references to it in his personal writings at the time were scant and oblique even where they did exist: like Maria herself he did not pass comment on the affair until long afterwards. A dozen years later Dickens wrote to an acquaintance called Thomas Powell:

> I broke my heart into the smallest pieces, many times between thirteen and three and twenty. Twice, I was very horribly in earnest; and once I really set upon the cast for six or seven long years, all the energy and determination of which I am the owner. But it went the way of nearly all such things at last, though I think it kept me steadier than the working of my nature was, to many good things for the time. If anyone had interfered with my very small Cupid, I don't know what absurdity I might have committed in assertion of his proper liberty; but having plenty of rope he hanged himself, beyond all chance of restoration.[7]

The "six or seven long years" was a naked exaggeration—it was in fact three years at the most—but it is clearly Maria Beadnell he is referring to here. When Maria contacted him again unexpectedly over twenty years later he would remember the end of the affair:

> I remember well that long after I came of age—I say long; well! It seemed long then—I wrote to you for the last time of all, with a dawn upon me of some sensible idea that we were changing into man and woman, saying would you forget our little differences and separations and let us begin again? You answered me very coldly and reproachfully,—and so I went my way.[8]

"[S]pring 1833 was notable . . . for . . . the final stage of his separation from Maria Beadnell," writes Peter Ackroyd:

> 'Separation' is perhaps not quite the right word, since they seem not to have been in any tangible sense together. It is a familiar story, but its familiarity does not render it any the less painful for the young men and women who experience it for the first time— passion on the one side and reserve on the other . . . for some three years Dickens had been paying court to Maria Beadnell. His advances were at first favoured and then neglected and finally rebuffed: there was a slow but steady falling off between them, and in the period towards the end of their acquaintance Dickens would, in the early hours of the morning, walk after work from the House of Commons to Lombard Street just to see the place in which she slept . . . That he was thwarted and stalled and frustrated and wounded there is no doubt: he was always afraid of being rebuffed and now, for the first time, he had been rejected. Three years marks a long period in the life of a young man, and now three years of courtship had come to nothing. Wasted. His heart laid bare, and also wasted. In later life he seemed to regard it as a traumatic event—one which he had 'locked up' in his own breast and which, he said, had led directly to a 'habit of suppression' which meant that he could never display his true feelings to anyone, not even to his children . . . the fact that [his rejection by Maria Beadnell] provoked such deep emotion in him suggests that it was in a sense an echo or reprise of earlier abandonments; those by his mother and by his sister were prominent in his own memories of his childhood, and there is every reason to suppose that the experience of female rejection determined much of his emotional life.[9]

Dickens did indeed go his way and buried himself in his work. "Dickens recovered from the blow," wrote William Robertson Nicoll in *Dickens's Own Story*, "but it did not leave him the same man, nor did he ever forget. He married, and was happy enough for a time. He began to feel a sense of 'one happiness I have missed in my life, and one friend and companion I have never made'. Decades later, just as he was laying plans for his most autobiographical novel *David Copperfield*, he began to write what was effectively his own autobiography but when he arrived at the period in his early manhood to which his infatuation with Maria Beadnell belonged, he 'lost courage and burned the rest'." Dickens's life went on, but both personally and professionally his relationship with Maria would alter him for ever.

III

In 1835 Dickens became engaged to Catherine Hogarth, the Scottish-born daughter of the writer George Hogarth: the two were married on the 2nd of April 1836. "How many men marry the first woman adored by them?" asked George Pierce Baker in his 1908 edition of the Dickens-Beadnell/Winter correspondence. "What possible criticism is it on the woman one marries, that one may already have been in love with another?"[10] Dickens had indeed been desperately in love with another and would never forget her. All the same, Catherine would be his wife for the next twenty-two sometimes stormy and difficult years and the mother of their ten children, nine of whom survived to adulthood. In 1842 Dickens and Catherine went to America on the first of his reading tours: Catherine's sister Georgina moved in to help manage the household and to look after the children left behind.

In the meantime Dickens was establishing himself, monthly instalment by monthly instalment, novel by novel, as the greatest writer in English of the nineteenth century and one of the greatest writers of all time. His industry was staggering: his was, as per the subtitle of Michael Slater's biography, truly a life defined by writing. In under twenty years he produced eleven major novels, many of them very lengthy, which have been endlessly adapted for stage, large and small screens and radio and which have been deeply loved by generations ever since: *Sketches by Boz* (1836), *The Pickwick Papers* (1837), *Oliver Twist* (1839), *Nicholas Nickleby* (1839), *The Old Curiosity Shop* (1841), *Barnaby Rudge* (1841), *A Christmas Carol* (1843), *Martin Chuzzlewit* (1844), *Dombey and Son* (1848), *David Copperfield* (1850), *Bleak House* (1853) and *Hard Times* (1854) to say nothing of sundry slighter works.

Yet if he was riding the crest of a professional wave, in private the early 1850s were a time of crisis for Dickens. In September 1848 his adored sister Fanny had died of consumption at the age of just thirty-eight. In April 1851 his ninth child, a beloved daughter named Dora Annie died aged just nine months: the following year his ineffectual but loved and loving father John passed away. There was the lesser but undoubtedly still stressful upheaval of moving house with a large family: in late November 1851 the Dickens family moved from Devonshire Terrace to Tavistock House in Marylebone, Charles's home for the next nine years in which he would write *Bleak House*, *Hard Times*, *Little Dorrit* and *A Tale of Two Cities*. In 1852, in which year his tenth and last child was born, he reached the milestone of forty, a landmark age which gives many people pause and compels them to stop and take stock of their lives past, present and future. Both Charles and Catherine themselves were frequently ill: in the absence of detailed symptoms it is almost impossible to reach a specific diagnosis but it seems very likely that in both cases their illnesses were primarily nervous and/or emotional in origin, the expression of prolonged stress, anxiety, grief and in Dickens's case relentless overwork. The term 'workaholic' was not coined until 1968, a century after his death, but it could have been made with men like Dickens in mind.

It would be trite simply to pass this off as a typically male mid-life crisis built out of nostalgia for the past (meaning youth and strength), an awareness of advancing age and mortality—

"The old days—the old days! Shall I ever, I wonder, get the frame of mind back as it used to be then? Something of it, perhaps, but never quite as it used to be," he wrote to his closest friend and, later, first biographer John Forster in 1856—but a crisis it certainly was and one relating specifically to his married life, for Charles and Catherine's marriage had been in trouble for some time and by now it was heading toward the rocks. In *Dickens and Women* Michael Slater argues that Dickens, for reasons best known to himself, seemed to have a vested interest in presenting to those few family members and particularly close friends he allowed to be party to his marital woes a picture of a marriage which had been deeply unhappy for many years, but as Slater himself shows firm evidence of any marital dissatisfaction and discord on Dickens's part dates only from around 1854 or so. Dickens undoubtedly exaggerated the length of serious marital discord. Still, it's undoubtedly true that while the early years were by all accounts happy and contented, as time wore on and more and more children arrived the relationship began to sour. The proximate cause (or at least one such according to his biographers) is that Dickens had all but accused Catherine of bearing so many children and placing severe strain on the family's finances, seemingly unaware that he was every bit as responsible himself for this situation. Catherine, though still considered pretty, had lost her youthful bloom and beauty and had grown plump (hardly surprising after giving birth to ten children). Dickens was a doting and affectionate father, especially when the children were very young, but he could also be demanding when they grew older and could not reach the exacting standards of behaviour and achievement that he demanded of them. It's quite clear that he resented, perhaps even only half-consciously to himself, such a tribe of children. After nearly twenty years of marriage it seems that Dickens, in short, had simply fallen out of love with his wife: visitors around this time noticed a tense, difficult, at times downright frigid atmosphere between the two. A separation was inevitable (it would finally come in June 1858) even if divorce was almost unthinkable: Dickens's good name would be irredeemably sullied by such a scandal. But it was becoming increasingly difficult for Charles and Catherine to share life in the same house.

Unsurprisingly all these things—advancing age; illness; a shattering series of deaths; a failing marriage—came as a series of body blows that drove Dickens in upon himself and instigated a period of deep self-examination and reflection. He started to write down an account of his life, perhaps partly as a distraction from his woes in the present but also as a means of making sense of it so far. It's unlikely that he ever seriously thought of publishing these memoirs in his lifetime: it seems largely to have been a private, personal and largely therapeutic exercise. He showed parts of the work in progress to Forster and possibly also to Catherine but eventually he abandoned these memoirs when he came to that part of his life where Maria Beadnell entered the story: at precisely this point he threw the project aside and it went no further. However, what Dickens could not do in the form of a memoir could be achieved if it was objectified and distanced from him by being fictionalised, so instead Dickens employed some of the salient details of his own real past in the construction of the next novel, his eighth, *David Copperfield*.

Dickens never forgot his first love. In *The History of Henry Esmond* (1852) Dickens's friend William Thackeray wrote: ". . . such a past is always present to a man; such a passion once felt forms a part of his whole being, and cannot be separated from it." It's also quite probable that writing the autobiography-that-never-was reawakened long-dormant memories of the first woman he had loved: by his own admission, as we have already seen, he was unable to proceed on the work past the point where he attempted to describe his young love for Maria Beadnell. Always an intensely autobiographical writer (which we will see similarly in later chapters with Scott Fitzgerald and Ernest Hemingway), throughout his career Dickens raided his own personal life for details which found their way into the lives of the dramatis personae of his many books. In particular it has long been regarded that Maria was the main inspiration for Dora Spenlow in *David Copperfield*, the most autobiographical of all Dickens's works and his personal favourite, possibly for the very reason that it was so nakedly personal a *Bildungsroman*. "He was about to make David fall in love in earnest," writes Dickens's biographer Michael Slater, "for which purpose he began mining memories of his own desperately ardent wooing of Maria Beadnell between the ages of eighteen and twenty-one."[11] In his biography of his friend (published in two volumes between 1872 and 1874) John Forster wrote:

> He too had his Dora at apparently the same hopeless elevation; striven for as the one only thing to be attained, and even more unattainable, for neither did he succeed nor happily [*sic*] did she die; but the one idol, like the other, supplying the motive to exertion for the time, and otherwise opening out to the idolater, both in fact and in fiction, a highly unsubstantial, happy, foolish time. I used to laugh and tell him I had no belief in any but the book Dora, until the incident of a sudden reappearance of the real one in his life, nearly six years after Copperfield was written, convinced me there had been a more actual foundation for those chapters of his book than I was ready to suppose.[12]

This was written in 1872: years earlier, in 1855, Forster had expressed to Dickens his doubts that the character of Dora Spenlow was an accurate representation of Dickens's early romance and that surely his friend was exaggerating how ardently he had felt all those years ago. Dickens replied:

> I don't quite apprehend what you mean by my overrating the strength of the feeling of five-and-twenty years ago. If you mean of my own feeling, and will only think what the desperate intensity of my nature is, and that this began when I was Charley's age [his son Charles Dickens Jr.]; that it excluded every other idea from my mind for four years, at a time of life when four years are equal to four times four; and that I went at it with a determination to overcome all the difficulties, which fairly lifted me up into that newspaper life, and floated me away over a hundred men's heads; then you are wrong, because nothing can exaggerate that. I have positively stood amazed at myself ever since—And so I suffered, and so worked, and so beat and hammered away at the maddest romances that ever got into any boy's head and stayed there, that to see the mere cause of it all, now, loosens my hold upon myself. Without for a moment sincerely believing that it would have been better if we had never got separated, I cannot see the occasion of much emotion as I should see anyone else. No one can imagine in the most distant degree what pain the recollection gave me in Copperfield. And, just as I can never open that book as I open any other book, I cannot see the face (even at four-and-forty), or hear the voice, without going wandering away over the ashes of all that youth and hope in the wildest manner.

Dickens himself was absolutely explicit on the point: when Maria contacted him again in 1855, five years after *David Copperfield*, he told her:

> . . . you may have seen in one of my books a faithful reflection of the passion I had for you, and may have thought that it was something to have been loved so well, and may have seen in little bits of 'Dora' touches of your old self sometimes . . .

These touches, says Michael Slater, include her shortness of stature, her abundant curls, her much doted-upon lapdog. "But, apart from these things, Dora is not physically presented in any solidly-realized way":

She enters the novel as a faery vision of loveliness, a vision fixed
for the reader by that unforgettable image of 'a straw hat and
blue ribbons, and a quantity of curls, and a little black dog being
held up, in two slender arms, against a bank of blossoms and
bright leaves'. For Dickens is not concerned to evoke Maria as she
actually was but as the 'Sun' that she had once been for him. She
must seem to the reader as to David 'everything that everybody
ever wanted' and to particularize her too closely would work
against this. Maria's eyebrows had had a tendency to join together,
Dickens fondly remembered, but to give this feature to Dora
could only distance her from the reader who would, of course,
have his own taste in eyebrows. So Dickens tactfully concentrates
on vague evocative phrases . . . leaving the reader's imagination
and own personal memories to do the rest.[13]

Nevertheless, even if the specifics are absent, there can be no
doubt whatever that Dickens's love for Maria is transcribed
wholesale into David Copperfield's love for Dora. When they
meet, the eponymous hero of the novel is working as a clerk at
the firm of Spenlow and Jorkins—Dora is the daughter of David's
employer, to whose home he has been invited:

We went into the house, which was cheerfully lighted up, and into
a hall where there were all sorts of hats, caps, great-coats, plaids,
gloves, whips, and walking-sticks. "Where is Miss Dora?" said
Mr Spenlow to the servant. "Dora!" I thought. "What a beautiful
name!"

We turned into a room near at hand . . . and I heard a voice
say "Mr Copperfield, my daughter Dora, and my daughter Dora's
confidential friend!" It was, no doubt, Mr Spenlow's voice, but I
didn't know it, and I didn't care whose it was. All was over in a
moment. I had fulfilled my destiny. I was a captive and a slave. I
love Dora Spenlow to distraction!

She was more than human to me. She was a Fairy, a Sylph, I
don't know what she was—anything that no one ever saw, and
everything that everybody ever wanted. I was swallowed up in an
abyss of love in an instant. There was no pausing on the brink; no

> looking down or looking back; I was gone, headlong, before I had
> sense to say a word to her.
>       . . .
> I could only sit down before my fire, biting the key of my carpet-
> bag, and think of the captivating, girlish, bright-eyed lovely
> Dora. What a form she had, what a face she had, what a graceful,
> variable, enchanting manner!

Dora, remarks Claire Tomalin, "has the body of an adult woman with the mental age of a three-year-old."[14] Nevertheless David is smitten to the point of the obsession that grips all passionate people in the throes of love—arguably never more so than the young experiencing first love—and if we accept that Maria Beadnell was the inspiration for the character of Dora we can take it that many of the details of David's ardent devotion to Dora echo the young Dickens's own feelings and actions all those years earlier:

> I don't remember who was there, except Dora. I have not the
> least idea what we had for dinner, besides Dora. My impression
> is, that I dined off Dora entirely, and sent away half-a-dozen
> plates untouched. I sat next to her. I talked to her. She had the
> most delightful little voice, the gayest little laugh, the pleasantest
> and most fascinating little ways, that ever led a lost youth into
> hopeless slavery. She was rather diminutive altogether. So much
> the more precious, I thought . . . To be allowed to call her 'Dora,'
> to write to her, to dote upon and worship her, to have reason to
> think that when she was with other people she was yet mindful
> of me, seemed to me the summit of human ambition—I am sure
> it was the summit of mine. There is no doubt whatever that I was
> a lackadaisical young spooney; but there was a purity of heart
> in all this still, that prevents my having quite a contemptuous
> recollection of it, let me laugh as I may.

David quickly exhibits all the frankly obsessional traits of the young person in love:

Within the first week of my passion, I bought four sumptuous waistcoats—not for myself; I had no pride in them; for Dora— and took to wearing straw-coloured kid gloves in the streets, and laid the foundations of all the corns I have ever had . . . wretched cripple as I made myself by this act of homage to Dora, I walked miles upon miles daily in the hope of seeing her. Not only was I soon as well known on the Norwood Road as the postmen on that beat, but I pervaded London likewise. I walked about the streets where the best shops for ladies were, I haunted the Bazaar like an unquiet spirit, I fagged through the Park again and again, long after I was quite knocked up. Sometimes, at long intervals, and on rare occasions, I saw her. Perhaps I saw her glove waved in a carriage window; perhaps I met her, walked with her and Miss Murdstone a little way, and spoke to her. In the latter case I was always very miserable afterwards, to think that I had said nothing to the purpose; or that she had no idea of the extent of my devotion, or that she cared nothing about me. I was always looking out, as may be supposed, for another invitation to Mr. Spenlow's house. I was always being disappointed, for I got none.

By and by David and are married. Though no less ardently in love with his new bride than before David (or 'Doady' as his wife refers to him) soon realises that he could scarcely have married a woman less capable of dealing with the demands and responsibilities of everyday married life.

"Will you call me a name I want you to call me?" inquired Dora, without moving.

"What is it?" I asked with a smile.

"It's a stupid name," she said, shaking her curls for a moment. "Child-wife."

I laughingly asked my child-wife what her fancy was in desiring to be so called. She answered without moving, otherwise than as the arm I twined about her may have brought her blue eyes nearer to me:

"I don't mean, you silly fellow, that you should use the name instead of Dora. I only mean that you should think of me that way. When you are going to be angry with me, say to yourself, 'it's only my child-wife!' When I am very disappointing, say, 'I knew, a long time ago, that she would make but a child-wife!' When you miss

what I should like to be, and I think can never be, say, 'still my
foolish child-wife loves me!' For indeed I do."

By now David is working hard at trying to become a writer—yet
another of Dickens's nakedly autobiographical references—and
though happy if exasperated by the domestic cluelessness of his
child-wife he is equally ill-suited at house-keeping, a fact also
true of a succession of either thieving or simply incompetent staff
that they take on.

After a couple of years or so of marriage Dora becomes
pregnant. However she suffers a miscarriage after which her
health goes into a steady and serious decline and it becomes clear
that she will not survive. At the very last Dora, who throughout
has been silly, vain, shallow, flippant, both child-like and childish,
develops some self-awareness:

> "I am going to speak to you, Doady. I am going to say something
> I have often thought of saying, lately. You won't mind?" with a
> gentle look.
> "Mind, my darling?"
> "Because I don't know what you will think, or what you may
> have thought sometimes. Perhaps you have often thought the
> same. Doady, dear, I am afraid I was too young."
> I lay my face upon the pillow by her, and she looks into my eyes,
> and speaks very softly. Gradually, as she goes on, I feel, with a
> stricken heart, that she is speaking of herself as past.
> "I am afraid, dear, I was too young. I don't mean in years only,
> but in experience, and thoughts, and everything. I was such a silly
> little creature! I am afraid it would have been better, if we had
> only loved each other as a boy and girl, and forgotten it. I have
> begun to think I was not fit to be a wife."

I try to stay my tears, and to reply, "Oh, Dora, love, as fit as I to be a husband!"

"I don't know," with the old shake of her curls. "Perhaps! But if I had been more fit to be married I might have made you more so, too. Besides, you are very clever, and I never was."

"We have been very happy, my sweet Dora."

"I was very happy, very. But, as years went on, my dear boy would have wearied of his child-wife. She would have been less and less a companion for him. He would have been more and more sensible of what was wanting in his home. She wouldn't have improved. It is better as it is."

"Oh, Dora, dearest, dearest, do not speak to me so. Every word seems a reproach!"

"No, not a syllable!" she answers, kissing me. "Oh, my dear, you never deserved it, and I loved you far too well to say a reproachful word to you, in earnest—it was all the merit I had, except being pretty—or you thought me so . . . Oh, Doady, after more years, you never could have loved your child-wife better than you do; and, after more years, she would so have tried and disappointed you, that you might not have been able to love her half so well! I know I was too young and foolish. It is much better as it is!"

. . .

The bright moon is high and clear. As I look out on the night, my tears fall fast, and my undisciplined heart is chastened heavily—heavily.

I sit down by the fire, thinking with a blind remorse of all those secret feelings I have nourished since my marriage. I think of every little trifle between me and Dora, and feel the truth, that trifles make the sum of life. Ever rising from the sea of my remembrance, is the image of the dear child as I knew her first, graced by my young love, and by her own, with every fascination wherein such love is rich. Would it, indeed, have been better if we had loved each other as a boy and a girl, and forgotten it? Undisciplined heart, reply!

How the time wears, I know not; until I am recalled by my child-wife's old companion [that is, Jip the dog]. More restless than he was, he crawls out of his house, and looks at me, and wanders to the door, and whines to go upstairs.

"Not tonight, Jip! Not tonight!"

He comes very slowly back to me, licks my hand, and lifts his dim eyes to my face.

"Oh, Jip! It may be, never again!"

He lies down at my feet, stretches himself out as if to sleep, and with a plaintive cry, is dead.

> "Oh, Agnes! Look, look, here!"—That face, so full of pity, and of
> grief, that rain of tears, that awful mute appeal to me, that solemn
> hand upraised towards Heaven!
> "Agnes?"
> It is over. Darkness comes before my eyes; and, for a time, all
> things are blotted out of my remembrance.

Dora, the child-woman, is dead. The real, live, flesh-and-blood Maria was still very much alive however but was just a distant and beautiful memory: gone from his life long ago and, it would seem, for ever. This was how things stood when the final double issue of *David Copperfield* was published in November 1850.

And then, over four years later, on Friday the 9th of February 1855, two days after his forty-third birthday and on the eve of a trip to Paris with his friend and fellow novelist Wilkie Collins, Dickens received a letter.

## IV

There was nothing remotely unusual about this in itself. Quite the opposite: Dickens was a tireless correspondent who was used to receiving and sending umpteen letters every day of his life. He had set the stack of letters to one side and had tried to read a book, but perplexingly he found his mind wandering again and again back to the past, to his first love Maria Beadnell especially, without at first being conscious why. He looked again at the scattering of envelopes by his side: what must have made his heart skip a beat as he sat by the fire that evening with that day's pile of correspondence was the sight of the handwriting on one particular envelope—a once very familiar handwriting, the script of someone from his distant and seemingly dead past which he now recognised. It was a letter from Maria Beadnell.

Out of the blue, after almost twenty-two years of separation, Maria had contacted him again in a letter which, in Peter Ackroyd's words, opened the floodgates of his past. How she knew where to write to him we cannot be quite sure. Maria's letters have not survived so we do not know exactly what she said and perhaps most intriguingly of all we can't know why she decided to resume contact with him again after so long. Dickens left behind more than 14,000 letters but we know that he destroyed a huge amount of his correspondence, especially that of a personal nature. On the 3rd of September 1860, as Dickens was in the process of moving from Tavistock House to Gad's Hill Place in Rochester, he decided to make a bonfire in a field at the back of the new house of all those private papers he wished to see destroyed. To William Henry Wills, sub-editor of *Household Words*, he wrote the following day: "Yesterday I burnt, in the field at Gad's Hill, the accumulated letters and papers of twenty years. They set up a smoke like the genie when he got out of the casket on the seashore; and as it was an exquisite day when I began, and rained very heavily when I finished, I suspect my correspondence of having overcast the face of the heavens." Some of his children helped him to carry basket after basket of letters and other papers from the house to the pyre, consigning everything to the flames. A few years later Dickens explained his rationale for such a conflagration. In December 1864 he wrote to the Dean of Rochester: "A year or two ago, shocked by the misuse of private letters of public men, which I constantly observed, I destroyed a very large and very rare mass of correspondence. It was not done without pain, you may believe, but, the first reluctance conquered, I have steadily abided by my determination to keep no letters by me, and to consign all such papers to the fire." The following year he told his friend, the actor William Charles Macready: "Daily seeing improper uses made of confidential letters in the addressing of them to a public audience that have no business with them, I made not long ago a great fire in my field at Gad's Hill, and burnt every letter I possessed. And now I always destroy every letter I receive not on absolute business, and my mind is so far at ease." Clearly Dickens felt that he had letters that he didn't want to see fall into other hands after his death, areas of his life that he wanted to hide from posterity. He had periodic purgings of this kind for the remaining decade of his life. In 1869, a year before his death, he again told Wills: "I have had a great burning of papers in your room—have destroyed everything not wanted." It's as good as certain that Maria's letters to him were among the victims of one such holocaust. That Dickens's letters to Maria—which of course he could not destroy—continued to be a source of distinct unease to those family members who survived him can be ascertained by the fact that in the early years of the twentieth century, well over three decades after Dickens's death, his sister-in-law Georgina Hogarth (who had been the editor of Dickens's selected letters published in several volumes in the early 1880s) successfully vetoed the publication of them in England, though she failed to suppress them in the United States:

> It was to be expected that Georgina would hold inviolable any details about Dickens's early romance with Maria Beadnell . . . What consternation, therefore, when in 1908 his letters to Maria appeared in an unauthorized publication by the Boston Bibliophile Society! In 1905, almost twenty years after Maria's death, her daughter Ella had sold the precious packet of correspondence tied up with a faded blue ribbon. Shocked by the printing of these intimate and tender missives, Georgina, with the concurrence of Harry, banned the Boston publication in England. But one copy passed the customs and came into the hands of B. W. Matz, then editor of the *Dickensian*, who could not understand why Georgina had always opposed his use of any letter to Maria in his journal. Even her name had been taboo. After he had shown Georgina his copy of the Boston book, she privately recorded her recollections of Maria and her husband. This note ultimately found its way into print when at long last the Beadnell letters were brought out in an English edition in 1934, seventeen years after Georgina's death.[15]

But this is to anticipate. Dickens's responses to Maria do survive and we do know what he said by way of reply to Maria's letters.

The following day he sat down and penned the following missive:

My Dear Mrs Winter—
                    I constantly receive hundreds of letters in great varieties of writing, all perfectly strange to me, and (as you may suppose) have no particular interest in the faces of such general epistles. As I was reading by my fire last night, a handful of notes was laid down on my table. I looked them over, and, recognising the writing of no private friend, let them lie there and went back to my book. But I found my mind curiously disturbed, and wandering away through so many years to such early times of my life, that I was quite perplexed to account for it. There was nothing in what I had been reading, or immediately thinking about, to awaken such a train of thought, and at last it came into my head that it must have been suggested by something in the look of one of those letters. So I turned them over again—and suddenly the remembrance of your hand came upon me with an influence that I cannot express to you. Three or four and twenty years vanished like a dream, and I opened it with the touch of my young friend David Copperfield when he was in love.

There was something so busy and so pleasant in your letter—so true and cheerful and frank and affectionate—that I read on with perfect delight until I came to your mention of your two little girls. In the unsettled state of my thoughts, the existence of these dear children appeared such a prodigious phenomenon, that I was inclined to suspect myself of being out of my mind, until it occurred to me, that perhaps I had nine children of my own! Then the three or four and twenty years began to rearrange themselves in a long procession between me and the changeless Past, and I could not help considering what strange stuff all our little stories are made of.

Believe me, you cannot more tenderly remember our old days and our old friends than I do. I hardly ever go into the City but I walk up an odd little court at the back of the Mansion House and come out by the corner of Lombard Street. Hundreds of times as I have passed the church there—on my way to and from the Sea, the Continent, and where not—I invariably associate it with somebody (God knows who) having told me that poor Anne [Maria's sister] was buried there. If you would like to examine me in the name of a good-looking Cornish servant you used to have (I suppose she has twenty-nine great grandchildren now, and walks with a stick), you will find my knowledge on the point, correct, though it was a monstrous name too. I forget nothing of those times. They are just as still and plain and clear as if I had never been in a crowd since, and had never seen or heard my own name out of my own house. What should I be worth, or what would labour and success be worth, if it were otherwise!

Your letter is more touching to me from its good and gentle associations with the state of Spring in which I was either much more wise or much more foolish than I am now—I never know which to think it—than I could tell you if I tried for a week. I will not try at all. I heartily respond to it, and shall be charmed to have a long talk with you, and most cordially glad to see you after all this length of time.

I am going to Paris to-morrow morning, but I propose being back within a fortnight. When I return, Mrs Dickens will come to you, to arrange a day for our seeing you and Mr Winter (to whom I beg to be remembered) quietly to dinner. We will have no intruder or foreign creature on any pretence whatever, in order that we may set in without any restraint for a tremendous gossip.

Mary Anne Leigh we saw at Broadstairs about fifty years ago. Mrs Dickens and her sister, who read all the marriages in the papers, shrieked to me when the announcement of hers appeared, what did I think of *that*? I calmly replied that I thought it was time. I should have been more excited if I had known of the old gentleman with seven thousand a year, uncountable grown-up children, and no English grammar.

My mother has a strong objection to being considered in the least old, and usually appears here on Christmas Day in a juvenile cap which takes an immense time in the putting on. The Fates seem to have made up their minds that I shall never see your Father when he comes this way. David Lloyd is altogether an imposter—not having in the least changed (that I could make out when I saw him at the London Tavern) since what I suppose to have been the year 1770, when I found you three on Cornhill, with your poor mother, going to St Mary Axe to order mysterious dresses—which afterwards turned out to be wedding garments. That was in the remote period when you all wore green cloaks, cut (in my remembrance) very round, and which I am resolved to believe were made of Merino. I escorted you with native gallantry to the Dress Maker's door, and your mother, seized with an apprehension—groundless upon my honour—that I might come in, said emphatically: 'And now, Mr Dickin' [*sic*]—which she always used to call me—'We'll wish *you* good morning.'

When I was writing the word Paris just now, I remembered that my existence was once entirely uprooted and my whole Being blighted by the Angel of my soul being sent there to finish her education! If I can discharge any little commission for you, or bring home anything for the darlings, whom I cannot yet believe to be anything but a delusion of yours, pray employ me. I shall be at the Hotel Meurice—locked up when within, as my only defence against my country and the United States—but a most punctual and reliable functionary, if you will give me any employment.

My Dear Mrs Winter, I have been much moved by your letter; and the pleasure it has given me has some little sorrowful ingredient in it. In the strife and struggle of this great world where most of us lose each other so strangely, it is impossible to be spoken to out of the old times without a softened emotion. You so belong to the days when the qualities that have done me most good since, were growing in my boyish heart that I cannot end my answer to you lightly. The associations my memory has with you made your letter more—I want a word—invest it with a more immediate address to me than such a letter could have from anybody else. Mr Winter will not mind that. We are all sailing away to the sea, and have a pleasure in thinking of the river we are upon, when it was very narrow and little.

Faithfully your friend,
Charles Dickens

Maria Beadnell, she had explained, was now Maria Winter. She had married Henry Louis Winter, the manager of a saw mill in Finsbury, on the 25th of February 1845 and as Dickens's reply reveals now had two daughters.

Dickens very likely already knew that Maria had married. In point of fact Dickens had not entirely lost all contact with the Beadnell family: he had kept up a sporadic correspondence with George Beadnell on and off ever since the end of his and Maria's romance which suggests that, whatever had happened all those years earlier, Maria's father had not harboured entirely negative feelings about him. It's improbable that Dickens had not heard about Maria's marriage from her own father as well as elsewhere. It's true that there is no explicit mention of it in any surviving correspondence but it beggars belief that old Mr Beadnell would have omitted to tell Dickens about his daughter's marriage or that he had not heard about it by other means. Additionally Dickens's sister Letitia and her husband Henry Austin remained on friendly terms with the Beadnells. By both of these routes, not to mention others, it's entirely possible that Dickens may have picked up here and there on the odd snippet of Maria's activities and her life including the facts of her marriage and subsequent children.

In 1906 Georgina Hogarth would claim that she, Catherine and Dickens had been guests of Maria and her husband not long after she, Maria, married. The three of them, she said, went to have "Tea and Supper with Mr and Mrs Winter who were living in Finsbury Crescent soon after their marriage"; Georgina went on to allege that in the carriage on the way home Dickens laughed about the callow earnestness of his ardent love for someone of whom Georgina would say "*I* could not see a trace even of the prettiness which seemed to have been her only attraction . . . [she was] a kind good natured woman but *fearfully* silly!!" But there is no firm evidence of this encounter at all, no way of corroborating it elsewhere and, as will be detailed below, there are good reasons to believe that this alleged encounter never took place. It is a curious anomaly but one can only conclude that Georgina was perhaps confused on specifics, dates especially. It is an odd claim to have made since if such a meeting really took place both Dickens and Maria themselves would surely have referred to it in their letters of 1855: in actuality Dickens stresses how long it had been since they were last in touch, even overestimating it by a year or two. Michael Slater takes the view that the meeting probably did happen but that "for all his merriment on the homeward journey, Dickens found purely social contact with this woman who had so strongly bewitched his younger self just too disturbing and so allowed it to 'die out'." Slater holds this view for two reasons: firstly that in one of his letters Dickens begged to be remembered to Mr Winter "which surely suggests that he had met him at least once," and secondly, ". . . what conceivable reason could Georgina have had to invent this anecdote?" Both points have force but are not in my opinion particularly compelling let alone persuasive. We do not need to accuse Georgina of conscious fabrication: in 1906 she was almost eighty years old—hazy memory about specific dates is surely a more likely explanation than the construction of a deliberate fiction. Slater himself goes so far as to allow that Georgina's recollection was "rather confused." If this encounter never happened, and in my opinion all indications are on balance against it, we have to conclude that before the letter that Dickens opened that Friday evening in February 1855 he and Maria had had no direct contact for very close to twenty-two years. His letters certainly read as such.

Maria's motivation in contacting Dickens again after twenty-two years is unknown. Her letters, as we've seen, do not survive so if she ever explained herself that confidence unfortunately has been lost. Nor does Dickens refer to it in any of his letters, so we cannot say with any certainty. Obviously in the intervening two decades the balance of their lives had shifted: rather than the hopeful but impecunious young parliamentary reporter that she had known so long before Dickens was now the most famous and best-loved writer in the English language, beloved and feted not only in the Anglophone world but also in countries where his works were known in translation, such as France. Dickens was, in short, all but a superstar as we would say now. By contrast Maria had settled down into quietly respectable married domesticity and obscurity.

Maria's letter had come out of nowhere at a turbulent and unhappy time in Dickens's private life. "Poor unsuspecting Maria," writes Michael Slater, "could hardly have chosen for her re-entry into his life a moment when his feelings were in a more combustible state."[16] Dickens's letters to his best friend and closest confidant John Forster of this time—the winter of 1854-5—are replete with expressions of his harried, careworn misery. "Am altogether in a dishevelled state of mind," he told Forster: "—motes of new books in the dirty air, miseries of older growth threatening to close upon me. Why is it, that as with poor David [Copperfield], a sense comes always crushing on me now, when I fall into low spirits, as of one happiness I have missed in life, and one friend and companion I have never made?" "*Restlessness*, you will say," he observed in another letter. "Whatever it is, it is always driving me, and I cannot help it. I have rested nine or ten weeks, and sometimes feel as if it had been a year—though I had the strangest nervous miseries before I stopped. If I couldn't walk fast and far, I should just explode and perish." Escape was on Dickens's mind, escape of a drastic nature: "I have had dreadful thoughts," he confessed, "of getting away somewhere altogether by myself . . . of living for half a year or so, in all sorts of inaccessible places." And again: "I have always felt that I must, please God, die in harness . . . However strange it is never to be at rest, and ever trying after something that is never reached, and always to be laden with plot and plan and care and worry, how clear it is that it must be, and that one is driven by an irresistible might until the journey is worked out . . . As to repose—for some men there's no such thing in this life." This mood goes some way toward explaining why Dickens reacted as he did to Maria, especially in the first three of the longest, most impassioned and most nakedly tender and personal letters sent before they met face-to-face for the first time in over twenty years.

Mrs Winter sent another letter but in his reply Dickens addressed her not by her formal title but as Maria—a very swift and rather telling shift of intimacy. "Clearly it was sent to a secret address," says Peter Ackroyd, "or sent privately to her by some other means, because only two days later he was addressing a perfectly discreet letter to 'My Dear Mrs Winter'; in other words, he was writing her a letter which could be shown to her husband without embarrassment."[17] The implication is clear: Dickens was already effectively writing two different sets of letters for two different pairs of eyes—'My Dear Mrs Winter' for those of her husband in case he should see them by accident or by design and 'Maria' purely for her own—which at least suggests that something more than a purely friendly association may already have been at the back of his mind.

That said, Dickens's ultimate intentions are far from easy to discern. In his biography Fred Kaplan is quite definite that Dickens was keen on building a purely platonic friendship with Maria and entertained no desire at all to rekindle any kind of romance. Ostensibly this seems to be borne out by the fact that

Dickens explicitly brought Catherine into the picture from the off: she is mentioned even in Dickens's first reply to Maria, for instance ("Mrs Dickens will come to you, to arrange a day for our seeing you") and the tone is light-hearted and chatty ("We will have no intruder or foreign creature on any pretence whatever, in order that we may set in without any restraint for a tremendous gossip"). For all that, his behaviour is in some respects contradictory: it was not entirely true, as Kaplan has it, that "their meetings would have to be public and mediated." In fact in the letter of the 22nd of February (reproduced below) Dickens makes it clear that he wants to meet Maria alone for the first time before the more formal meeting with their respective spouses. "Who knows what airy castles were building in Dickens's mind?" ponders Michael Slater. Who knows indeed.

Dickens and Collins crossed the Channel to Paris. On the 15th Dickens wrote to Maria another very long, intimate if not downright flirtatious letter from the Hôtel Meurice. Something unspoken, indeed unknown but clearly profound happened to Dickens in the five days between his first reply and his second, something which can only be associated with his memories of his youthful love for Maria: the floodgates of the past are now wide open and from the very first sentence it is clear that Dickens's intimacy is deepening:

My Dear Mrs Winter—
(I had half a mind when I dipped the pen in the ink, to address you by your old natural Christian name).

The snow lies so deep on the Northern Railway, and the Posts have been so interrupted in consequence, that your charming note arrived here only this morning. I reply by return of post—with a general idea that Sarah [possibly a servant of the Beadnells'] will come to Finsbury Place with a basket and a face of good-humoured compassion, and carry the letter away, and leave me as desolate as she used to do.

I get the heartache again when I read your commission, written in the hand which I find now to be not in the least changed, and yet it is a great pleasure to be entrusted with it, and to have that share in your gentler remembrances which I cannot find it still my privilege to have, without a stirring of the old fancies. I need not tell you that it shall be executed to the letter—with as much interest as I once matched a little pair of gloves for you which I recollect were blue ones. (I wonder whether people generally wore blue gloves when I was nineteen, or whether it was only you!). I am very very sorry you mistrusted me in not writing before your little girl was born [in 1846]; but I hope now you know me better you will teach her, one day, to tell her children, in times to come when they may have some interest in wondering about it, that I loved her mother with the most extraordinary earnestness when I was a boy.

I have always believed since, and always shall to the last, that there never was such a faithful and devoted poor fellow as I was. Whatever of fancy, romance, energy, passion, aspiration and determination belong to me, I never have separated and never shall separate from the hard hearted little woman—you—whom it is nothing to say I would have died for, with the greatest alacrity! I can never think, and I never seem to observe, that other young people are in such desperate earnest, or set so much, so long, upon absorbing one hope. It is a matter of perfect certainty to me that I began to fight my way out of poverty and obscurity, with one perpetual idea of you. This is so fixed in my knowledge that to the hour when I opened your letter last Friday night, I have never heard anybody addressed by your name, or spoken of by your name, without a start. The sound of it has always filled me with a kind of pity and respect for the deep truth that I had, in my silly hobbledehoyhood, to bestow upon one creature who represented the whole world to me. I have never been so good a man since, as I was when you made me wretchedly happy. I shall never be half so good a fellow any more.

This is all so strange now both to think of, and to say, after every change that has come about; but I think, when you ask me to write to you, you are not unprepared for what it is so natural to me to recall, and will not be displeased to read it. I fancy,—though you may not have thought in the old time how manfully I loved you—that you may have seen in one of my books a faithful reflection of the passion I had for you, and may have thought that it was something to have been loved so well, and may have seen in little bits of 'Dora' touches of your old self sometimes, and a grace here and there that may be revived in your little girls, years hence, for the bewilderment of some other young lover—though he will never be as terribly in earnest as I and David Copperfield were. People used to say to me how pretty all that was, and how fanciful it was, and how elevated it was above the little foolish loves of very young men and women. But they little thought what reason I had to know it was true and nothing more nor less.

These are things that I have locked up in my own breast, and that I never thought to bring out any more. But when I find myself writing to you again 'all to yourself', how can I forbear to let as much light in upon them as will shew you that they are there still! If the most innocent, the most ardent, and the most disinterested days of my life had you for their Sun—as indeed they had—and if I know that the Dream I lived in did me good, refined my heart, and made me patient and persevering, and if the Dream were all of you—as God knows it was—how can I receive a confidence from you, and return it, and make a feint of blotting all this out!

As I have said, I fancy that you know all about it quite as well as I do, however. I have a strong belief—there is no harm in adding hope to that—that perhaps you have once or twice laid down that book, and thought, 'How dearly that boy must have loved me, and how vividly this man remembers it!'

I shall be here until Tuesday or Wednesday. If the snow allows this letter to come to you in the meantime, perhaps it would allow one to come to me, 'all to myself,' if you were to try it. A number of recollections came into my head when I began, and I meant to have gone through a string of them and to have asked you if they lived in your mind too. But they all belong to the one I have indulged in—half pleasantly, half painfully—and are all swallowed up in that, so let them go.

My dear Mrs. Winter,
Ever affectionately yours,
Charles Dickens


P. S. I wonder what has become of a bundle of letters I sent you back once (according to order) tied with a blue ribbon, of the colour of the gloves!

Dickens and Collins had originally floated the idea of making a trip to Bordeaux but this plan soon fell by the wayside: Michael Slater makes the by no means improbable claim that Dickens's impatience to get back to England to see Maria may have been partly or even largely responsible. Dickens and Collins left Paris on Tuesday the 20th of February. On the 22nd Dickens, safely back in England and at Tavistock House once more, wrote another long and noticeably even more heartfelt letter, in keeping with the increasingly ardent tone of the correspondence with each passing missive. Though Maria's letters are no longer thought to exist we can see at least some of her comments reflected in Dickens's responses:

> My dear Maria,—
>
> The old writing is so plain to *me* that I have read your letter with great ease (though it is just a little crossed), and have not lost a word of it. I was obliged to leave Paris on Tuesday morning before the Post came in; but I took such precautions to prevent the possibility of any mischance, that the letter came close behind me. I arrived at home last night, and it followed me this morning. No one but myself has the slightest knowledge of my correspondence, I may add, in this place. I could be nowhere addressed with stricter privacy or in more absolute confidence than at my own house.
>
> Ah! Though it is so late to read in the old hand what I never read before, I have read it with great emotion, and with the old tenderness softened to a more sorrowful remembrance than I could easily tell you. How it all happened as it did, we shall never know on this side of Time; but if you had ever told me then what you tell me now, I know myself well enough to be thoroughly assured that the simple truth and energy which were in my love would have overcome everything. I remember well that long after

I came of age—I say long; well! It seemed long then—I wrote to you for the last time of all, with a dawn upon me of some sensible idea that we were changing into man and woman, saying would you forget our little differences and separations and let us begin again? You answered me very coldly and reproachfully,—and so I went my way.

But nobody can ever know with what a sad heart I resigned you, or after what struggles and what a conflict. My entire devotion to you, and the wasted tenderness of those hard years which I have ever since half loved, half dreaded to recall, made so deep an impression on me that I refer to it a habit of suppression which now belongs to me, which I know is no part of my original nature, but which makes me chary of showing my affections, even to my children, except when they are very young. A few years ago (just before Copperfield) I began to write my life, intending the manuscript to be found among my papers when its subject should be concluded. But as I began to approach within sight of that part of it, I lost courage and burned the rest. I have never blamed you at all, but I have believed until now that you never had the stake in that serious game which I had.

All this mist passes away upon your earnest words; and when I find myself to have been in your mind at that thoughtful crisis in your life which you so unaffectedly and feelingly describe, I am quite subdued and strangely enlightened. When poor Fanny died (I think she always knew that I never could bear to hear of you as of any common person) we were out of town, and I never heard of your having been in Devonshire Terrace—least of all in my room! I never heard of you in association with that time until I read your letter to-day. I could not, however,—really could not—at any time within these nineteen years, have been so unmindful of my old truth, and have so set my old passion aside, as to talk to you like a person in any ordinary relation towards me. And this I think is the main reason on my side why the few opportunities that there have been of our seeing one another again have died out.

All this again you have changed and set right—at once so courageously, so delicately and gently, that you open the way to a confidence between us which still once more, in perfect innocence and good faith, may be between ourselves alone. All that you propose, I accept with my whole heart. Whom can you ever trust if it be not your old lover! Lady Olliffe asked me in Paris the other day (we are, in our way, confidential you must know) whether it was really true that I used to love Maria Beadnell so very, very, very much? I told her that there was no woman in the world, and there were very few men, who could ever imagine how much.

You are always the same in my remembrance. When you say you are 'toothless, fat, old, and ugly' (which I don't believe), I fly away to the house in Lombard Street, which is pulled down, as if it were necessary that the very bricks and mortar should go the way of my airy castles, and see you in a sort of raspberry coloured dress with a little black trimming at the top—black velvet it seems to be made of—cut into Vandykes—an immense number of Vandykes—with my boyish heart pinned like a captured butterfly on every one of them. I have never seen a girl play the harp, from that day to this, but my attention has been instantly arrested, and that drawing room has stood before me so plainly that I could write a most accurate description of it. I remember that there used to be a tendency in your eyebrows to join together; and sometimes in the most unlikely places—in Scotland, America, Italy—on the stateliest occasions and the most unceremonious—when I have been talking to a strange face and have observed even such a slight association as this in it, I have suddenly been carried away at the rate of a thousand miles a second, and have thought 'Maria Beadnell!' When we were falling off from each other, I came from the House of Commons many a night at two or three o'clock in the morning, only to wander past the place you were asleep in. And I have gone over that ground within these twelve months, hoping it was not ungrateful to consider whether any reputation the world can bestow is repayment to a man for the loss of such a vision of his youth as mine. You ask me to treasure what you tell me, in my heart of hearts. O see what I have cherished there, through all this time and all these changes!

In the course of Saturday I will write to you at Artillery Place, sending the little brooches and telling you when Catherine will come—not forgetting the little niece, though I don't expect her to remind me of Somebody or Anybody. And now to what I have reserved for the last.

I am a dangerous man to be seen with, for so many people know me. At St. Paul's, the Dean and the whole chapter know me. In Paternoster Row of all places, the very tiles and chimney pots know me. At first, I a little hesitated whether or no to advise you to forego that interview or suggest another—principally because what would be very natural and probable a fortnight hence, seems scarcely so probable now. Still I should very much like to see you before we meet when others are by—I feel it, as it were, so necessary to our being at ease—and unless I hear from you to the contrary, you may expect to encounter a stranger whom you may suspect to be the right person if he wears a moustache.

You would not like better to call here on Sunday, asking first
for Catherine and then for me? It is almost a positive certainty
that there will be no one here but I, between 3 and 4. I make this
suggestion, knowing what odd coincidences take place in streets
when they are not wanted to happen; though I know them to be
so unlikely, that I should not think of such a thing if any one but
you were concerned. If you think you would not like to come here,
make no change. I will come there.

I cannot trust myself to begin afresh, or I should have my
remembrances of our separation, and think yours hard to me.
I remember poor Anne writing to me once (in answer to some
burst of low-spirited madness of mine), and saying 'My dear
Charles, I really cannot understand Maria, or venture to take the
responsibility of saying what the state of her affections is'—and
she added, I recollect, God bless her, a long quotation about
Patience and Time. Well, well! It was not to be until Patience and
Time should bring us round together thus.

Remember, I accept all with my whole soul, and reciprocate all.
Ever your affectionate friend,
Charles Dickens

Dickens's indication that he wanted to meet up with Maria again
for the first time alone rather than in company indicates that there
may well have been things he wished to say to her that were for
her ears only. Once again, what those things may have been are
unknown and were locked up in Dickens's breast. Small wonder
that in George Pierce Baker's 1908 edition of the letters between
Dickens and Maria he wrote that this second letter must in Maria's
mind have read "very much like a love letter . . . Surely this seems
like dangerous ground and drifting rapidly away from the region
of calm, common-sense middle-age."[18]

Be that as it may Dickens and Maria finally met up again,
almost certainly for the first time in well over twenty years, at

some still unspecified time and place (not at Tavistock House; possibly at Maria's own home in Finsbury) between Thursday the 22nd of February and Saturday the 24th. Meeting up with someone not seen for twenty years previously can only ever be a memorable event, whether for good or ill: meeting up with an old flame, a former love whose embers never quite lost their heat, is momentous. Yet Dickens was aghast. Maria's description of herself as "toothless, fat, old and ugly" was, as far as he was concerned, entirely accurate—she (apparently to him) really *was* fat, old and ugly. (Not just in his eyes alone it would seem: Georgina later rather sniffily described Maria as having "become *very* fat! And quite commonplace"). The beautiful young woman Dickens had adored as a young man was, in his eyes at least, an overweight, blowsy middle-aged matron. The maiden's coquettish laugh which had been music in the young Dickens's ears was now the irritatingly silly giggle of a forty-something frump. There are hints from several different sources that she was known to have a fondness for the bottle and may even have made the first approach for that reason, writing her letter in an impulsive access of drink-sodden sentimentality and nostalgia: according to Thomas Wright's 1935 biography Dickens later quietly but firmly distanced himself from Maria at least partially because "Further acquaintance with Mrs Winter increased his disillusionment.

She drank brandy in her tea!" Decades later a nursemaid in the Winter household (quoted below) left a rather pathetic account of Mrs Winter's behaviour when in her cups. From the pathetic to the bathetic, according to some reports at the time of their meeting she had had a cold which Dickens promptly caught. The disparity between what Dickens might have hoped and expected to see in the present based on his memories of twenty-odd years past and what he actually found before him was terrible. "He clearly expected, at some level, that the Mrs Winter of now would be the Maria of yesterday," wrote one Dickens scholar, "and the visual evidence of his fatuity brought his dreams (whatever, precisely, they were) and the potential relationship to an abrupt, if not unkindly managed, conclusion."[19] In fact we do know what Dickens's dreams were for he had said so quite explicitly: "When you say you are 'toothless, fat, old, and ugly' (which I don't believe), I fly away to the house in Lombard Street, which is pulled down, as if it were necessary that the very bricks and mortar should go the way of my airy castles, and see you in a sort of raspberry coloured dress with a little black trimming at the top—black velvet it seems to be made of—cut into Vandykes—an immense number of Vandykes—with my boyish heart pinned like a captured butterfly on every one of them." Dickens expected a Maria who was, though twenty-two years older, still the beautiful pocket Venus in a raspberry coloured dress with black trimming: this she could not possibly be in reality, only in memory, and Dickens could not cope with the difference between the two. He cannot seriously have expected his first love to have remained unchanged in any way by the "toils of time, her lauded beauties carried off from her" (in Thomas Hardy's phrase) and one is forced to conclude that in many respects part of the reason why Dickens rejected Maria was the same as part of the reason why he rejected Catherine: both had lost their youthful beauty and slimness and had grown older and fatter. Catherine was described at this stage as still pretty but after ten children stout, just like Maria. In short, they had merely grown older with all that that entails for their physical appearance and Dickens seemed simply unable to cope with that ineluctable fact. The violence of Dickens's reaction alone would seem to disprove Georgina's account that she, her sister and Dickens had met the Winters some time after their marriage in 1845: if Dickens had seen Maria in 1845 and then again ten years later he cannot have been quite as shocked by any change in her appearance as might have been the case if he had not seen her at all between 1833 and 1855, on top of which we have Dickens's own words that when he opened her letter "three or four and twenty years vanished like a dream." It was actually twenty-two years—as we've already seen Dickens was apt to be somewhat slipshod with his dates in this manner—but if he had seen Maria ten years earlier he would most certainly have remembered it and would have said so: he would surely have written "ten years vanished like a dream." In any case the change in Maria was so shocking to Dickens that he resolved to break off any further association between them gently but decisively. Though the letters continued a little while longer they were for the most part limp and perfunctory efforts on his part and after their meeting they had nothing much more to do with each other again. This reflects badly on Dickens but he simply could not being himself to carry on an association. George Pierce Baker opined:

> The author does not expose himself to unfavourable comment . . . surely Dickens loses nothing from these letters, particularly the second set [i.e. the letters of 1855 and after]. Both sets are as human as the man always was, and in the end they are chivalrous and, as a whole, tactful. Reading them, one cannot respect Dickens less; rather one knows him better, seeing the kindliness and the deep regard he had for friendship, even when past, and how patient he was willing to be for its sake.[20]

Chivalrous and tactful, possibly: but surely Dickens *does* lose from these letters and loses much. In almost nothing else does Dickens come across as so shallow and superficial as he does in his turning away from the Maria of 1855, and in this regard he comes over as someone simply unable to accept with good grace the passage of time and the changes it effects in other people as the years and decades pass. Maria had given him fair notice that she had changed drastically in the intervening years: he had been fully forewarned. Even so Michael Slater claims that ". . . enough of the lost girl's appearance and demeanour survived, however altered, in the mature woman to move Dickens profoundly every time he set eyes on her."

However moved he may have been, Dickens's next letter to Maria after their first meeting in twenty-two years, written on the 10th of March, exhibits a subtle but very definite shift in tone. She is still addressed as 'My Dear Maria' but the letter is distinctly cooler and less effusive (not to mention very considerably shorter). Even though Dickens, in pointedly reminding her that "in writing to me, you write to no one else", is perhaps still inviting her to share confidences, the truly personal, soul-baring element of his first few letters is now absent, never to return. Although Maria clearly wishes to see Dickens again, that he says that he cannot guarantee that he will be at home as he may be on business certainly sounds like an excuse:

> My dear Maria,—
> Your letter was delivered here yesterday evening at half past seven. Being out, I did not receive it until I returned home at midnight. This answer is necessarily very short, for I have a fear that it may not reach you otherwise.
> I think we are pretty sure to be at home before three tomorrow. I cannot positively speak for myself, as I am one of a committee

on some public literary business, which may have to make an official representation some time tomorrow. I have undertaken to say what is necessary to be said, whenever the interview comes off; and it is not impossible (the matter pressing), that Sunday may be profaned for the purpose. I do not think it is very likely, however.

Your cold is a very well-disposed one, to improve in such weather, and it has my warmest commendation for being so good. I am so busy that I have not had time to consider whether I took it by sympathy on Wednesday evening—but I think I heard somebody sneezing at my desk half the day yesterday, who sounded Uke the incomparable author.

You make me smile when you picture to yourself how weak I might be, and what poor thoughts I might have, and in what unworthy lights it might be my spoiled nature to shew myself. With faults enough to answer for, I believe I have never been that kind of person for a day.

Little Ella shall hear from me on Monday.

In the ghostly unrest of going to begin a new book, my time is like one of the Spirits in Macbeth, and 'will not be commanded'— even by me.

You may be perfectly sure that in writing to me, you write to no one else.

Ever affectionately yours,

C. D.

The gaps between letters become longer; the next was written on the 3<sup>rd</sup> of April:

My dear Maria,—

Going down to Ashford this day week, already with a bad cold, I increased it so much by getting into the intense heat consequent upon a reading of three hours and then coming up in the night (which I was obliged to do, having business in town next morning), that I was very unwell all the week, and on Friday night was so completely knocked up that I came home at 9 o'clock to bed. A necessity is upon me now—as at most times— of wandering about in my own wild way, to think. I could no more resist this on Sunday or yesterday, than a man can dispense with food, or a horse can help himself from being driven. I hold my inventive capacity on the stern condition that it must master my whole life, often have complete possession of me, make its own demands upon me, and sometimes for months together put everything else away from me. If I had not known long ago that my place could never be held, unless I were at any moment ready to devote myself to it entirely, I should have dropped out of it very soon. All this I can hardly expect you to understand—or the restlessness and waywardness of an author's mind. You have never seen it before you, or lived with it, or had occasion to think or care about it, and you cannot have the necessary consideration for it. 'It is only half an hour'—'it is only an afternoon'—'it is only an evening'—people say to me over and over again—but they don't know that it is impossible to command one's self sometimes to any stipulated and set disposal of five minutes—or that the mere consciousness of an engagement will sometimes worry a whole day. These are the penalties paid for writing books. Whoever is devoted to an Art must be content to deliver himself wholly up to it, and to find his recompense in it. I am grieved if you suspect me of not wanting to see you, but I can't help it; I must go my way, whether or no.

I thought you would understand that, in sending the card for the box, I sent an assurance that there was nothing amiss. I am pleased to find that you were all so much interested with the play. My ladies say that the first part is too painful and wants relief. I have been going to see it a dozen times, but have never seen it yet, and never may. Madame Celeste is injured thereby (you see how unreasonable people are!) and says in the Green Room, with a very tight cheek, '*M. Dickens est artiste! Mais il n'a jamais vu Janet Pride!*'

It is like a breath of fresh spring air to know that that unfortunate baby of yours is out of her one close room and has about half a pint of very doubtful air per day. I could only have become her godfather on the condition that she had 500 gallons of open air at any rate, every day of her life. And you would soon see a rose or two in the face of my other little friend, Ella, if you opened all your doors and windows throughout the whole of all fine weather, from morning to night.

I am going off, I don't know where or how far, to ponder about I don't know what. Sometimes I am half in the mood to set off for France, sometimes I think I will go and walk about on the sea shore for three of four months, sometimes I look towards the Pyrenees, sometimes Switzerland. I made a compact with a great Spanish authority last week, and vowed I would go to Spain. Two days afterwards Layard and I agreed to go to Constantinople when Parliament rises. To-morrow I shall probably discuss with somebody else, the idea of going to Greenland or the North Pole. The end of all this, most likely, will be that I shall shut myself up

in some out of the way place I have never yet thought of, and go
desperately to work there.

Once upon a time I didn't do such things, you say. No, but I
have done them through a good many years now, and they have
become myself and my life.

Ever affectionately,

C. D.

Dickens's surprisingly blunt "I am grieved if you suspect me of not
wanting to see you, but I can't help it; I must go my way, whether
or no" indicates that Maria must have made some comment
to that effect. "This letter," wrote George Pierce Baker, "shows
even more clearly than its predecessor the completely changed
attitude of Dickens toward Mrs. Winter. This is the writing of a
man in whom all ardency of feeling for the person addressed is
forever dead, but who yet wishes to remain on terms of pleasant
and even of intimate acquaintanceship, provided the intimacy
is not exacting."[21] Dickens signed himself "Yours affectionately"
and there is no reason to think that this affection was anything
other than unfeigned, but however genuine it may have been it
seemed to be cooling rapidly. The next letter on the 11th of June is
little more than a perfunctory note:

My dear Maria,—

I answered your last letter, but one, almost as
soon as I received it, to let you know that I should be out of town
that Sunday, and for several Sundays in succession. This note of
mine must have gone astray somehow or somewhere, for I posted
it myself. It has happened on a former occasion—but only on

one—that a letter of mine failed to reach its destination. How this comes to be missing, I cannot comprehend.

Your account of your poor little child is distressing indeed, and makes me heartily sorry for your fatigues and anxieties. I have never had any faith in the homoeopathic system and therefore have never tried it. I am inclined to think that it is principally successful with people who have nothing the matter with them, and that active diseases where there is a vigorous action for evil going on, require more decided remedies. Still, it is indubitably successful m some violent cases even.

I shall be very happy to receive your little token of remembrance, when you have less care on your mind, and have set your baby up—as I hope and trust you soon will—twenty times stronger than before. Take care of your baby's mother, and God bless her.

Ever faithfully yours,
C. D.

But tragedy was about to befall Maria. Her child did not get better but died. Dickens, who had been devastated by the death of his own daughter just a few years previously, wrote to her on the 13th of June:

My dear Mrs. Winter,—

I am truly grieved to hear of your affliction in the loss of your darling baby. But if you be not, even already, so reconciled to the parting from that innocent child for a little while, as to bear it gently and with a softened sorrow, I know that that not unhappy state of mind must soon arise. The death of infants is a release from so much chance and change—from so many casualties and distresses—and is a thing so beautiful in its serenity and peace—that it should not be a bitterness, even in a mother's heart. The simplest and most affecting passage in all the noble history of our Great Master, is his consideration for little children. And in reference to yours, as many millions of bereaved mothers poor and rich will do in reference to theirs until the end of time, you may take the comfort of the gracious words "And he took a child, and set it in the midst of them."

In a book by one of the greatest English writers [Henry Fielding], called *A Journey from this World to the Next* [1834], a parent comes to the distant country beyond the grave, and finds the little girl he had lost so long ago, engaged in building a bower to receive him in, when his aged steps should bring him there at last. He is filled with joy to see her—so young—so bright—so full of promise—and is enraptured to think that she never was old, wan, tearful, withered. This is always one of the sources of consolation in the deaths of children. With no effort of the fancy, with nothing to undo, you will always be able to think of the pretty creature you have lost, as a child in Heaven.

A poor little baby of mine lies in Highgate Cemetery—and I laid her, just as you think of laying yours, in the catacombs there, until I made a resting-place for all of us in the free air.

It is better that I should not come to see you. I feel quite sure of that, and will think of you instead.

God bless and comfort you! Mrs Dickens and her sister send their kindest condolences to yourself and Mr Winter. I add mine with all my heart.

Affectionately your friend
Charles Dickens

Dickens's first (and to at least one biographer, greatest) love had contacted him again after well over twenty years: a brief but passionate flurry of letters ensued: yet upon their first meeting in two decades Dickens was horrified by the ravages—to him at least—that time had wrought in his former sweetheart. Inevitably Dickens did what he had always done: he turned the experience into copy and turned Maria Winter as she now was into the faded, fat, faintly absurd and in some respects rather pathetic Flora Finching in *Little Dorrit*, his eleventh novel published in instalments between 1855 and 1857. Arthur Clennam and Flora Casby had been childhood sweethearts but due to circumstances beyond their control their romance was broken off, after which

Arthur went to China for twenty years with his father. Following his father's death Arthur returns to London to see his mother; in the capital he is reacquainted with Flora, the sweetheart he had loved and lost so many years before. Flora is now a widow: she had married a Mr Finching who subsequently died. The change in her after twenty years or more is a shocking one:

The return of Mr Casby with his daughter Flora, put an end to these meditations. Clennam's eyes no sooner fell upon the subject of his old passion than it shivered and broke to pieces.

Most men will be found sufficiently true to themselves to be true to an old idea. It is no proof of an inconstant mind, but exactly the opposite, when the idea will not bear close comparison with the reality, and the contrast is a fatal shock to it. Such was Clennam's case. In his youth he had ardently loved this woman, and had heaped upon her all the locked-up wealth of his affection and imagination. That wealth had been, in his desert home, like Robinson Crusoe's money; exchangeable with no one, lying idle in the dark to rust, until he poured it out for her. Ever since that memorable time, though he had, until the night of his arrival, as completely dismissed her from any association with his Present or Future as if she had been dead (which she might easily have been for anything he knew), he had kept the old fancy of the Past unchanged, in its old sacred place . . .

Flora, always tall, had grown to be very broad too, and short of breath; but that was not much. Flora, whom he had left a lily, had become a peony; but that was not much. Flora, who had seemed enchanting in all she said and thought, was diffuse and silly. That was much. Flora, who had been spoiled and artless long ago, was determined to be spoiled and artless now. That was a fatal blow.

This is Flora!

'I am sure,' giggled Flora, tossing her head with a caricature of her girlish manner, such as a mummer might have presented at her own funeral, if she had lived and died in classical antiquity, 'I am ashamed to see Mr Clennam, I am a mere fright, I know he'll find me fearfully changed, I am actually an old woman, it's shocking to be found out, it's really shocking!'

He assured her that she was just what he had expected and that time had not stood still with himself.

'Oh! But with a gentleman it's so different and really you look so amazingly well that you have no right to say anything of the kind, while, as to me, you know—oh!' cried Flora with a little scream, 'I am dreadful!'

"Was it possible," Arthur wonders, "that Flora could have been such a chatterer in the days she referred to? Could there have been anything like her present disjointed volubility in the fascinations that had captivated him?" In spite of his shock Arthur politely pretends that she has barely changed at all in the intervening years, a dismal subterfuge enacted without conviction that Flora sees through at once:

'My dear Mrs Finching,' Arthur began, struck by the good tone again.

'Oh not that nasty ugly name, say Flora!'

'Flora. I assure you, Flora, I am happy in seeing you once more, and in finding that, like me, you have not forgotten the old foolish dreams, when we saw all before us in the light of our youth and hope.'

'You don't seem so,' pouted Flora, 'you take it very coolly, but however I know you are disappointed in me, I suppose the Chinese ladies—Mandarinesses if you call them so—are the cause or perhaps I am the cause myself, it's just as likely.'

'No, no,' Clennam entreated, 'don't say that.'

'Oh I must you know,' said Flora, in a positive tone, 'what nonsense not to, I know I am not what you expected, I know that very well.'

This is a rather cruel portrait of the real-life Maria, the girl he had "left a lily, [who] had become a peony" (why are peonies not beautiful in their own right?) and one dreads to think what Maria made of it if she ever read it. George Pierce Baker believed that "It is most likely, however, that with the blessed power we have not to see ourselves as others see us . . . Mrs. Winter never dreamed that Flora owed anything to her," and one can only hope that he was right. Admittedly in Dickens's characterisation Flora, if flighty, empty-headed, silly and somewhat laughable in her refusal to accept that Arthur no longer has any romantic feelings for her, is also shown to be a genuinely warm, caring, large-hearted and good-natured woman which is in accord with what we know about the real Maria. Admittedly Dickens himself was pleased if his readers found Flora a likeable and sympathetic character rather than the butt of a rather cruel joke; to the Duke of Devonshire he wrote: "I am so glad you like Flora. It came into my head one day that we have all had our Floras (mine is living, and extremely fat), and that it was a half serious, half ridiculous truth which had never been told. It is a wonderful gratification to find that everybody knows her." All the same if Maria ever read *Little Dorrit*—and we don't know that she ever did so but it is quite possible—she would surely have been hurt and insulted at the disparity between the way she had been portrayed as Dora and then as Flora several years later. Michael Slater calls the Flora Finching episode a "benignly comic portrait" about which Maria, if she read it, "was perhaps more flattered than hurt." Again, one hopes so.

That Maria may well have seen herself fictionalised as Flora is quite probable given that we know that she had a large collection of Dickens's books. In March 1912 the *Daily Chronicle* published the recollections of a Mrs Warren who, decades earlier, had been a young nursemaid in the employ of the Winters. Maria's weakness for drink is again alluded to, as is her enduring affection for Dickens:

> She would be sweet and kindly in the early part of the day, but after, and often before luncheon, her addiction to nips of drinking would render her like another woman. All her refinement and restraint seemed then to break down, and it would be during these times, induced, I think, by the recollection of the past, that she would refer to Dickens. She had a tremendous collection of his books by that time. They were to be found all about the house. When excited she would take them from the shelves and run through their pages, commenting on their contents, interspersing them with references to the author. At other times she would lie on her couch and say, 'Nurse, it was here that he used to sit'; and I have seen her, in one of these moods, actually kiss the place on the couch, and recall something that Charles Dickens had said to her . . . while I was in her service I was satisfied that her heart was still upon the 'poor reporter' whom her father would not tolerate.

If there is something both comically touching and rather pathetic in this there is also something rather dark hovering in the background. A radical change of personality when inebriated is more the hallmark of a genuine alcoholic rather than someone who tipples a little too much every now and again (as we shall see later with Scott Fitzgerald): and Mrs Warren's account suggests if not explicitly states that Maria's feelings for Dickens were no mere residual affection for an old flame but something considerably deeper and more intense and, on that account, more heartbreaking. Years later Georgina Hogarth remembered that Maria was "always romantic, and used to talk a great deal about her early love." Such details make it sound very much as though, in spite of her marriage and children and new life elsewhere, Maria remained in the grip of something very close to a romantic infatuation if not obsession which she never got over. Her letters to Dickens may have advertised something of this, which was perhaps just one more reason why he felt it best to obliterate all trace of them and to distance himself from her as far as possible.

That Maria Winter was the model for Flora Finching has always been common knowledge but Michael Slater goes much further in suggesting that she was also the inspiration for the cool and cruelly aloof Estella in *Great Expectations* (1861). Most Dickens scholars and biographers have taken it that Estella was inspired at least in part by Ellen ('Nelly') Ternan, the young actress whose relationship with Dickens in the final thirteen years of his life inspires much comment and interesting if ultimately fruitless speculation to this day. Some regard the relationship that Dickens and Ternan enjoyed as a merely platonic friendship; others have speculated not only that the two had a sexual affair but that Dickens fathered a child with Nelly which subsequently died. The facts and fancies of Dickens's relationship with Nelly are outside of the scope of the present work and interested readers should consult almost any of the significant number of biographies of Dickens and especially Claire Tomalin's *The Invisible Woman: The Story of Nelly Ternan* (1990). To return to the point at hand: Michael Slater suggests that we should look not to Nelly Ternan but to Maria Beadnell Winter for the model for Estella. "Biographers have long associated Estella in *Great Expectations* exclusively with the great love of Dickens's last years, Ellen Ternan," he writes in *Dickens and Women*, "and Pip's unhappy passion for her with Dickens's supposed miseries in loving Ellen. This is mere speculation, however, impure but simple . . . It is not, I believe, to Ellen that we owe the powerful vision of frustrated love that Dickens gives us in the most perfectly achieved of all his novels but to Maria, making her last and most haunting appearance on the Dickens stage. This time, however, she appears neither as a radiant vision of her younger self (Dora) nor as a comic version of her mature self (Flora) but as an ice-maiden, Estella, who is, as her name suggests, as cold and as beautiful and as desolatingly unattainable as a star."[22]

As those familiar with this beloved novel will recall, Estella is a young girl who has been adopted by the deeply eccentric Miss Havisham, who was jilted at the altar as a young woman many years previously and who ever since that day has locked herself in the crumbling Satis House, still wearing the remnants of her wedding dress, with the decaying remains of the wedding cake on the table and with all the clocks in the mansion stopped at the exact moment—twenty minutes to nine—that she learned of her jilting. Because of this decades-earlier abandonment Miss Havisham adopted Estella and raised her to be cold, distant and aloof to males generally (and to Pip specifically, brought to Satis House ostensibly to be a playmate for Estella but actually for Miss Havisham to carry out her bitter plan) and to inspire hopeless unrequited love in them which she will cruelly crush as an act of vicarious revenge against the whole of mankind (literally):

> Estella was always about, and always let me in and out, but never told me I might kiss her again. Sometimes, she would coldly tolerate me; sometimes, she would condescend to me; sometimes, she would be quite familiar with me; sometimes, she would tell me energetically that she hated me. Miss Havisham would often ask me in a whisper, or when we were alone, "Does she grow prettier and prettier, Pip?" And when I said yes (for indeed she did), would seem to enjoy it greedily. Also, when we played at cards Miss Havisham would look on, with a miserly relish of Estella's moods, whatever they were. And sometimes, when her moods were so many and so contradictory of one another that I was puzzled what to say or do, Miss Havisham would embrace her with lavish fondness, murmuring something in her ear that sounded like "Break their hearts my pride and hope, break their hearts and have no mercy!"

Reading between the lines however there are certain subtle indications that Estella harbours feelings towards Pip which are not quite as uniformly negative as Miss Havisham would have wished. As a grown woman Estella marries Bentley Drummle—Pip's hated rival—who turns out to be a violent and abusive husband. Estella's misery is relatively short-lived: by the end of the book it transpires that Drummle has died, leaving Estella a widow. In Dickens's original version of the novel Pip hears that Estella has married a second time to a doctor from Shropshire. By chance he and Estella meet briefly in the street and exchange pleasantries but little more. This ending received sufficient negative criticism (from his friend Wilkie Collins amongst others) that Dickens was moved to pen a second, open-ended but potentially hopeful version (now considered the definitive conclusion, one that pleased Dickens himself better according to his letters) in which Pip goes to see the ruins of Satis House one last time and runs across Estella, where the two experience a sort of reconciliation:

> I knew . . . that I secretly intended to revisit the site of the old house that evening, alone, for her sake. Yes, even so. For Estella's sake . . .
>
> I could trace out where every part of the old house had been, and where the brewery had been, and where the gates, and where the casks. I had done so, and was looking along the desolate garden walk, when I beheld a solitary figure in it.
>
> The figure showed itself aware of me, as I advanced. It had been moving towards me, but it stood still. As I drew nearer, I saw it to be the figure of a woman. As I drew nearer yet, it was about to turn away, when it stopped, and let me come up with it. Then, it faltered, as if much surprised, and uttered my name, and I cried out,—
>
> "Estella!"

"I am greatly changed. I wonder you know me."

The freshness of her beauty was indeed gone, but its indescribable majesty and its indescribable charm remained. Those attractions in it, I had seen before; what I had never seen before, was the saddened, softened light of the once proud eyes; what I had never felt before was the friendly touch of the once insensible hand.

We sat down on a bench that was near, and I said, "After so many years, it is strange that we should thus meet again, Estella, here where our first meeting was! Do you often come back?"

"I have never been here since."

"Nor I."

The moon began to rise, and I thought of the placid look at the white ceiling, which had passed away. The moon began to rise, and I thought of the pressure on my hand when I had spoken the last words he had heard on earth.

Estella was the next to break the silence that ensued between us.

"I have very often hoped and intended to come back, but have been prevented by many circumstances. Poor, poor old place!"

The silvery mist was touched with the first rays of the moonlight, and the same rays touched the tears that dropped from her eyes. Not knowing that I saw them, and setting herself to get the better of them, she said quietly,—

"Were you wondering, as you walked along, how it came to be left in this condition?"

"Yes, Estella."

"The ground belongs to me. It is the only possession I have not relinquished. Everything else has gone from me, little by little, but I have kept this. It was the subject of the only determined resistance I made in all the wretched years."

"Is it to be built on?"

"At last, it is. I came here to take leave of it before its change. And you," she said, in a voice of touching interest to a wanderer,— "you live abroad still?"

"Still."

"And do well, I am sure?"

"I work pretty hard for a sufficient living, and therefore—yes, I do well."

"I have often thought of you," said Estella.

"Have you?"

"Of late, very often. There was a long hard time when I kept far from me the remembrance of what I had thrown away when I was quite ignorant of its worth. But since my duty has not been incompatible with the admission of that remembrance, I have given it a place in my heart."

"You have always held your place in my heart," I answered.

And we were silent again until she spoke.

"I little thought," said Estella, "that I should take leave of you in taking leave of this spot. I am very glad to do so."

"Glad to part again, Estella? To me, parting is a painful thing. To me, the remembrance of our last parting has been ever mournful and painful."

"But you said to me," returned Estella, very earnestly, 'God bless you, God forgive you!' And if you could say that to me then, you will not hesitate to say that to me now,—now, when suffering has been stronger than all other teaching, and has taught me to understand what your heart used to be. I have been bent and broken, but—I hope—into a better shape. Be as considerate and good to me as you were, and tell me we are friends."

"We are friends," said I, rising and bending over her, as she rose from the bench.

"And will continue friends apart," said Estella.

I took her hand in mine, and we went out of the ruined place; and, as the morning mists had risen long ago when I first left the forge, so the evening mists were rising now, and in all the broad expanse of tranquil light they showed to me, I saw no shadow of another parting from her.

Dickens's depiction of Estella-as-Maria is not the literal truth but an imaginative reconstruction by a great writer of fiction. There is no suggestion whatever that the real Maria treated the young Dickens with the same kind of deliberately stony-hearted cruelty with which the fictional Estella maltreats young Pip: the truth of such a recreation can be found rather in Pip's *reaction* to Estella's perceived emotional sadism, which surely mirrored Dickens's own feelings as a young man. The ambiguous and possibly happy ending (in which some sort of future relationship is implied in Pip's claim that he sees no shadow of parting from Estella again) allowed Dickens's alter ego Pip to have what he, Dickens, was denied in real life as a young man: the continuance of a friendship if not a romantic union. If Slater is correct and Maria really was the model for Estella, which is entirely plausible, the writing of this second ending to *Great Expectations* seems to have written Maria out of him once and for all at least in terms of his fiction. "All Pip's dreaming love," writes Slater, "all his passion and romance, is thrown away upon a beautiful monster, an utterly heartless woman trained from her babyhood to entrap and torture men. Maria becomes at last fully mythologized and thereafter appears no more in Dickens's fiction."[23]

If the fictionalized Maria never made another appearance in Dickens's books the real one continued to correspond with him, even if in an even more scrappy and desultory fashion on his part especially. Following the death of her child there seem to have been no further letters between Maria and Dickens for the next three years (none that survive at any rate) although it seems that she maintained friendly contact with the Dickens family. She was on intimate terms with Georgina, Dickens's sister-in-law: it was Georgina who wrote to Maria in 1857 to relate that Dickens's fourth child and second son, Walter Landor Dickens, had at the age of just sixteen gone out to India as a cadet of the East India Company. Dickens went down to Southampton to see off his son not realising that he would never set eyes on him again:

sadly Walter would die in a Calcutta hospital six years later in 1863, aged just twenty-two. Maria must surely have realised that Dickens no longer wanted to maintain a relationship on almost any terms, not even in the form of an entirely platonic friendship, yet still she hoped to stay in cordial contact: she wrote to him hoping that she would be able to see him in Liverpool where she was going to be at just the time that Dickens was giving one of his public readings. This brought forth Dickens's next letter to her on the 16th of August 1858 in which he made his excuses as to why it would be impossible for him to do so. (The mention of Anne is also certainly a reference to Maria's sister of that name who had married Dickens's old friend Henry Kolle and who had died in May 1836).

My dear Mrs. Winter,—
               I have read poor dear Anne's prayer with great sorrow, and with many emotions of sadly affectionate remembrance. It was written, no doubt, under a presentiment of Death; but it must always be remembered that such a presentiment often exists when it fails to be fulfilled; and it is very commonly engendered in the state of mind belonging to the condition in which she composed the prayer.

  It would give me great pleasure to see you at Liverpool, if I had the least confidence in my own freedom for a moment under the circumstances which will take me there. But I have so much business to transact at times, and have to keep myself so quiet at other times, and have so many people to give directions to, and make arrangements with (four travel with me), that I see no one while I am on this Tour, and have to be always grimly self-denying and heroic. So I shall hope to see you in London, at some time when I am in a less virtuous, and less hurried and worried condition.

With my love to Ella, and kindest regards to Mr Winter,
Ever affectionately yours,
Charles Dickens

It is another perfunctory missive and the 'Charles Dickens' is rather stiffly formal if not downright cool.

In 1858 Charles and Catherine Dickens finally separated. The few previous years of growing estrangement and disaffection (more on the husband's part than that of the wife, it has to be said) came to a head in the summer of that year when Catherine and her son Charley moved out of the family home to a new home in Gloucester Crescent, supported by a very substantial allowance from Charles. Surprisingly, Georgina sided with Charles throughout and remained at Tavistock House to look after the children with him and to keep house (although Mary Dickens was old enough to be considered mistress of the household), an act that led to predictable if entirely unfounded rumours of an incestuous relationship between Dickens and his sister-in-law. It was Georgina who wrote to Maria on the last day of May—a letter which Dickens possibly may have simply dictated, according to Peter Ackroyd—to let her know that Dickens and Catherine had separated:

I am now going to tell you something which will, I am sure, surprise you, and, at the first, shock and distress you. It is that Charles and his wife have agreed to live apart, in future. Believe me when I assure you that I am perfectly convinced that this plan will be for the happiness of all. I worked hard to prevent it, as long as I saw any possibility, but latterly I have come to the conviction that there was no other way out of the domestic Misery of this house. For my sister and Charles have lived un- happily for years—they were totally unsuited to each other in almost every respect—and as the children grew up this unsuitability developed itself more strongly, and disagreements and Miseries which used to be easily kept out of sight have forced themselves into notice . . . for many years, although we have put a good face upon it, we have been very miserable at home. My sister has often expressed a desire to go and live away, but Charles never agreed to it on the girls' account; but latterly he thought it must be to their advantage as well as to his own and Catherine's, to consent to this and remodel their unhappy home. So, by mutual consent and for the reasons I have told you, and no other, they have come to this arrangement. She is to have a house of her own in London, and her eldest son (at his father's request and not taking any part or showing any preference in doing it) is to live with and take care of her. The other children remain with their father—his eldest daughter naturally taking her mother's place, as mistress of the house.

In 1858 Henry Winter's financial affairs collapsed. The specific details are unclear but Henry and Maria found themselves all but destitute after he was declared bankrupt in March of 1859. This seems to have been the event that precipitated a complete change of Winter's course of life: while Maria and their surviving daughter stayed behind in London, in February 1860 he enrolled as a Fellow Commoner at Queen's College, Cambridge, and began reading for Holy Orders. While Mr Winter was presumably not interested in laying up for himself treasure on earth his wife was rather more practically minded and she threw herself on Dickens's mercy, swallowing her pride and asking him for help in getting her husband back on his financial feet. Dickens's refusal in his letter of the 13th of November was politely couched but firm:

My dear Mrs. Winter,—

I have been so constantly and rapidly changing from place to place during the past week, that I am only just now in receipt of the intelligence of your misfortune. With the utmost sincerity and earnestness of which my heart is capable, I condole with you upon it, and assure you of my true sympathy and friendship. It has distressed me greatly. Not because I am so worldly or so unjust as to couple the least reproach or blame with a reverse that I do not doubt to have been unavoidable, and that I know to be always easily possible of occurrence to the best and most fortunate of men, but because I know you feel it heavily.

I wish to Heaven it were in my power to help Mr Winter to any new opening in life. But you can hardly imagine how powerless I am in any such case. My own work in life being of that kind that I must always do it with my own unassisted hand and head, I have such rare opportunities of placing any one, that for years and years I have been seeking in vain to help in this way a friend of the old days when the old house stood unchanged in Lombard Street. To this hour, I have not succeeded, though I have strenuously tried my hardest, both abroad and at home. Commercial opportunities, above all, are so far removed from me, that I dare not encourage a hope of my power to serve Mr Winter with my good word, ever coming within a year's journey of my will and wish to do it.

But I really think that your father, who could do much in such a case without drawing at all heavily upon his purse, might be induced to do, what—I may say to you, Maria—it is no great stretch of sentiment to call his duty. Has not Margaret great influence with him? Have not you some? And don't you think that if you were to set yourself steadily to exert whatever influence you can bring to bear upon him, you would do the best within your reach for your husband, your child, and yourself? Is it not all important that you should try your utmost with him, at this time?

Forgive my recommending this, if you have so anticipated the recommendation as to have done all that possibly can be done to move him. But what you tell me about George seems so strange, so hard, and so ill balanced, that I cannot avoid the subject.

I write in the greatest haste, being overwhelmed by business here. On Monday I hope to be at Gad's Hill, and to remain either there or at Tavistock House for months to come. I enclose a few lines to Mr Winter, and am ever,

                           Your faithful friend,
                           Charles Dickens


## Dickens wrote to Henry Winter directly on the same day:


My dear Mr. Winter, —
                In the hope that a friendly word of
remembrance in season may not be unacceptable to you, I write
to assure you of my sympathy with you in your trouble. Pray
do not let it cast you down too much; what has happened to
you, has happened to many thousands of good and honourable
men, and will happen again in a like manner, to the end of all
things. If you should feel the bitterness of losing belief in any
nature you had previously trusted in, consider that the truth is
always better than falsehood, even though the truth involves
the detection of such skin-deep friendships as that which can
cool towards a man in temporary misfortune. It is better lost
than kept, as all things worthless are.
   Be strong of heart for yourself, and look forward to a better
time. You will not think, I know, that I obtrude myself upon you
in asking to be borne in mind among the friends who feel truly
towards you.
                           Faithfully yours always,
                           Charles Dickens


## Dickens again went abroad to Paris and it was here that he heard of the death, on the 5th of November, of Maria's father George Beadnell at the age of eighty-nine. On the 17th of November he wrote to Maria sending her his condolences:


My dear Maria, —
                I had read in Galignani that your poor father
was dead, before I received your touching account of his last
moments. Of course I could not be surprised, knowing his great
age, by the wearing out of his vitality; but—almost equally of
course—it was a shock too, for all the old Past comes out of its
grave when I think of him, and the Ghosts of a good many years
stand about his memory.

He died among his children, and could have died with no better words and no better hopes. God be thanked for it, and may such mercy and comfort be in store for us!

Always yours affectionately
Charles Dickens

Pray give my kind regard to Margaret and your brother.

Mr Beadnell had left behind an estate of some £40,000 which temporarily assuaged the Winters' financial straits.

Further communication between Dickens and Maria was sporadic and perfunctory: as time passed he came to view her more and more with mild irritation as a figure of annoyance and regrettably someone to be rather spitefully mocked behind her back. Henry Winter had taken his degree at the age of forty-eight, had been ordained, had entered the ministry and become the curate at Little Eversham in Cambridgeshire in 1866 and afterwards the vicar of Alnmouth in Northumberland where he would die in March 1871. In 1866 Dickens was again on another reading tour of Scotland and the north of England: he found himself in Newcastle—about thirty-five miles south of Alnmouth—from where he wrote cattily to Georgina: "No news yet of the Winter family. I live in a tremble." A couple of days later when he had moved on to Leeds he said: "Thank heaven, there have been no signs either of Mrs. Winter or 'dear Mr. W.'." Clearly by now Maria was somebody he thought best avoided altogether and whose foibles could be lampooned with impunity.

Prematurely aged by year after year of relentless overwork, though only in his fifties Dickens's health began to fail. He looked far older than his years, with a face etched with deep lines and with his beard and what was left of his hair turning white. Physically and also mentally he was increasingly unwell, suffering from a host of individually relatively minor but troublesome ailments both physical—neuralgia, bleeding piles, headaches, stomach pains and digestive upsets, flatulence, renal colic, a swollen and extremely painful left foot which left him walking with a stick, colds and catarrh, the skin condition erysipelas, insomnia, failing eyesight—and psychological, particularly an increasingly deep depression and a pervasive anxiety: he may well have suffered from panic attacks with or without agoraphobia. "I have sudden vague rushes of terror," he wrote in 1868, "even when riding in a hansom cab, which are perfectly unreasonable but quite insurmountable"; his children later recalled symptoms of sudden, inexplicable and extreme terror in him consistent with panic attacks. This seems to be traceable directly to the fact that Dickens was involved in the Staplehurst rail crash in Kent in June 1865 when the 2:38 from Folkestone to London was derailed, killing ten and injuring forty. Dickens was himself physically unharmed in the tragedy but was left so psychologically disturbed by it that there is every indication that he was afflicted by something very much like post-traumatic stress disorder. There is a compelling body of evidence that just after another trip to Paris in 1865 he had suffered a relatively slight but ominous stroke from which he made a more or less complete and fairly rapid recovery—he himself dismissed the episode to a friends as 'sunstroke'—but which was, with the benefit of hindsight, a disturbing omen. His strength was deserting him: he was growing increasingly exhausted and even enfeebled. He was, in short, a deeply tired man whose decades of overwork, nervous strain and poor health had left him a burnt-out case.

But Dickens had always been a driven man in his professional life and letting up the pace even at this stage was all but unthinkable. For some time he had been in the habit of giving dramatic, highly theatrical readings from his own works, at first to small, select groups of friends and family for the sheer pleasure of doing so and later on to larger paying audiences for charitable purposes. These readings were so popular that he decided that he could make a commercial venture out of them, which he began to do in 1858. In the ten months between April of that year and February 1859 he gave 108 such readings, earning in the first month alone no less than £1,025. To put this into context his average earnings from his literary productions had formerly been less than £3,000 *per year*. The readings were massively popular, so much so that these public events became in the final years of his life more profitable than the books from which they were taken. Dickens was close to what we might now term a megastar. He was phenomenally popular and very rich but the demands that the punishing schedule of travelling and reciting placed on him both physically and mentally were severe to the point of brutality. In spite of his failing health in November 1867 he sailed from Liverpool to embark upon his second reading tour of America.

Back at home he continued to write, principally on *Our Mutual Friend* and then on his final, unfinished, novel *The Mystery of Edwin Drood*. His last public readings were in the manner of a farewell tour, conducted in such a way which suggests that Dickens knew full well he was not long for the world and that he may have entertained intimations that he would never make old bones: it is difficult to read the later pages of almost any biography of Dickens and the litany of physical and psychological health problems he endured and not feel not just that he was a man living under sentence of death but one who knew it.

On the 8th of June 1870 he started another full day's work on *Edwin Drood* in his working chalet at Gad's Hill. He came into the house for lunch and smoked a cigar in the conservatory before returning to the chalet for the second session on the book. He came back into the house in the evening about an hour before dinner: he seemed tired and distracted but this was quite usual after a day of concentrated labour. In the library, waiting for dinner, he wrote his last two letters before taking his place at the dining table: at this point, just as they were sitting down, only his sister-in-law Georgina was present and she noticed that he looked dreadfully unwell. She asked if he felt ill. "Yes, very ill," he replied. "I have been very ill for the last hour." She wanted to send for the doctor immediately but Dickens refused. At this point, out of nowhere, his speech became slurred and then incoherent and he seemed to suffer some sort of fit. Georgina pleaded with him to lie down. "Yes, on the ground," he slurred. They were his last words: he collapsed into Georgina's arms and then crashed to the floor.

At the dinner table he had just suffered a massive brain haemorrhage. Not wanting to move him, a couch was brought into the dining room and he was lifted onto it. Georgina, his daughters and two doctors kept a vigil by its side all night but he never regained consciousness and at about a quarter past six in the evening of the following day, the 9th of June 1870, he died. He was fifty-eight years old. The greatest English writer of his day belonged, finally, to the ages. It had been Dickens's stated desire to be buried in Rochester Cathedral "in an inexpensive, unostentatious, and strictly private manner" but his wish was roundly ignored: on the 14th of June he was laid to rest in the Poet's Corner of Westminster Abbey.

We can only imagine how Maria took the news. Maria Winter *née* Beadnell lived on for another sixteen years. Georgina Hogarth kept up an occasional correspondence with her, rather dutifully if Arthur A. Adrian's *Georgina Hogarth and the Dickens Circle* is to be believed: "With three women who had figured prominently in Dickens's life Georgina maintained occasional contact. Of the three—Maria Beadnell Winter, Mary Boyle, and Ellen Ternan—it was Mrs. Winter, least valued by Dickens in his later years, who was the least regarded by his sister-in-law."[24] Little is known about her later life. Maria survived her husband by fifteen years: she died in 1886 at the age of seventy-six and is buried in the Highland Road Cemetery, Portsmouth.

The story of Charles Dickens and Maria Beadnell is a touching but fundamentally unhappy tale of hopeful young love, rejection, a reunion many years afterwards and another rejection, this time by the other party. Maria was the first cut that wounded Dickens the earliest and deepest but in so being became one of the most important inspirations for some of the most perennially fascinating characters in his deathless novels. Indeed, in *Dickens and Women* Michael Slater explicitly states: "It is true to say, I believe, that Dickens never loved any other woman as he loved Maria." Almost certainly the same could be said, in reverse, of Maria herself.

# Two:
## Living Too Long with a Single Dream

"At any rate, let us love for a while, for a year or so, you and me. That's a form of divine drunkenness that we can all try." —F. Scott Fitzgerald, *The Diamond as Big as the Ritz*

The worst things: To be in bed and sleep not, to want for one who comes not, to try to please and please not.—Egyptian proverb, copied into Fitzgerald's notebook.

### I

Francis Scott Key Fitzgerald was born in St. Paul, Minnesota, on the 24th of September 1896, the first surviving child born into a middle class family. (Two girls had died in infancy before Scott's birth and another daughter born in 1900 lived for just an hour. His one surviving sister Annabel was born in July 1901). He was named after a distant relative on his father's side, Francis Scott Key (1779-1843), best remembered as the author in 1814 of the lyrics to 'The Star Spangled Banner,' the American national anthem. Scott's maternal grandfather Philip F. McQuillan had come to America aged just nine in 1843 from County Fermanagh in Ireland, first to Illinois and then in 1857 to St. Paul where he became a successful grocery wholesaler: when he died in 1877 (of kidney disease, aged only forty-three) he left an estate of well over a quarter of a million dollars. His eldest child, a daughter named Mollie—Scott's mother—, was born in 1860. Mollie probably met her husband-to-be, Edward Fitzgerald, in St. Paul but they were married in Washington in February 1890.

Scott's upbringing was fairly rootless—the family moved often—but secure and modestly financially comfortable. As already noted there was money after a fashion on Mollie's side of the family whereas Edward was a quiet, affable, easy-going man without much drive or ambition. In the early 1890s he was president of his own willow and rattan furniture company but he was not a natural businessman and the firm was soon in financial trouble. After the company collapsed in 1898 Edward took a job as a wholesale grocery salesman with Procter & Gamble in Buffalo, New York, meaning that the family were uprooted once again. However in March 1908 Edward, aged fifty-five, lost his job, an experience that Scott never forgot. "That morning he had gone out a comparatively young man, a man full of strength, full of confidence. He came home that evening an old man, a completely broken man. He had lost his essential drive, his immaculateness of purpose. He was a failure the rest of his days." Years later he would tell his literary agent, "His own life after a rather brilliant start back in the seventies has been a 'failure'—he's always lived in mother's shadow and he takes an immense vicarious pleasure in any success of mine." The family went back to St. Paul where Edward tried to maintain a business as a grocery salesman but without conspicuous success, although Mollie's money supplemented by other inheritances meant that they continued to move from one rented house to another on an almost yearly basis. Edward was not allowed to forget that he was being kept. "Where would we be," Mollie said regularly, "if it wasn't for grandfather McQuillan?"

Scott's talent for writing manifested itself early. He was spoiled by Mollie but she would worry about letting her son became a writer: she wanted him to become the successful businessman her husband had never managed to be. Edward Fitzgerald was more supportive: he instilled a deep love of literature in his son by reading Byron and Poe to him from the cradle. As a young man Edward himself had nursed some literary aspirations and had even collaborated on an unpublished novel so he viewed his son's clear talent in that direction with a favourable eye even though he wanted Scott to become an army officer. Scott did later join the army briefly but from an early age it was clear that he had set his heart and mind on his vocation as a writer. At the age of just twelve Scott published his first surviving literary effort, a detective story, in a school newspaper. Despite his evident prowess with language he was not particularly academically inclined and four years later he was expelled for neglecting his studies. His exam results at the Newman prep school in New Jersey, designed to get him into Princeton, were dismal: he nevertheless secured an interview at the illustrious Ivy League university and somehow managed to talk his way in. He was scarcely more studious afterwards: he only managed to stay there according to one biographer "by luck and by all-night cramming sessions with wet towels and pots of coffee."[1]

It was more than just Scott's way with words that showed itself early in his life: so did his capacity for alcohol. Scott discovered drink early and it would be fair to say that he never escaped from its grip for most of the remainder of his short life. In this he was more likely than not influenced by his father—by no means an alcoholic but certainly a boozer on the sly. "Father used to drink too much and then play baseball in the back yard," he recalled in the journal that he called his *Ledger* in 1905. At Princeton he was not considered to be a particularly heavy drinker, no more so than his fellows at least, but before many more years had passed he would become well known for being able to consume large quantities of booze: eventually he would become a chronic alcoholic and with occasional but relatively brief periods of sobriety would remain one almost for the rest of his days, only conquering his addiction finally within a year or so of his premature death. Unfortunately Scott's personality changed when under the influence and not for the better. A normally quiet, polite, affable and likeable man he became assertive, confrontational, cruel then verbally and even physically aggressive depending on the amount of alcohol he had imbibed: stories of his outrageous behaviour when in his cups are legion. In 1978, in conversation with Scott Donaldson, Fitzgerald's daughter Scottie asked: "Did liquor have a drastically unhealthy effect on one's life? Did one's personality change as a result of drinking? In the case of F. Scott Fitzgerald, she'd decided that the answer to both questions was yes. When sober he was a thoughtful and gentle and kind, if somewhat over-solicitous, father" but he ". . . was a totally different person when drunk: not just gay or tiddly, but *mean*."[2] In a way reminiscent of the classic alcoholic, the morning after another one of his benders, horrifically hung-over and more or less sober for the time being, Scott was full of contrition and consumed by remorse for things he could barely even remember. According to fellow writer Anita Loos, Scott was always "dangerous when drunk and eating humble pie when sober."

All this was in the future, though. The meeting of Scott and Ginevra King came about through Marie Hersey, an old flame of Scott's who was a classmate of Ginevra at Westover school in Middlebury, Connecticut. Marie invited Ginevra to visit St. Paul three hundred and fifty miles away for the 1914-1915 Christmas holidays and it was then that Scott Fitzgerald and Ginevra King first met at a dinner dance at the Town and Country Club on the 4th of January 1915. (This is according to Matthew J. Bruccoli's definitive biography of Fitzgerald and also Scott Donaldson in *Fool for Love*; James West in *The Perfect Hour* has their first meeting at a party at Marie Hersey's home). Scott had been due to leave to go back to Princeton that very day but postponed the trip in order to attend the event. He was eighteen, she was sixteen.

Ginevra King was born in Chicago in 1898, the eldest of the three daughters of Charles Garfield King and Ginevra Fuller King. The unusual first name, shared by Ginevra's mother and grandmother, came from Leonardo's c. 1474 portrait of the Florentine aristocrat Ginevra de' Benci, painted possibly to celebrate her marriage. Charles King was a successful mortgage banker and stockbroker and his wife also came from a moneyed background so, like her Renaissance namesake, Ginevra was raised in surroundings of great wealth, privilege and prestige. Charles King was a keen golfer and polo player (his daughter would inherit a similar love for sport) and with his wife was a keen socialite in the upper echelons of Chicago society. The Kings were natives of Lake Forest, one of the most affluent suburbs of Chicago in the North Shore area bordering Lake Michigan. At the time of Ginevra's birth Mr and Mrs King were living with Mr Fuller in Chicago but Charles King later took over the expansive (and, needless to say, expensive) summer residence called Kingdom Come Farm in Lake Forest which had been built by his father. Charles King subsequently also built a four-storey mansion in the city.

In summer 1914 Ginevra and three close girlfriends labelled themselves the 'Big Four,' that is, the four wealthiest, most beautiful and desirable girls in Chicago. "They had not consulted anyone about this," writes one biographer: "they had simply anointed themselves."[3] For all that this sounds like a disagreeably egotistical act Professor James L.W. West III, professor of English at Pennsylvania State University, a noted Fitzgerald scholar and biographer of the Scott-Ginevra romance, paints an appealing portrait of an attractive young woman:

> Ginevra herself was lovely. She was small, about five feet four inches in height, with refined features and a good profile. She had a slim figure, pretty legs and ankles, and small, graceful hands. Her hair was dark and curly; her eyes, deep brown in colour, were lively and sparkling. Ginevra's voice was her most unusual attribute—low and expressive, with a slight roughness of texture. She liked to sing and laugh: if something truly amused her she would produce a snort. She loved parties, adored dancing, and was adept in social situations, relying on her looks and instincts to see her through . . . She was intensely competitive and did not like to lose at anything—golf, tennis or even basketball (for which she was undersized). She loved athletics and was a good enough golfer to hold her own against Edith Cummings, who later won two national titles in the sport. Ginevra was reasonably diligent about her schoolwork but was terribly interested in it. She preferred athletics and parties, and she liked to sit up late talking with her friends. She was direct in speech and self-confident in behaviour: there was little that was studied or calculated in what she did or said. She was

not especially interested in discussing the shortcomings of others and was not much inclined to introspection or self-analysis.[4]

At the time the two young people met Ginevra was, as already noted, a pupil at Westover School in Middlebury, Connecticut. Westover was still new — it had been founded only in 1910 by two ladies, Miss Mary Robbins Hilliard and Miss Theodate Pope — but had already acquired a reputation of being a small (about 150 girls) and rather exclusive finishing school. Conditions were spartan though not severely so. Only five or six or so of the forty-odd graduates each year went on to college: it was expected that most of the girls would find wealthy husbands, the future course of their lives mapped out as wives and mothers and stolidly respectable upper class citizens. Ginevra disliked the stuffy, repressive atmosphere at school although she could not be said to have been desperately unhappy: apart from sporting activities for the most part she felt merely bored and stifled.

Ginevra's diary for the 4th of January records: "Got dressed for dinner. Larry, Betty, Midge, Kit, Mary, Frank H., Scott Fitzgerald. Reuben, Jimmie Johnston, Bobbie Schirmer, Bill Lindsee. Sat between Scott + Reuben, danced for a while afterwards. Scott perfectly darling." This is a cursory sketch which tells us very little but the first meeting between these two young people would be fictionalised in more detail in chapter two of Fitzgerald's wildly successful (and like many first novels deeply autobiographical) novel *This Side of Paradise*, published a few years later. In the book Ginevra became Isabelle Borgé.

> "Did any one ever tell you, you have keen eyes?" she said. Amory attempted to make them look even keener. He fancied, but he was not sure, that her foot had just touched his under the table. But it might possibly have been only the table leg. It was so hard to tell. Still it thrilled him. He wondered quickly if there would be any difficulty in securing the little den up-stairs.

Scott himself became Amory Blaine. Both the real Scott and the fictional Amory were from the Midwest; both attended Princeton; both joined the army; both had failed relationships with a debutante and so forth.

> Amory was now eighteen years old, just under six feet tall and exceptionally, but not conventionally, handsome. He had rather a young face, the ingenuousness of which was marred by the penetrating green eyes, fringed with long dark eyelashes. He lacked somehow that intense animal magnetism that so often accompanies beauty in men or women; his personality seemed rather a mental thing, and it was not in his power to turn it on and off like a water-faucet. But people never forgot his face.

The attraction between the two was immediate and intense.

> "Isabelle," he said suddenly, "I want to tell you something." They had been talking lightly about 'that funny look in her eyes,' and Isabelle knew from the change in his manner what was coming— indeed, she had been wondering how soon it would come. Amory reached above their heads and turned out the electric light, so that they were in the dark, except for the red glow that fell through the door from the reading-room lamps. Then he began:

"I don't know whether or not you know what you—what I'm going to say. Lordy, Isabelle—this *sounds* like a line, but it isn't."

"I know," said Isabelle softly.

"Maybe we'll never meet again like this—I have darned hard luck sometimes." He was leaning away from her on the other arm of the lounge, but she could see his eyes plainly in the dark.

"You'll meet me again—silly." There was just the slightest emphasis on the last word—so that it became almost a term of endearment. He continued a bit huskily:

"I've fallen for a lot of people—girls—and I guess you have, too—boys, I mean, but, honestly, you—" he broke off suddenly and leaned forward, chin on his hands: "Oh, what's the use— you'll go your way and I suppose I'll go mine."

Even in 1938, eighteen years after the publication of *Paradise* and only two years before his death, Scott could still say in a letter that in that novel he had been writing "about a love affair that was still bleeding as fresh as the skin wound on a hemophile."[5]

For Scott, Ginevra "matched his dreams of the perfect girl: beautiful, rich, socially secure, and sought after. The last qualification was important. His ideal girl had to be one pursued by many men; there had to be an element of competition."[6] According to another biographer her name "had become associated with a reputation for what passed, in those days, as sexual daring. It was rumored that Ginevra had kissed dozens of boys, and that almost all of them had fallen desperately in love with her."[7] All the same, the day after they first met Ginevra and Scott spent the afternoon squashed next to each other in the back of a friend's car before going out to a dance in the evening; it must have been a heady day for later that night Ginevra confided to her diary: "Am absolutely gone on Scott!" There are certain indications, made much later and long after-the-fact, that the attraction was stronger on his side than on hers: her daughter Ginevra Mitchell Hunter explicitly stated that her mother as a young woman was never in love with Scott. Ginevra was not only beautiful but coy and maddeningly flirtatious: many years later she admitted that as a young woman she was "definitely out for quantity not quality in beaux . . . there were a lot of boys back then . . . I still wasn't serious enough not to want plenty of other attention" and claimed that her love affair with Scott was merely a "silly passing romance," although for the time being he was still 'top man.' "I hear you had plans for kissing me goodbye publicly," she wrote in January 1915. "My goodness, I'm glad you didn't. I'd have had to be severe as anything with you! (*Ans. this—Why didn't you? (KISS ME).*" And again later on, asking Scott to find a chaperone, she slyly counselled that "a dumb and blind one is best." In later life Ginevra—just as Agnes von Kurowsky did with Ernest Hemingway—seemed to wish to rewrite her past and minimise the true extent and intensity of her feelings for Scott.

The surviving documentary evidence tells a very different story. It was the first mature relationship of their adult lives for both of them and whatever picture of the romance Ginevra wanted to paint many decades later the two young people really were deeply in love. After their first encounter they were able to see each other in person relatively infrequently. Scott had no car and in any case Westover girls were rarely allowed outside the school grounds and while male visitors were allowed the girls were strictly chaperoned. Scott planned to visit Westover on the 20th of February. "I would simply *adore* to have you come," Ginevra wrote when the subject was broached. "The difficulty is that you can only come on Saturdays—from four till six . . . The worst thing is that you must sit in a glass case," Ginevra's reference to the fact that male visitors could only see Westover girls in drawing rooms with large glass doors so that they could be observed by staff sitting nearby to ensure that propriety was observed at all times. Kissing was expressly forbidden, though if the two parties were careful a very discreet and fleeting holding of hands might be managed. Scott nevertheless visited Ginevra as planned: though he chafed at the restrictions and was disappointed that they could spend no time together Ginevra later told her diary: "*Scott came in afternoon. Oh it was so wonderful to see him again. I am madly in love with him. He is so wonderful . . . marvelous time.*"

Future meetings were few and far between. Fitzgerald invited Ginevra to the Princeton Sophomore Prom but a girl of her age and social position was once again expected to be chaperoned at such an occasion (usually by her mother) and in this instance Mrs King couldn't make it. "I'm so disap. about the dance I cant see straight," Ginevra bitterly told him. By way of compensation Scott and Ginevra were allowed to meet up in Manhattan on the 8th of June. Like any couple in love they went out for dinner (at the roof garden of the Ritz, no less—Scott had a taste for the high life, the ostentatious gesture and spending way beyond his means even then) before going to see a play and then a Ziegfeld show on 42nd Street. Understandably it would prove to be an unforgettable night for both of them; in 1932 Scott would draw upon the experience for his essay 'My Lost City' in which he wrote: ". . . she to whom I fatuously referred as 'my girl' was a Middle Westerner, a fact which kept the warm centre of the world out there, so I thought of New York as essentially cynical and heartless—save for one night when she made luminous the Ritz Roof on a brief passage through."

Scott managed to see Ginevra again later that same month but those kinds of meetings were exceptional events. Indeed they met face to face so rarely that Ginevra was able to tot up just how much time they had spent in each other's company; on the 25th of August, well over eight months after they had first met, she wrote: "Why couldn't we have chosen places nearer to each other? . . . I told you, didn't I, that I figured out that we have seen each other for exactly *15* hours." To make up for this they exchanged photographs and conducted a voluminous and intense epistolary relationship, writing to each other frequent and some exceedingly long and passionate letters. "Boys in their teens typically do not excel at the epistolary arts," writes Prof. West. "Scott Fitzgerald, however, quickly proved himself to be a wonderful correspondent."[8] Scott wrote to her almost every day, penning letters of such inordinate length that some of them had to be split and sent in two separate envelopes, each thrilling arrival duly noted breathlessly in Ginevra's diary—". . . a *sweet* one from Scott," "Wonderful letter from Scott again today!", "Long wonderful letter from Scott this morn.," "marvelous wonderful heavenly letter from Scott . . . cheered me up immensely," "24 pages from Scott. *Thrills*" and so forth. "I hope the fact that I never write over 4 pages to anybody else is appreciated," Ginevra pointedly told him in a letter of her own.

It was. Yet as 1915 wore on Scott began to see for himself the true scale of the social and financial gulf that separated his world from Ginevra's. By her standards—those of the well-off Chicago smart set—Scott, a middle-class boy, was comparatively speaking all but a pauper and it was little wonder that he soon began to nurse a growing sense of inferiority about his perceived lack of money and social status. The other boys with which Ginevra mingled were scions of hugely wealthy old money families, the sons of eminent physicians and judges and the like: Scott's father was merely a grocery salesman and not a successful one at that. The overall tone of the letters that Scott and Ginevra sent to each other begins to shift during the summer of 1916. Her letters to him become less frequent, less hectic, less ardently affectionate. That summer she writes practically nothing about Scott in her diary. If the element of competition had been an attracting factor for Scott in the beginning it now became a double-edged sword: Ginevra's numerous other suitors began to play on his mind and jealousy was beginning to make ever greater inroads into his letters. He was fearful that his position as Ginevra's 'top man' was about to be usurped. Admittedly this was partly Ginevra's doing: she saw no reason not to tell Scott of these potential rivals (as he saw them) and which boys she liked and who had escorted her where and when and so forth. "I'm perfectly fascinated with some boys, I'm willing to admit," she told him candidly. During their time apart Fitzgerald imagined Ginevra in the company of "some 'unknown Chicagoan' with crisp dark hair and glittering smile." By her own frank admission much of the time she was stepping out with some other handsome young man and though these were social occasions, parties and dances and the like and entirely innocent, she was beginning to find Scott's jealousy tiresome. Occasionally there were even flashes of anger or something very close to it: "Never say again that I'm going to marry Deering!" she wrote in November 1915, referring to Deering Davis, a mutual friend.

There is no indication that Ginevra's parents placed any overt pressure on her regarding her relationship with Scott but she cannot possibly have failed to be aware that like all other girls of her class she would be expected to marry a certain kind of husband and Scott was simply not that kind of husband. He had not distinguished himself academically—far from it; he came from a middle-class Roman Catholic family; he was the son of a grocery salesman of all things and was of Irish immigrant stock. Intelligence, wit, good looks and a way with words were simply not enough. In August 1916 Scott wrote in his journal the famous phrase 'Poor boys shouldn't think of marrying rich girls.' Understandably some have surmised that these words were spoken to Scott by Ginevra's father or that Scott had overheard these words spoken by another: whether they were or not or were simply indicative of how he had come to see the situation he was in, the substance of them perfectly encapsulates Scott's growing unease about the chasm between himself and Ginevra. Scott had been granted partial admission into a social circle of vast wealth and ostentation and, frankly, colossal snobbery: in summer 1915, having taken Ginevra to a Broadway show and then to the Ritz for a dance, an acquaintance volunteered to take Ginevra home

in his 'electric'—that is, an electrically-powered automobile of a

kind then considered to be a new-fangled novelty and extremely

expensive. In spite of this Scott was solemnly informed by another

friend that the possessor of the electric was "as poor as a church

mouse." If the owner of an expensive electric car was "as poor as

a church mouse" what did that make Scott? Increasingly he came

to feel himself to be on the outside of the world in which Ginevra

and her kind moved so effortlessly and comfortably. That Scott

carried a chip on his shoulder about the 'them-and-us' difference

between the vastly rich and the comparatively poor is a recurring

theme that appears again and again throughout his writings all

his life; it can be gauged from a representative passage on this

theme from his 1926 novelette *The Rich Boy*, written just after *The

Great Gatsby*:

> Let me tell you about the very rich. They are different from you
> and me. They possess and enjoy early, and it does something to
> them, makes them soft where we are hard, and cynical where
> we are trustful, in a way that, unless you were born rich, it is
> very difficult to understand. They think, deep in their hearts,
> that they are better than we are because we had to discover the
> compensations and refuges of life for ourselves. Even when they
> enter deep into our world or sink below us, they still think that
> they are better than we are. They are different.

"That was always my experience—," he would say in 1938, "a

poor boy in a rich town; a poor boy in a rich boy's school; a poor boy in a rich man's club at Princeton . . . I have never been able to forgive the rich for being rich and it has colored my entire life and works."[9] One of Fitzgerald's biographers implies that not only was the disparity one of the major reasons for the failure of the romance but that this was known to and admitted by Ginevra herself since she was "a child of wealth and in selecting her serious suitors, she probably couldn't consider a middle-class boy from St. Paul, no matter how charming and clever he was."[10] It is also possible that Scott's Irish heritage and Roman Catholicism were additional factors. Perhaps Ginevra simply grew away from him: even in the short span of their romance it is quite noticeable in her letters and diary that she grew up fast and demonstrated by the end of the relationship a degree of seriousness and maturity not evident at the beginning. In any case much later Scott would allege (to his daughter Scottie) that Ginevra dumped him "with the most supreme boredom and indifference." Many decades later Ginevra's granddaughter Ginevra King Chandler offered a similar observation: "She knew he was a great writer, but I don't think she ever considered herself a big part of the story . . . She was quite coy about it. She told me they had a lovely little romance but it wasn't a big deal."[11] But the available evidence suggests that this was simply not the case by any means. Ginevra certainly did consider herself to be passionately and seriously in love with Scott, if only for a relatively brief period. On the 22$^{nd}$ of February 1915 she told her diary: "I am madly in love with him. He is wonderful." On another occasion she wrote: "Oh Scott why aren't we . . . somewhere else to-night? Why aren't we at a dance in summer now with a full moon a big lovely garden and soft music in the distance. I don't want to be here!" These are hardly the declarations of someone for whom a romantic relationship is no big deal.

Things were not going well for Scott academically. As autumn 1915 wore into winter he continued to cut classes and his grades continued to slide. Finally in December 1915 he dropped out of Princeton for the remainder of the academic year and went back home to St. Paul—not something that would have improved his already somewhat suspect standing in the eyes of Mr and Mrs King and their milieu and perhaps even Ginevra herself. In fairness Scott was also in indifferent health: he claimed that he was beginning to develop tuberculosis and rather than being a hypochondriacal dodge there does seem to be sound evidence that Fitzgerald was indeed tubercular.

Ginevra was not faring much better at Westover either. In May 1916 she and a couple of her friends were caught leaning out of their dormitory windows to talk to some boys who were at the school for a senior dance. The headmistress, Miss Hilliard, took a dim view of this and called the three girls into her office for a carpeting during which (according to Ginevra's account to Scott) they were labelled as "bold, bad hussies" and "adventuresses" whose "honour was stained." Miss Hilliard told the trio that they would be expelled after their exams though this must have struck even the headmistress as extreme and was later retracted. Nevertheless after Charles King became involved he withdrew Ginevra from Westover in high dudgeon and installed her at Miss McFee's finishing school on West 72nd Street in Manhattan for her senior year.

Meanwhile back in St. Paul Scott was passing his time writing, concentrating specifically on two short stories based on himself and Ginevra which were his first attempts—the first of many, stretching all the way almost to the end of his life—to bring Ginevra alive in his writing and fictionalise their romance. The two stories are now lost, presumably discarded when Ginevra destroyed Scott's letters to her when their relationship ended, but we do know a few sketchy details about them and especially about the first which Scott titled 'The Perfect Hour.' The phrase came from Ginevra: it recurs throughout her letters and refers to her idealised picture of the relationship she wished they could have:

> What would it be like, she had wondered, if the two of them could be truly alone for one perfect hour? What if there were

no glass-enclosed parlors or bothersome chaperones or curious
parents or desirous suitors or Lake Forest friends or loud football
crowds? . . . "Honestly and truly," Ginevra had written him on
January 31st [1915], "it would be wonderful to have that perfect
hour, sometime, someday and somewhere." But they never did.
Scott, by now, must have realized that such perfect moments only
exist in fiction.[11]

"Someday—Scott—some day. Perhaps in a year—two—three—
We'll have that perfect hour! I want it—and so we'll have it!"

Scott was not the only one to write: his stories prompted
Ginevra to try her hand at a very brief (untitled) short story of her
own which she sent to him on the 6th of March, diffidently telling
him in the accompanying letter: "Enclosed you'll find out my idea
of a 'Perfect Hour' is [sic]. So you see my idea is quite different
from yours. It isn't a bit clever, so don't expect anything." James
L.W. West suggests that Ginevra's rather breathless little vignette,
naïve and unformed as it is (and reproduced in full in Professor
West's book The Perfect Hour), exerted a significant influence on
the development of Fitzgerald's most famous work, The Great
Gatsby, nearly a decade later:

Her story, like Fitzgerald's novel, is about a reunion. Her 'Ginevra'
character, like Daisy Buchanan, is married to a wealthy man with
whom she is unhappy. Jewels, furs, and a luxury car have not
satisfied her; she wants love and emotional fulfillment. 'Ginevra'
seeks out an old flame named 'Scott Fitz-Gerald'—apparently she
has kept up with him and knows where he lives (as Gatsby has
kept up with Daisy). 'Scott' is now a celebrity, connected in some
way with the movie industry and the stage. He lives in elaborately
decorated quarters and is looked after by a somber servant. He

wears a brown-and-white-checked outfit that might have hung in Jay Gatsby's closet, right next to the famous pink suit. Certain details in the story catch the eye: the clock in the sitting, room, for example, brings to mind the clock on the mantel in Nick Carraway's bungalow—an important detail in the reunion scene between Daisy and Gatsby . . . Daisy Buchanan resembles Ginevra physically; her voice, full of money, seems to be Ginevra's voice . . . the correspondences between Ginevra's story and Fitzgerald's novel are close enough to suggest that her story might have had an influence, perhaps even an important one, on the genesis of the novel.[12]

In November 1916 Scott told Ginevra that he was writing about her again in a short story called 'Babes in the Wood' for the *Nassau Literary Magazine*, the Princeton campus literary magazine. "It would be slick to have you write a story about me," Ginevra told him in early November. The story, not published until May 1917 (by which time Scott and Ginevra's relationship was over), included a fictionalised version of their first encounter and would be reworked for inclusion in Scott's first novel *This Side of Paradise* a few years later.

Slick or not Ginevra had been tiring of Scott for some time and now she decided that their relationship must come to an end, which it did in or at least by the end of January 1917 in which month he wrote in his *Ledger*: "Final break with Ginevra." There is no detailed account of exactly what happened: in October of that year Scott published another story in the *Nassau Lit.* entitled 'The Pierian Spring and the Last Straw' which intimates that he and Ginevra had had some form of furious argument, but even in a writer as consistently autobiographical as Fitzgerald we can't say for sure that this actually happened: it may have simply been a fictional plot device. Whatever the final straw may have been, after almost exactly two years Scott and Ginevra's romance, limping along as it had been for some time, was over. She continued to appear sporadically in his *Ledger* nonetheless. "Ginevra engaged?" he wrote quizzically in June and in the same month, "Girl at show resembled G.K."

In October 1917, six months after America had entered the Great War, Scott joined the army. He was commissioned as a second lieutenant and spent the next nine months in training camps across the Unites States: in Kansas, Kentucky and Georgia. As letters to his mother show he portrayed himself as blithely cavalier about the prospect of death, almost expecting to be killed in action: "I went into this perfectly cold-bloodedly and don't sympathize with the 'Give my son to country' etc. etc. etc. or 'Hero stuff,' because I just went and for purely social reasons. If you want to pray, pray for my soul and not that I won't be killed—the last doesn't seem to matter particularly and if you are a good Catholic the first ought to. To a profound pessimist about life, being in danger is not depressing. I have never been more cheerful."[13] Yet he was evidently disturbed by the fear that he would die without having given to the world some sign of his budding genius. In snatches in the officer's mess in the evening and at weekends he quickly wrote a novel which he called *The Romantic Egotist* which a few years later would in a dramatically revised version form the basis of *This Side of Paradise*, his first published novel. (His work rate was remarkable: he wrote *The Romantic Egotist*, a novel of some 120,000 words, in about three months). He clearly wished his novel to live on after him but not the numerous lengthy letters he had written to Ginevra. To a certain extent we can never know the full truth about Scott's feelings during their all too brief romance since Scott's side of the story is missing from his biography. Six months after the end of their relationship he asked Ginevra to destroy all his letters to her, a request with which she complied albeit with some puzzlement and dismay. In April 1915 she had told him, "Yes, I certainly do save letters! I wouldn't throw yours away for the world, and have them at present locked up in my strong-box—only there are so many that they dont all quite go in! Every now and then, when I feel blue, I pull out a nice, long, fat one, and read it through." Now he wanted every last one consigned to the flames. Exactly why he wanted so many beautifully crafted missives, many of them very long, to be obliterated is unknown but he asked Ginevra to do so all the same. "I have destroyed your letters—so you needn't be afraid that they will be held up as incriminating evidence," she told him on the 17th of July 1917.

"They were harmless—have you a guilty conscience? I'm sorry you think that I would hold them up to you as I never did think they meant anything." Ginevra likewise requested that Scott destroy her side of the correspondence ("If it isn't too much trouble you might destroy mine too") but not only did Scott fail to do so, he kept all of her letters and some years later had them typed up to serve as source material for some of the stories he was writing at the time. The originals do not survive so presumably after having them typed Scott destroyed them. Professor West surmises that Scott had the letters copied partly for practical reasons—Ginevra's handwriting was sometimes difficult to decipher and not always conspicuously easy on the eye—but also because a neatly clinical typescript was a way of distancing himself from the handwritten originals and the acutely painful emotions they would have aroused in him even so many years later. "Having them typed," West claims, "allowed him to objectify the letters in a way that he couldn't have done if he'd held the actual letters that she'd held and written."[14]

His military training took him to Camp Sheridan in Alabama and it was at a dance at the Country Club of Montgomery that he met the beautiful, eccentric, brilliant, eighteen-year-old Zelda Sayre, a native of the state capital. Scott met Zelda in the same month that Ginevra announced her engagement, sufficiently quickly for us to be able to say that he fell in love with Zelda very much on the rebound. Yet if his own account is to be believed it was hardly love at first sight: in his journal for September 1917 Scott noted "Fell in love on the 7th" — two months after their first encounter.

Zelda was born in Montgomery in July 1900, the daughter of Judge Anthony and Minnie Machen Sayre:

> At eighteen she was a celebrated belle with a domain that extended over Alabama and Georgia. She was like nobody else and practiced a don't-give-a-damn code. Even more dramatically than Ginevra, Zelda possessed the qualities that Fitzgerald required in a girl. She was beautiful, independent, socially secure (but not wealthy), and responsive to his ambitions. More than any girl he had ever known, Zelda shared his romantic egotism. She and Fitzgerald wanted the same things — metropolitan glamour, success, fame . . . She was not well-read, but her mind had a brilliant quality in its ability to make unlikely connections and express itself in fresh or startling ways . . . She was unconventional and even wild, but she maintained her reputation within the boundaries of Southern feminine conduct . . . Her hair was a dark-blond honey colour — like a chow's, as Fitzgerald described it. She had blue eys, thin lips, and a straight nose that gave her an almost hawklike profile. Standing two or three inches shorter than Fitzgerald's five feet seven, her erect posture made her seem taller than she was, and she moved with a dancer's grace . . . Zelda was one of the most popular girls in town because she was known as a good sport who would do anything for the fun of it . . . Like Fitzgerald, Zelda had an exhibitionistic streak. But there was a difference: Fitzgerald wanted admiration or at least attention; Zelda did not care what people thought. His behaviour indicated insecurity: hers seemed to display defiance.[15]

After a couple of months Scott and Zelda's relationship was clearly deepening into something serious but in spite of this fact it was far from the end of Scott and Ginevra's association. Their romance might have been over in any formal sense but they had parted without overt bitterness and recrimination and they kept in touch for a time after January 1917 even if on an intermittent basis. Because it had been difficult for the young couple to meet in person as regularly as they would have wished they had come to depend upon letters as a means of communication and clearly it proved to be a habit which was impossible to shake off even after Ginevra had rejected him romantically. In July 1918 Scott wrote to Ginevra once again: Prof. West speculates that in spite of his burgeoning relationship with Zelda Sayre, Scott wanted to rekindle his epistolary relationship with Ginevra. She wrote back on the 15th of July to inform him ("I've got a piece of very wonderful news for you that I'm sure will be a great surprise") that she was engaged to be married to William Hamilton (Bill) Mitchell, a wealthy young man who was the son of a business associate of her father—the Mitchells and the Kings knew each other personally; Ginevra had known Bill all her life. He was intelligent, good looking and charming: he had left Harvard to join the naval aviation corps where he excelled as a flyer to such an extent that he soon became a flight instructor in Key West, Florida. It was on one of his periods of home leave that he proposed to Ginevra. Her prominent position in the upper echelons of American social life meant that Scott could easily have discovered the news for himself from its announcement in the newspapers soon enough but she pointedly told Scott that she wanted him to be the first to know. "To say that I am the happiest girl on earth would be expressing it mildly," she wrote, "and I wish you knew Bill so that you could know how very lucky I am." (In keeping with her desire to rewrite the past, much later Ginevra would claim: "I'm surprised I remembered to write him. I had quite a few other letters to write, because I was engaged to two other people then. That was very easy during the war because you'd never get caught. It was just covering yourself in case of a loss"). A week later on the 21st of July Scott wrote back from Camp Sheridan to offer his warmest congratulations in what remains his sole surviving letter to her. "This is to congratulate you—I don't know Billy Mitchell, but from all I've heard of him he must be one of the best ever—Doesn't it make you sigh with relief to be settled and think of all the men you escaped marrying?" (In fact Scott did know Mitchell, albeit very slightly: he had even met him briefly during one of his visits to Lake Forest, possibly in August 1916). His pleasure was genuine and his cordiality unfeigned: his largesse does him credit. But it was only half the story: that Ginevra's marriage cut him deeply and desperately painfully can be ascertained by the fact that Scott pasted her photograph and the newspaper article announcing the marriage into his scrapbook, which also contained one of her handkerchiefs, a few stray sad tokens of his love for the woman who was now joined to another man. Underneath the cuttings he scrawled in large, untidy letters: "The end of a once poignant story." In this he was sorely mistaken: it would turn out to be very far from the end.

Bill Mitchell and Ginevra King were married in Chicago's St Chrysostom's church on the 4th of September 1918, honeymooning in Florida where they also lived for a time before returning to Lake Forest after the end of the war two months later to live in a spacious Tudor-style home on Rosemary Avenue (bought for them by Bill's father) that they shared for the remainder of their married life. We know that Scott was invited to the wedding—his invitation was pasted into his scrapbook—and whether the invitation came from Ginevra or her husband-to-be or both the gesture again does her, or them, credit. But there is no record that he actually attended. James West notes that at the time Scott was at Camp Sheridan and would have found it difficult to get away to attend the wedding, but in all probability even if he had been perfectly free to go he still could not have done so. To have the woman he loved marry another man was a hard enough blow to take: to be physically present in the same room while the ceremony was conducted would have been unendurable to almost any man.

Scott was preparing to go overseas to see military action for the first time. Early in November 1918 he was sent to Camp

Mills on Long Island, the embarkation point for US troops bound for the trenches and battlefields of Europe. However the war came to an end just a few days later on the 11th and Scott went back to Alabama to await his discharge without ever having been abroad or having fired a shot in anger. In Montgomery he carried on courting Zelda and at some point proposed to her. Zelda accepted. Yet even at this stage Ginevra continued to occupy his mind. An occasional poet, in the *Nassau Lit* in 1919 Scott published a poem which clearly referred to her:

> All my ways she wove of light
> Wove them half alive,
> Made them warm and beauty-bright . . .
> So the shining, ambient air
> Clothes the golden waters where
> The pearl fishers dive.
> When she wept and begged a kiss
> Very close I'd hold her,
> Oh I know so well in this
> Fine, fierce joy of memory
> She was very young like me
> Tho' half an aeon older.
>
> Once she kissed me very long,
> Tip-toes out the door,
> Left me, took her light along,
> Faded as a music fades . . .
> Then I saw the changing shades,
> Color-blind no more.

In February 1919 Scott was discharged from the army and went to New York to work for a time for the Barron Collier advertising agency, though he travelled regularly down to Montgomery to see Zelda. Scott and Zelda's romance was passionate but this proved to be a double-edged sword: from the off their relationship was fractious and unpredictable, marked by furious and bitter arguments, jealousy, threats and recriminations on both sides, not to mention Scott's long-standing sense of financial and social inferiority. Matters came to a head in June 1919 when Zelda broke off their engagement. In New York a self-pitying, self-dramatising but undeniably deeply wounded Scott went on an extended drinking binge throughout the rest of the summer (a period in which he said to a friend of Zelda: "I wouldn't care if she died, but I couldn't stand to have anybody else marry her") after which he climbed aboard the wagon and went back to his parents in St. Paul where, with their financial support, he continued to work on his writing: on various short stories which he tried to sell with almost no success but more substantially on the revision of *The Romantic Egotist,* Scott's idea being that if he could finish and publish his first novel he might be able to win over Zelda. The gamble worked: in this he was absolutely correct. After comprehensively recasting the book in six feverish weeks of maniacal hard work and renaming it as *This Side of Paradise* (the title taken from a poem by Rupert Brooke) Scott submitted it to Scribners in September 1919 who accepted it for publication within days. With literary success just around the corner Scott returned triumphantly to Zelda and in November 1919 their engagement was resumed.

*This Side of Paradise* was published in March 1920. It was both a critical and commercial success, earning glowing plaudits from most reviewers and selling well: the initial print run sold out in just three days. The *Chicago Tribune* declared that "it bears the impress . . . of genius," while the acerbic H.L. Mencken, a man not often given to fulsome praise, declared that it was the best American novel he had seen of late. Today, when viewed next to *Tender is the Night* and especially *The Great Gatsby*—arguably his masterpiece—, it is probably fair to say that it is generally considered to be one of the slighter works in the Fitzgerald canon but in its day it was something of a sensation and was certainly the most popular of all his books in his lifetime. Scott had arrived, a new star in the American literary firmament. He was now a published novelist whose book had sold well, earning him nationwide fame, a significant amount of money and had garnered the praise of the critics. Thus he was in a position to marry Zelda, which he did in a chapel of New York's St. Patrick's Cathedral on the 3rd of April 1920, soon afterwards moving to Westport, Connecticut before moving back to New York in October. Their only child, a beloved daughter they named Frances Scott Fitzgerald but always called Scottie, was born in St. Paul in October 1921.

Marriage to Zelda, the birth of their daughter and the publication of his first novel marked the advent of the 1920s and of what soon became known as the Roaring Twenties or the Jazz Age of which Fitzgerald was the leading literary exponent in the US. The first half of the decade was far and away the most productive era of Fitzgerald's writing career, but unfortunately marriage, fatherhood, literary success and a certain amount of disposable income went hand in hand with a dramatic worsening of Scott's abuse of alcohol. The high sales of *This Side of Paradise* did not make Scott a rich man: such money as it did earn was extremely welcome of course but his profligate ways meant that he still needed to borrow heavily and widely. This and the much more lucrative sales of his numerous shorter fiction pieces enabled the Fitzgeralds to live a life of ostentatious extravagance and excess throughout much of the 1920s which for Scott particularly meant drinking ceaselessly, although in fairness he was and remained a supremely disciplined craftsman. Zelda drank much more than her share too but without the desperate and compulsive element or the furtive secrecy which characterises the incipient alcoholic which by now Scott certainly was. (When Scott hired a new secretary in Los Angeles in 1939 one of her first duties was to gather up the empty gin bottles in a sack and discreetly take them out to throw them over the side of a canyon). Zelda's own behaviour was outrageous but not conspicuously more so than had become the norm for other people in her position. Years later Sheilah Graham, Scott's girlfriend for his final three years, remembered:

> . . . the 20s were a crazy time, what with Tallulah and John Barrymore making spectacles of themselves, so that Zelda in its context was simply 'an original.' Those plunges into the Plaza fountain—today she would have been carted off to Bellevue. The undressing at the Follies—well, that at least might be countenanced today as streaking. But streakers seem tame compared to Zelda. She was flamboyantly wild in an era when even little old ladies were seen staggering across the lobby of the old Waldorf Astoria.[16]

As already noted Scott had been a drinker since his student days but several factors—among them the demands of supporting a wife and child, the need to follow up *This Side of Paradise*, the constant pressure to create familiar to any artist and possibly some genetic tendency inherited from his father—meant that he eventually became a full-blown and chronic alcoholic. Several people around him noted that in the beginning his tolerance for alcohol was extremely low: Ernest Hemingway—known, it's fair to say, as a major league drinker himself—noted with contempt that even in the early 1920s that Fitzgerald "would pass out cold at the number of drinks that would just make you feel good" while Louis Bromfield recalled: "One cocktail and he was off. It seemed to affect him as much as five or six drinks affected Hemingway or myself." However year after year after year of wall-to-wall boozing meant that his tolerance for alcohol increased steadily throughout the 1920s until by the early to mid-1930s he was consuming at least two pints of gin every day and if not gin he was easily putting away twenty or thirty bottles of beer daily. On the other hand more than a few people felt that Fitzgerald actually acted drunker than he really was as a means of showing off and being the centre of attention. The words put into the mouth of Dick Ragland in the 1931 short story 'A New Leaf' were nakedly autobiographical: "About the time I came into some money I found that with a few drinks I got expansive and somehow had the ability to please people, and the idea turned my head. Then I began to take a whole lot of drinks to keep going and have everybody think I was wonderful." We can only be grateful that he didn't come into more money than he actually did: in 1935 he told his friend Laura Guthrie that if he'd inherited more money he would have killed himself with dissipation years earlier.

The Fitzgeralds lived a largely rootless existence much as Scott and his parents had. They never truly owned their own home or sunk roots in one particular spot for long: they travelled across Europe and across America staying in rented accommodation or the most luxurious of hotels in such a manner as to suggest an anxious, almost desperate wanderlust, shuttling back and forth between New York, Paris, Long Island, the French Riviera, Rome, drinking and partying and eating up money as they went. Scott was almost constantly in debt but equally regularly back out of it—just. He published two further novels in the 1920s, *The Beautiful and Damned* in 1922 and *The Great Gatsby* three years later; neither were bestsellers as *This Side of Paradise* had been but they sold well enough though Scott earned much more money from his short fiction, much of which appeared in the *Saturday Evening Post* and other mass circulation magazines known in their day as 'slicks.' By 1929 the *Post* was paying him $4,000 per short story, added to which subsidiary rights of adaptations brought in even more money so the disastrous Wall Street crash of that year and the subsequent years of economic depression barely affected the Fitzgeralds, not least because of the fact that they did not lose any savings because they had none to lose. At least some of this material was, to be blunt, hackwork churned out at high speed simply for the money but a writer of his calibre was almost incapable of writing an inelegant sentence: Dorothy Parker observed that while Scott could write a bad story, he couldn't write badly.

Bill and Ginevra Mitchell had similarly mixed fortunes throughout the decade. They were financially secure: like his father-in-law, Bill Mitchell became a successful stockbroker cofounding the firm of Mitchell, Hutchins & Co. Tragically his parents died in a road accident in October 1927: Bill's very substantial inheritance as well as shrewd investments meant that like the Fitzgeralds they lived on in comfort but unlike the Fitzgeralds in permanent financial security. Bill was an astute businessman who saw the way that things were going economically and in February 1929 he withdrew all their money from both the New York and Chicago stock exchanges thus protecting their assets from the crash in October. Unlike the Fitzgeralds who were often in the public eye and very happy to be so, most very wealthy people during the Depression years tried to maintain as low a profile as possible: robberies and even kidnapping for ransom were commonplace—the Mitchells were in fact the target of a bungled armed burglary in November 1931. Nevertheless they were aware of how lucky they had been and were sensible of their obligations, opening a soup kitchen in their own home serving hot food to the unemployed of the area. As befitted a Westover girl Ginevra settled into comfortably respectable domesticity, active in all manner of charitable causes. She was a dedicated sportswoman, making herself a good golfer, and a keen horsewoman and hunter.

There was also heartache in what must have seemed to the world at large like a charmed existence. The second of their three children, Charles King Mitchell but always known as Buddy, was born in June 1921 with what we now call Down Syndrome. In those days he would have been referred to—even or especially by doctors and not with any malicious intent—as a mongoloid idiot, the standard term for such a child decades before the actual cause of the condition (an extra chromosome) was identified in 1959. Easily the majority of Down children were committed to institutions where most died in infancy or in early adult life at the latest, succumbing to the manifold health problems associated with the condition. Bill and Ginevra had the wealth to be able to spare Buddy this unhappy fate and he was cared for at home, living with a nurse on the top floor of the family mansion. In common with Down children generally his sister, five years his junior, remembered him as a sweet-natured and gentle little boy.

The romance between Scott and Ginevra was long since dead and buried in any formal sense but their relationship, using the word loosely, never really came to an end on his side. He never forgot her. A married family man though he now was Scott continued to be haunted, at times perhaps even tormented by the memory of Ginevra. Recreating her, albeit in fictional form to serve artistic ends, became and clearly remained an almost compulsive need throughout his writing career: while Zelda was certainly a model for his most famous female characters so was Ginevra, either singly or in parallel to Zelda. Most of his characters were composites—it was comparatively rare for him to base one of his creations on just one real-life individual—but Ginevra was certainly there throughout his writing life, always ready to be invoked. As his biographer Scott Donaldson puts it, Fitzgerald always had more than one female model in mind when he was creating his female characters: though a great many of them were certainly composites drawn from various different people Ginevra was always a primary inspiration. Like so many creative artists he needed a muse, a model to write about, or for, or to, and in this regard there was no more urgent spur than Ginevra and the desperate hurt she had caused him. "The rejection devastated Fitzgerald, even as it supplied him with the basic subject matter of much of his fiction. There are probably more characters in his stories and novels modelled on Ginevra than on Zelda, who caught him on the rebound."[17] How closely the real Ginevra King and the fictional characters she inspired coincided is open to debate. "I don't know that Fitzgerald ever captured the real Ginevra in his fiction," says Prof. West, "but then he wasn't really trying to. Rather, he was creating a character— by beginning with the young girl he had known but amplifying her personality, giving it flaws, and letting his imagination play over the possibilities for the woman she might become." Even so, West continues, "Ginevra is arguably the most important romance Fitzgerald ever experienced, more than Zelda. He lost her, but the ideal of her remained throughout his life." Wholly or partially she became Isabelle Borgé and Rosalind Connage in *This Side of Paradise*; Kismine Washington in 'The Diamond as Big as the Ritz'; Judy Jones in 'Winter Dreams'; Nicole Diver in *Tender is the Night*; Josephine Perry in the 'Josephine' stories and most famously of all Daisy Buchanan in *The Great Gatsby* to name but a few. Fitzgerald was quite open about this to anybody who cared to listen. In 1935 he was asked to comment on Judy Jones in 'Winter Dreams'; he responded that she had been based on "my first girl 18-20 whom I've used over and over and never forgotten." Using Ginevra as a model for female characters either wholly or in part spanned his writing career almost in its entirety, all the way from 1917's 'Babes in the Woods' right up to 'Three Hours Between Planes' in 1939 and all points in between:

> He turned to Ginevra repeatedly in his short fiction, and most often in those stories that he chose *not* to include in the four cloth-bound collections that he published during his career— *Flappers and Philosophers* (1920), *Tales of the Jazz Age (1922)*, *All the Sad Young Men* (1926) and *Taps at Reveille* (1935). In many of these uncollected (and therefore lesser-known) stories, Fitzgerald wrote about a failed romance between a poor boy and rich girl, often followed by a reunion between the two characters years later. In the early stories, the ones he published during the 1920s, the man is usually taken away by the war. Sometimes he returns as a damaged battlefield hero and is reunited with a heroine whose social status has fallen. In other narratives the hero leaves

to make his fortune through business derring-do, then returns as a wealthy man and is reunited with the rich girl. Sometimes a new love springs up, more mature and realistic than the first infatuation; more often the reunion generates no sparks, suggesting that first love cannot be recaptured and repeated. These patterns are found also in stories that Fitzgerald wrote during the 1930s, though now the plot device that separates the young lovers is the Depression, not the war. Otherwise the mechanics of the stories are the same.[18]

'Winter Dreams', first published in the *Metropolitan Magazine* in December 1922 (and collected in 1926's *All the Sad Young Men*) in particular deserves scrutiny. Not only considered one of Fitzgerald's finest short stories and on that account widely anthologised, it is one of those pieces of short fiction from the early 1920s which rehearses the themes which would be given their fullest and finest expression in *The Great Gatsby* three years later. Matthew J. Bruccoli is quite right to regard 'Winter Dreams' as "virtually a preview" of *Gatsby*.

Dexter Green is a middle-class boy, the son of a grocery store owner in Keeble, Minnesota who dreams of joining the ranks of the old money elite. Dexter becomes a teenaged golf caddy at Black Bear Lake golf club working for Mortimer Jones. Dexter meets Mortimer's eleven-year-old daughter Judy and promptly develops a massive crush on her, but when one day he is assigned to be her caddy wounded pride takes over and he quits his job, unwilling to be her servant.

A dozen years later, after college and starting on a business career, Dexter meets Judy again on the golf course. She is now twenty-three and has become a stunningly beautiful young woman. Judy invites Dexter to dinner and they begin an affair but later Dexter discovers that he is just one of a number of men that Judy is stringing along simultaneously. She also turns out to be materialistic and rather shallow. "I've just had a terrible afternoon," she tells him after dinner. "There was a man I cared about, and this afternoon he told me out of a clear sky that he was poor as a church-mouse. He'd never even hinted it before." While Judy is away in Florida, Dexter becomes engaged to a girl called Irene Scheerer who seems to be the polar opposite of Judy: warm, kind-hearted but not slender or graceful and rather plain. Yet even with his marriage to Irene set for the near future it is Judy who continues to occupy his thoughts:

> Summer, fall, winter, spring, another summer, another fall—so much he had given of his active life to the incorrigible lips of Judy Jones. She had treated him with interest, with encouragement, with malice, with indifference, with contempt. She had inflicted on him the innumerable little slights and indignities possible in such a case—as if in revenge for having ever cared for him at all. She had beckoned him and yawned at him and beckoned him again and he had responded often with bitterness and narrowed eyes. She had brought him ecstatic happiness and intolerable agony of spirit. She had caused him untold inconvenience and not a little trouble. She had insulted him, and she had ridden over him, and she had played his interest in her against his interest in his work—for fun. She had done everything to him except

to criticise him—this she had not done—it seemed to him only because it might have sullied the utter indifference she manifested and sincerely felt toward him.

When autumn had come and gone again it occurred to him that he could not have Judy Jones. He had to beat this into his mind but he convinced himself at last. He lay awake at night for a while and argued it over. He told himself the trouble and the pain she had caused him, he enumerated her glaring deficiencies as a wife. Then he said to himself that he loved her, and after a while he fell asleep. For a week, lest he imagined her husky voice over the telephone or her eyes opposite him at lunch, he worked hard and late, and at night he went to his office and plotted out his years.

Time moves on. Judy goes away to Florida for long enough for Dexter's emotions to begin to settle:

> For the first time in over a year Dexter was enjoying a certain tranquility of spirit. Judy Jones had been in Florida, and afterward in Hot Springs, and somewhere she had been engaged, and somewhere she had broken it off. At first, when Dexter had definitely given her up, it had made him sad that people still linked them together and asked for news of her, but when he began to be placed at dinner next to Irene Scheerer people didn't ask him about her any more—they told him about her. He ceased to be an authority on her.

This relative equanimity does not last. Dexter's ostensibly dormant passion for Judy proves to be irresistible: when she returns from Florida they meet up once more at a dance and instantly he is captivated all over again. In fact Judy asks Dexter not only to pick up where they left off but asks to marry him; for this reason he breaks off his engagement to Irene but just a month later Judy spurns him for a second time offering the specious excuse that she doesn't want to "take him away" from Irene. All the same

Dexter cannot bring himself to hate Judy. "He loved her, and he would love her until the day he was too old for loving—but he could not have her. So he tasted the deep pain that is reserved only for the strong, just as he had tasted for a little while the deep happiness." Devastated, having lost not one but the two women in his life, Dexter joins the army to fight in the Great War. "He was one of those young thousands who greeted the war with a certain amount of relief, welcoming the liberation from webs of tangled emotion."

Seven years later, long after the war, Dexter has become a highly successful and immensely rich businessman in New York City. He hasn't been home in years and has kept his former life—Judy Jones included—locked away in some secret part of himself. Or so he believes. One day a man named Devlin from Detroit visits Dexter on business: by an incredible coincidence it transpires that Devlin knows Judy, now married to a man named Lud Simms (Devlin was an usher at Judy's wedding) with children but unhappily married. Her looks have apparently faded:

> "So you're from the Middle West," said the man Devlin with careless curiosity. "That's funny—I thought men like you were probably born and raised on Wall Street. You know—wife of one of my best friends in Detroit came from your city. I was an usher at the wedding."
> Dexter waited with no apprehension of what was coming.
> "Judy Simms," said Devlin with no particular interest; "Judy Jones she was once."

"Yes, I knew her." A dull impatience spread over him. He had heard, of course, that she was married—perhaps deliberately he had heard no more.

"Awfully nice girl," brooded Devlin meaninglessly, "I'm sort of sorry for her."

"Why?" Something in Dexter was alert, receptive, at once.

"Oh, Lud Simms has gone to pieces in a way. I don't mean he ill-uses her, but he drinks and runs around."

"Doesn't she run around?"

"No. Stays at home with her kids."

"Oh."

"She's a little too old for him," said Devlin.

"Too old!" cried Dexter. "Why, man, she's only twenty-seven."

. . .

"Go on, then. Go on."

"What do you mean?"

"About Judy Jones."

Devlin looked at him helplessly.

"Well, that's, I told you all there is to it. He treats her like the devil. Oh, they're not going to get divorced or anything. When he's particularly outrageous she forgives him. In fact, I'm inclined to think she loves him. She was a pretty girl when she first came to Detroit."

A pretty girl! The phrase struck Dexter as ludicrous.

"Isn't she—a pretty girl, any more?"

"Oh, she's all right."

"Look here," said Dexter, sitting down suddenly, "I don't understand. You say she was a 'pretty girl' and now you say she's 'all right.' I don't understand what you mean—Judy Jones wasn't a pretty girl, at all. She was a great beauty. Why, I knew her, I knew her. She was—"

Devlin laughed pleasantly.

"I'm not trying to start a row," he said. "I think Judy's a nice girl and I like her. I can't understand how a man like Lud Simms could fall madly in love with her, but he did." Then he added: "Most of the women like her."

Dexter looked closely at Devlin, thinking wildly that there must be a reason for this, some insensitivity in the man or some private malice.

"Lots of women fade just like that," Devlin snapped his fingers. "You must have seen it happen. Perhaps I've forgotten how pretty she was at her wedding. I've seen her so much since then, you see. She has nice eyes."

Dexter, unlike the eponymous Gatsby three years later, realises with horror that his dream has died:

> He had thought that having nothing else to lose he was invulnerable at last—but he knew that he had just lost something more, as surely as if he had married Judy Jones and seen her fade away before his eyes.
>
> The dream was gone. Something had been taken from him. In a sort of panic he pushed the palms of his hands into his eyes and tried to bring up a picture of the waters lapping on Sherry Island and the moonlit veranda, and gingham on the golf-links and the dry sun and the gold colour of her neck's soft down. And her mouth damp to his kisses and her eyes plaintive with melancholy and her freshness like new fine linen in the morning. Why, these things were no longer in the world! They had existed and they existed no longer.
>
> For the first time in years the tears were streaming down his face. But they were for himself now. He did not care about mouth and eyes and moving hands. He wanted to care, and he could not care. For he had gone away and he could never go back any more. The gates were closed, the sun was gone down, and there was no beauty but the gray beauty of steel that withstands all time. Even the grief he could have borne was left behind in the country of illusion, of youth, of the richness of life, where his winter dreams had flourished.

There is something within hailing distance of obsession in the sheer number of times that Fitzgerald returned to and worried at the theme of ultimately doomed love between the rich upper-class girl and the comparatively poor middle-class boy. Perhaps in writing about Ginevra and what she meant to him then and now, hidden behind a succession of invented names and other characteristics, he sought to exorcise her memory but if this was his intention it backfired: dwelling upon her to such an extent raked up all the worst and most painful as well as the happiest memories of their brief but, for Scott, unforgettable romance. There was undoubtedly an element of idealisation in play here. For Scott, Ginevra "eventually became an abstraction . . . he did not watch her grow older; in his mind the sadnesses and blows of life did not touch her. Zelda, on the other hand, was always before him. He observed her as she lost her youthful bloom, then watched her drift through the 1920s with little direction or purpose . . . Fitzgerald watched Zelda lose her mental equilibrium and documented that decline in *Tender is the Night*. Ginevra, however, remained impervious to change, preserved within his memories."[19] Writing, like memory, freezes time. Especially when drawing upon his own life the writer of fiction can halt the march of time and keep the past alive in permanent stasis the way things really were or were preferred to be. Until they met for the last time in 1937 in some way perhaps Ginevra remained in Scott's memory exactly as she had been when he left her, still eighteen, still young, still beautiful. We have the example of Charles Dickens and Maria Beadnell to warn us just how fraught with danger to the heart nurturing such memories can be.

Staying in touch with her undoubtedly kept the wounds open. More than three years after the end of their romance he wrote to Ginevra shortly before the publication of *This Side of Paradise*, proudly sending her a copy of his first novel and informing her of his forthcoming marriage. She wrote back on the 17$^{th}$ of April telling him of the son she had had and congratulating him on his marriage and on the appearance of his book. Her reply makes it clear that although Scott had informed her that he was to be married he had been cagey about the specifics and had not even mentioned Zelda by name:

> Dear Scott,
>
> Your very nice present was a-waiting me on my return from California last Saturday, and I haven't written to thank you as I wished to read some of your book before I sent my congratulations to you . . . the book is a great success, I personally think. Also everyone seems to be speaking of it, and you have made a name for yourself. Not that I didn't think for a moment but that you eventually would . . . I cannot begin to tell you how really pleased I am at your success, so try to read between these incoherent lines and gather that I'm proud to know you!
>
> When next you are in Chicago, please come and see us. Telephone conversations are very unsatisfactory, especially as the last one we had was rudely interrupted by the yelling of my young son! He's quite a boy. You had better come up to see him, anyway, also to meet Bill—By the way, who are you going to marry so shortly? Why didn't you tell me her name n'everything instead of mere insinuations? You're a funny one—
>
> Many, many thanks to you, Scott, for remembering me, and I do wish you all the success in the world!

According to Prof. James West, Scott never ceased to wonder after Ginevra and her life. "He probably kept up with the major events of her life through mutual friends, but he carefully avoided seeing her so that his illusions would remain undisturbed," which last he openly admitted to his daughter Scottie shortly before seeing

Ginevra face to face for the final time in 1937, three years before his death. Clearly for a very long time—twenty years in fact—the memory of Ginevra and the part that she had played and still played in his inner life was so sacrosanct that Scott dared not risk it being sullied by prosaic reality. For her part, "[Ginevra] would surely have been aware of Scott's fame as a writer, and she must have seen reviews, photographs, and interviews with him in newspapers and magazines. Perhaps she kept up with the progress of his life through friends in St. Paul. How much of his work she read is not known. She was not a literary person; people who knew her do not remember her as a regular reader of fiction, nor do they recall her ever discussing Fitzgerald's work. Probably she was unaware of how important, to Fitzgerald, his memories of her had become."[20] Caroline Preston's fictionalised version of the Scott-Ginevra romance in her 2006 novel *Gatsby's Girl* has the older Ginevra keenly interested in the writing career of her former beau but there is no evidence that this was ever the case for the real Ginevra. On the other hand in 1948 she told Arthur Mizener during the research for his biography of Fitzgerald that she had read *This Side of Paradise, The Beautiful and Damned, The Great Gatsby* and *The Crack-Up*. Says Professor West:

> Perhaps he truly was only one among many former admirers. But the intensity of her letters to him in 1915 and the feelings that she

recorded in her diary suggest otherwise . . . During the earliest, best months of their romance, his letters touched her heart, and her love for him was fresh and new. As an adult she did not attempt to capitalize on her romance with Scott Fitzgerald, but it must have pleased her, at least a little, to know that he had become a major writer, that she had been his first love, and that he had never forgotten her.[21]

## II

In the spring of 1924 the Fitzgerald family were again on the move, heading to France where Scott worked hard on *The Great Gatsby*, a novel he had started to write in June of 1922, during the summer and autumn of that year. Progress on the novel was slow and it was written in various places both in America and Europe: it would be published finally on the 10th of April 1925.

Set in 1922 but recalled a couple of years after that date *The Great Gatsby* is narrated by Nick Carraway, a young bachelor from a wealthy Midwestern family. After graduating from Yale in 1915 and serving in the Great War he returns to America, working eventually in New York City where he learns the bond business. Despite his wealth Nick lives relatively simply in a modest bungalow at West Egg on Long Island, thinly-fictionalised version of Kings Point and Sands Point on the well-heeled North Shore of Long Island where he, Zelda and Scottie lived between October 1922 and May 1923 and where he made slow progress on *Gatsby*. West Egg is the *nouveau riche* counterpart of its neighbour East Egg, the haunt of those of old money stock. East Egg happens to be the home of Daisy Buchanan, Nick's second cousin once removed, and her husband Tom and their baby daughter Pammy:

> I looked back at my cousin who began to ask me questions in her low, thrilling voice. It was the kind of voice that the ear follows up and down as if each speech is an arrangement of notes that will never be played again. Her face was sad and lovely with bright things in it, bright eyes and a bright passionate mouth—but there was an excitement in her voice that men who had cared for her found difficult to forget: a singing compulsion, a whispered 'Listen,' a promise that she had done gay, exciting things just a while since and that there were gay, exciting things hovering in the next hour.

Tom Buchanan has been taken by some to have been modelled in at least some particulars on Bill Mitchell; for others (such as Scott Donaldson) Ginevra's father Charles was the more likely inspiration. Tom is an arrogant, boorish, overbearing, a rather unintelligent and unimaginative millionaire with an passion for polo (this last characteristic was certainly shared by Mr King), hypocritical, a white supremacist and also on one occasion violent towards women, hitting his mistress so hard in the face that he breaks her nose. There is no suggestion that the real-life Bill Mitchell or Charles King shared these attributes apart from the adoration of polo but the fact that Fitzgerald attributed them to Mitchell's fictional counterpart is telling if hardly surprising. In the book's opening chapter Nick drives over to East Egg one evening to have dinner with Tom and Daisy where he meets Daisy's friend Jordan

Baker, a professional golfer modelled on Edith Cummings, herself a real-life professional golfer and close friend of Ginevra King. It is clear from the outset that in spite of their wealth and privilege the Buchanans are trapped in a loveless marriage: Daisy is pampered but bored and unfulfilled, a rather distant mother to her daughter, and Jordan reveals to Nick that Tom has a mistress. Nick also learns that his near neighbour at West Egg is the eponymous Gatsby, an allegedly phenomenally rich man about whom nobody seems to know anything of any substance. His background, the source of his wealth, his personal life are all unknown beyond that he lives in a very large mansion, apparently alone apart from his domestic staff. To fill in the gaps in their knowledge people gossip that he might have been a cousin of the Kaiser or that he may have been a German spy in the war or that he once killed a man and other far-fetched speculations. What is known for sure about Gatsby that he regularly throws wild, lavish, boozy parties attended by crowds of hundreds of flappers or what in England at the time were being called bright young things—technically illegal gatherings given that between 1920 and 1933 Prohibition was in force. "His lavish parties are monuments to bad taste and conspicuous display," writes Scott Donaldson; "he thinks them splendid gatherings of the best and brightest." The first time that Gatsby shows Daisy around his mansion he asks her:

"Do you like it?"
"I love it, but I don't see how you live there all alone."
"I keep it always full of interesting people, night and day. People who do interesting things. Celebrated people."

To one of these parties Nick is himself invited one Saturday evening where he meets Gatsby, who turns out to be not the fat, complacent, middle-aged self-made man he had expected but a rather diffident man of about Nick's own age. It turns out that there is already a slight connection between them:

"Your face is familiar," he said, politely. "Weren't you in the Third Division during the war?"
"Why, yes. I was in the Ninth Machine-Gun Battalion."
"I was in the Seventh Infantry until June nineteen-eighteen. I knew I'd seen you somewhere before."

A curious sort of friendship springs up between the mysterious Gatsby and Nick and the former tells the latter some of the details of his life: that his family had all died (which by the book's end turns out to be a lie), that he hailed originally from San Francisco (another lie), that he had gone to Oxford university (true), that he had made his fortune in drugstores (only semi-true) and in oil and that he had "lived like a young rajah in all the capitals of Europe—Paris, Venice, Rome—collecting jewels, chiefly rubies, hunting big game, painting a little, things for myself only, and trying to forget something very sad that had happened to me long ago." Crucially for the plot only this last point is absolutely and unequivocally true. He is cagey about his current business affairs:

> I think he hardly knew what he was saying, for when I asked him what business he was in he answered "That's my affair," before he realized that it wasn't the appropriate reply.
> "Oh, I've been in several things," he corrected himself. "I was in the drug business and then I was in the oil business. But I'm not in either one now."

Having taken both Nick and Jordan Baker into his confidence to this limited extent Gatsby asks Nick to help him with a plan he has in mind. Gatsby refuses to tell Nick himself anything about it and leaves it to Jordan to explain all.

Jordan tells Nick that five years earlier, in 1917, back in Louisville, Daisy Fay (as she then was) met and fell in love with a handsome first lieutenant in the Army—a man by the name of Jay Gatsby. "The officer looked at Daisy while she was speaking, in a way that every young girl wants to be looked at sometime," Daisy recalled, "and because it seemed romantic to me I have remembered the incident ever since. His name was Jay Gatsby and I didn't lay eyes on him again for over four years—even after I'd met him on Long Island I didn't realize it was the same man." The romance was forbidden by Daisy's mother: Gatsby disappeared and Daisy went on to marry Tom Buchanan some nine months later. Gatsby hinted to Nick on another occasion that the end of the romance with Daisy left him suicidal and that he deliberately courted death in battle. "Then came the war, old sport. It was a great relief and I tried very hard to die but I seemed to bear an enchanted life." Gatsby survived and was unable to forget Daisy: it becomes clear that he has found out where she lives and has followed her to West Egg merely to be near her again in the hope that their romance could be rekindled. Jordan Baker tells Nick:

> "Well, about six weeks ago, she heard the name Gatsby for the first time in years. It was when I asked you — do you remember? — if you knew Gatsby in West Egg. After you had gone home she came into my room and woke me up, and said 'What Gatsby?' and when I described him — I was half asleep — she said in the strangest voice that it must be the man she used to know. It wasn't until then that I connected this Gatsby with the officer in her white car . . . "
>
> "It was a strange coincidence," I said.
>
> "But it wasn't a coincidence at all."
>
> "Why not?"
>
> "Gatsby bought that house so that Daisy would be just across the bay."
>
> Then it had not been merely the stars to which he had aspired on that June night. He came alive to me, delivered suddenly from the womb of his purposeless splendour.
>
> "He wants to know —" continued Jordan " — if you'll invite Daisy to your house some afternoon and then let him come over."
>
> The modesty of the demand shook me. He had waited five years and bought a mansion where he dispensed starlight to casual moths so that he could 'come over' some afternoon to a stranger's garden.
>
> "Did I have to know all this before he could ask such a little thing?"
>
> "He's afraid. He's waited so long. He thought you might be offended. You see he's a regular tough underneath it all."
>
> Something worried me.
>
> "Why didn't he ask you to arrange a meeting?"
>
> "He wants her to see his house," she explained. "And your house is right next door."

"Oh!"

"I think he half expected her to wander into one of his parties, some night," went on Jordan, "but she never did. Then he began asking people casually if they knew her, and I was the first one he found. It was that night he sent for me at his dance, and you should have heard the elaborate way he worked up to it . . ."

"And Daisy ought to have something in her life," murmured Jordan to me.

"Does she want to see Gatsby?"

"She's not to know about it. Gatsby doesn't want her to know. You're just supposed to invite her to tea."

"She doesn't understand," Gatsby tells Nick when the two finally discuss his plan. "She used to be able to understand. We'd sit for hours—":

> "I wouldn't ask too much of her," I ventured. "You can't repeat the past."
>
> "Can't repeat the past?" he cried incredulously. "Why of course you can!"
>
> He looked around him wildly, as if the past were lurking here in the shadow of his house, just out of reach of his hand.
>
> "I'm going to fix everything just the way it was before," he said, nodding determinedly. "She'll see."
>
> He talked a lot about the past and I gathered that he wanted to recover something, some idea of himself perhaps, that had gone into loving Daisy. His life had been confused and disordered since then, but if he could once return to a certain starting place and go over it all slowly, he could find out what that thing was . . .

"Neither the realities of time nor the contingencies of human character discourage him," Fitzgerald's first biographer, Arthur Mizener wrote. "When he discovers that in the five years since he has last seen Daisy Fay she has married and had a child, Gatsby decides that he will take her back to Louisville to the place—*and* the time, he obviously believes—where they had left off, and that they will start their life over again from there."[22]

The tea party goes ahead: Gatsby and Daisy meet up again for the first time in five years. The initial meeting is somewhat clumsy and awkward but Daisy and Gatsby resume their romance, embarking on a clandestine affair. Meanwhile rumours about Gatsby continue to swirl in New York: a reporter arrives at his mansion hoping to interview him. The reporter doesn't get his interview but Nick finally uncovers something of the truth about Gatsby's past. He was in fact born James Gatz into humble if not downright poor circumstances on a North Dakota farm. He went to college in St Olaf's, Minnesota but dropped out after just two weeks because he hated the menial janitorial work he had to do to pay his way. The following summer, aged just seventeen, he took a job on Lake Superior fishing for salmon and clam-digging: one day he spotted the yacht of Dan Cody, a wealthy alcoholic copper magnate and rowed out to the yacht to warn him about an approaching storm. Cody took Jimmy Gatz, now reinvented—reborn, even—as Jay Gatsby, under his wing and introduced him to a lifestyle of fantastic wealth and affluence for which Gatsby soon developed a taste. When Cody died he left Gatsby $25,000 but Cody's mistress prevented Gatsby from receiving his inheritance. Nevertheless Gatsby had set his sights upon the future course of his life: becoming a wealthy self-made man. Jimmy Gatz from the North Dakota farm was dead: long live the millionaire Jay Gatsby.

The characters now move toward their doom with something of the ominous inevitability of a Greek tragedy of which Nick is the chorus. The parties at Gatsby's mansion cease and his staff are dismissed. It has become clear to Nick that they were merely a highly elaborate ploy staged in the hope that one night Daisy would appear: now that Daisy and Gatsby have met and resumed their romance the parties have served their purpose. On the hottest day of the year Nick drives over to Tom and Daisy's house: there he is surprised to find Gatsby and Jordan as well. Exacerbated by the heat and fuelled by alcohol the mood in the room, already tense and oppressive, deteriorates: noticing telling looks between Daisy and Gatsby, Tom is beginning to suspect that something may be going on between them. Daisy suggests that they all go to New York: Nick rides with Jordan and Tom in Gatsby's car while Daisy and Gatsby travel in Tom's car. The quintet takes a suite at the Plaza hotel and endures a tense and ugly showdown:

"Wait a minute," snapped Tom, "I want to ask Mr. Gatsby one more question."
"Go on," Gatsby said politely.
"What kind of a row are you trying to cause in my house anyhow?"
They were out in the open at last and Gatsby was content.

> "He isn't causing a row." Daisy looked desperately from one to the other. "You're causing a row. Please have a little self control."
>
> "Self control!" repeated Tom incredulously. "I suppose the latest thing is to sit back and let Mr. Nobody from Nowhere make love to your wife. Well, if that's the idea you can count me out . . . "

With the already fraught situation worsened by still more alcohol (Scott Donaldson says that while Gatsby is never drunk and Nick rarely the book is "saturated with liquor") it finally falls out that Daisy and Gatsby knew each other before her marriage to Tom and had a romantic attachment. Tom reveals that he has been making discreet but thorough enquiries into Gatsby's background (hence the reference to Mr Nobody from Nowhere) and his present activities and tells the assembled company that Gatsby has made his fortune as a bootlegger, intimating that Gatsby has also been involved in illegal gambling:

> "I found out what your 'drug stores' were." He turned to us and spoke rapidly. "He and this Wolfshiem bought up a lot of side-street drug stores here and in Chicago and sold grain alcohol over the counter. That's one of his little stunts. I picked him for a bootlegger the first time I saw him and I wasn't far wrong . . . Walter could have you up on the betting laws too, but Wolfshiem scared him into shutting his mouth" . . . "That drug store business was just small change," continued Tom slowly, "but you've got something on now that Walter's afraid to tell me about."

The truth is now finally out: not just about the source of Gatsby's fortune but his affair with Daisy. Gatsby applies emotional pressure to Daisy, encouraging her to say that she had never loved Tom and that instead she had loved him all along:

"Your wife doesn't love you," said Gatsby. "She's never loved you. She loves me."

"You must be crazy!" exclaimed Tom automatically.

Gatsby sprang to his feet, vivid with excitement.

"She never loved you, do you hear?" he cried. "She only married you because I was poor and she was tired of waiting for me. It was a terrible mistake, but in her heart she never loved any one except me!"

At this point Jordan and I tried to go but Tom and Gatsby insisted with competitive firmness that we remain—as though neither of them had anything to conceal and it would be a privilege to partake vicariously of their emotions.

"Sit down Daisy." Tom's voice groped unsuccessfully for the paternal note. "What's been going on? I want to hear all about it."

"I told you what's been going on," said Gatsby. "Going on for five years—and you didn't know."

Tom turned to Daisy sharply.

"You've been seeing this fellow for five years?"

"Not seeing," said Gatsby. "No, we couldn't meet. But both of us loved each other all that time, old sport, and you didn't know. I used to laugh sometimes—" but there was no laughter in his eyes, "to think that you didn't know."

"Oh—that's all." Tom tapped his thick fingers together like a clergyman and leaned back in his chair.

"You're crazy!" he exploded. "I can't speak about what happened five years ago, because I didn't know Daisy then—and I'll be damned if I see how you got within a mile of her unless you brought the groceries to the back door. But all the rest of that's a God damned lie. Daisy loved me when she married me and she loves me now."

"No," said Gatsby, shaking his head.

"She does, though. The trouble is that sometimes she gets foolish ideas in her head and doesn't know what she's doing." He nodded sagely. "And what's more, I love Daisy too. Once in a while I go off on a spree and make a fool of myself, but I always come back, and in my heart I love her all the time."

"You're revolting," said Daisy. She turned to me, and her voice, dropping an octave lower, filled the room with thrilling scorn: "Do you know why we left Chicago? I'm surprised that they didn't treat you to the story of that little spree."

Gatsby walked over and stood beside her.

"Daisy, that's all over now," he said earnestly. "It doesn't matter any more. Just tell him the truth—that you never loved him—and it's all wiped out forever."

She looked at him blindly. "Why,—how could I love him—possibly?"

"You never loved him."

She hesitated. Her eyes fell on Jordan and me with a sort of appeal, as though she realized at last what she was doing—and as though she had never, all along, intended doing anything at all. But it was done now. It was too late.

"I never loved him," she said, with perceptible reluctance.

"Not at Kapiolani?" demanded Tom suddenly.

"No."

From the ballroom beneath, muffled and suffocating chords were drifting up on hot waves of air.

"Not that day I carried you down from the Punch Bowl to keep your shoes dry?" There was a husky tenderness in his tone. ". . . Daisy?"

"Please don't." Her voice was cold, but the rancour was gone from it. She looked at Gatsby. "There, Jay," she said—but her hand as she tried to light a cigarette was trembling. Suddenly she threw the cigarette and the burning match on the carpet.

"Oh, you want too much!" she cried to Gatsby. "I love you now—isn't that enough? I can't help what's past." She began to sob helplessly. "I did love him once—but I loved you too."

Gatsby's eyes opened and closed.

"You loved me *too*?" he repeated.

"Even that's a lie," said Tom savagely. "She didn't know you were alive. Why,—there're things between Daisy and me that you'll never know, things that neither of us can ever forget."

The words seemed to bite physically into Gatsby.

"I want to speak to Daisy alone," he insisted. "She's all excited now—"

"Even alone I can't say I never loved Tom," she admitted in a pitiful voice. "It wouldn't be true."

"Of course it wouldn't," agreed Tom.

She turned to her husband.

"As if it mattered to you," she said.

"Of course it matters. I'm going to take better care of you from now on."

"You don't understand," said Gatsby, with a touch of panic. "You're not going to take care of her any more."

"I'm not?" Tom opened his eyes wide and laughed. He could afford to control himself now. "Why's that?"

"Daisy's leaving you."

"Nonsense."

"I am, though," she said with a visible effort.

The situation is at breaking point. In spite of Daisy's assertion that she is leaving her husband, when Tom sends her back home she complies:

> "You two start on home, Daisy," said Tom. "In Mr. Gatsby's car."
> She looked at Tom, alarmed now, but he insisted with magnanimous scorn.
> "Go on. He won't annoy you. I think he realizes that his presumptuous little flirtation is over."

A distraught Daisy flees the scene and runs outside to Gatsby's car. Gatsby wants to drive her home but Daisy, despite having drunk a considerable amount of alcohol, insists on taking the wheel as she thinks it will calm her down. Tom, Jordan and Nick follow in Tom's car. Tom's braggadocio and his ostensibly magnanimous gesture in allowing Daisy to ride home with Gatsby indicate that in revealing Gatsby's criminal activities he has irreparably damaged and demeaned him in Daisy's eyes: in short, that he had won.

But this will be a game without winners. Before reaching home Gatsby's car is involved in a hit-and-run accident. Daisy runs into and kills a woman standing by the roadside who happens to be Myrtle Wilson—her husband's mistress. In a panic Daisy and Gatsby flee but Tom, Jordan and Nick stop to join the crowd gathering at the scene. It later transpires that Tom, in a fit of rage, grief and revenge ("The God damned coward!" he whimpered. "He didn't even stop his car"), tells Myrtle's husband that a man named Gatsby knocked down his wife—it was after all Gatsby's car which struck Myrtle although Tom wasn't to know that his wife was behind the wheel and would presumably have continued to insist that Gatsby was driving even if he had known. Back at Tom's house Nick discovers Gatsby skulking in the bushes outside: Gatsby tells Nick that he has been waiting there in order to make sure that Tom did not hurt Daisy. He tells Nick that Daisy was driving when the car ploughed into Myrtle but that he himself will shoulder all responsibility for the accident for Daisy's sake. Still worried about Daisy, Gatsby sends Nick to check on her. Through the window Nick sees Tom and Daisy eating and talking. They have apparently patched up their differences. Nick leaves Gatsby outside the house.

After a sleepless night Nick calls on Gatsby early the following morning: Gatsby tells him that he waited outside the house until four o'clock but nothing happened. Nick urges Gatsby to leave Long Island and to go far away for a while, forgetting Daisy and giving up all hope of ever winning her back, but Gatsby says that this is impossible: he has waited for five years to see her again and he is not going to go anywhere without her or at least not without final confirmation that his dream is truly dead. The past can still be repeated.

> "You ought to go away," I said. "It's pretty certain they'll trace your car."
>
> "Go away *now*, old sport?"
>
> "Go to Atlantic City for a week, or up to Montreal."
>
> He wouldn't consider it. He couldn't possibly leave Daisy until he knew what she was going to do. He was clutching at some last hope and I couldn't bear to shake him free.

## Over breakfast Gatsby's memory ranges back into the past:

She was the first 'nice' girl he had ever known. In various unrevealed capacities he had come in contact with such people but always with indiscernible barbed wire between. He found her excitingly desirable. He went to her house, at first with other officers from Camp Taylor, then alone. It amazed him—he had never been in such a beautiful house before. But what gave it an air of breathless intensity was that Daisy lived there—it was as casual a thing to her as his tent out at camp was to him. There was a ripe mystery about it, a hint of bedrooms upstairs more beautiful and cool than other bedrooms, of gay and radiant activities taking place through its corridors and of romances that were not musty and laid away already in lavender but fresh and breathing and redolent of this year's shining motor cars and of dances whose flowers were scarcely withered. It excited him too that many men had already loved Daisy—it increased her value in his eyes. He felt their presence all about the house, pervading the air with the shades and echoes of still vibrant emotions.

But he knew that he was in Daisy's house by a colossal accident. However glorious might be his future as Jay Gatsby, he was at present a penniless young man without a past, and at any moment the invisible cloak of his uniform might slip from his shoulders. So he made the most of his time. He took what he could get, ravenously and unscrupulously—eventually he took Daisy one still October night, took her because he had no real right to touch her hand.

He might have despised himself, for he had certainly taken her under false pretenses. I don't mean that he had traded on his phantom millions, but he had deliberately given Daisy a sense of security; he let her believe that he was a person from much the same stratum as herself—that he was fully able to take care of her. As a matter of fact he had no such facilities—he had no comfortable family standing behind him and he was liable at the whim of an impersonal government to be blown anywhere about the world.

But he didn't despise himself and it didn't turn out as he had imagined. He had intended, probably, to take what he could and go—but now he found that he had committed himself to the following of a grail. He knew that Daisy was extraordinary but he didn't realize just how extraordinary a 'nice' girl could be. She vanished into her rich house, into her rich, full life, leaving Gatsby—nothing. He felt married to her, that was all.

. . .

"I can't describe to you how surprised I was to find out I loved her, old sport. I even hoped for a while that she'd throw me over, but she didn't, because she was in love with me too. She thought I knew a lot because I knew different things from her . . . Well, there I was, way off my ambitions, getting deeper in love every minute, and all of a sudden I didn't care. What was the use of doing great things if I could have a better time telling her what I was going to do?"

Gatsby still nurses the hope—some may say the delusion—that Daisy's heart had always been with him and not with Tom:

"I don't think she ever loved him." Gatsby turned around from a window and looked at me challengingly. "You must remember, old sport, she was very excited this afternoon. He told her those things in a way that frightened her—that made it look as if I was some kind of cheap sharper. And the result was she hardly knew what she was saying."

He sat down gloomily.

"Of course she might have loved him, just for a minute, when they were first married—and loved me more even then, do you see?"

Suddenly he came out with a curious remark:

"In any case," he said, "it was just personal."

What could you make of that, except to suspect some intensity in his conception of the affair that couldn't be measured?

He came back from France when Tom and Daisy were still on their wedding trip, and made a miserable but irresistible journey to Louisville on the last of his army pay. He stayed there a week, walking the streets where their footsteps had clicked together through the November night and revisiting the out-of-the-way places to which they had driven in her white car. Just as Daisy's house had always seemed to him more mysterious and gay than other houses so his idea of the city itself, even though she was gone from it, was pervaded with a melancholy beauty.

Though loth to go into the city to do a day's work Nick tears himself away from Gatsby with the promise to call him on the telephone at noon. Gatsby expresses the hope that Daisy will call too: to the very last he clings on still to the vestiges of his hope that she will come back to him—or does he, Nick wonders:

> At two o'clock Gatsby put on his bathing suit and left word with the butler that if anyone phoned word was to be brought to him at the pool. He stopped at the garage for a pneumatic mattress that had amused his guests during the summer, and the chauffeur helped him pump it up. Then he gave instructions that the open car wasn't to be taken out under any circumstances—and this was strange because the front right fender needed repair.
> Gatsby shouldered the mattress and started for the pool. Once he stopped and shifted it a little, and the chauffeur asked him if he needed help, but he shook his head and in a moment disappeared among the yellowing trees.
> No telephone message arrived but the butler went without his sleep and waited for it until four o'clock—until long after there was any one to give it to if it came. I have an idea that Gatsby himself didn't believe it would come and perhaps he no longer cared.

Demented with grief and fury Wilson, armed with a gun, has disappeared in search of Gatsby, the man that he wrongly believes has killed his wife. Wilson has tied the car and the identity of its owner together and he now discovers Gatsby idly floating on the air mattress in his swimming pool. Wilson shoots Gatsby, killing him instantly before turning the gun on himself, "and the holocaust was complete."

Gatsby's funeral is sparsely attended: only Nick, Gatsby's father who comes up from Minnesota and a couple of others attend. With Gatsby dead the group disintegrates. Tom and Daisy disappear, presumably to start a new life together elsewhere. Jordan tells Nick that she is engaged to be married; Nick goes back permanently to the Midwest. Before his departure Nick makes one last trip to New York where he runs into Tom Buchanan on Fifth Avenue. Tom confesses that he told Wilson that Gatsby had mown down his wife:

> "What if I did tell him? That fellow had it coming to him. He threw dust into your eyes just like he did in Daisy's but he was a tough one. He ran over Myrtle like you'd run over a dog and never even stopped his car."
> There was nothing I could say, except the one unutterable fact that it wasn't true.

Gatsby's mansion, when Nick leaves, stands empty, its lawn overgrown. Obscene graffiti is already starting to appear on its steps. The dereliction and decay of the house so recently filled with music and laughter indicates that the Gatsby dream is finally well and truly dead, yet the end of the novel points up the enormous disparity between Gatsby on the one hand and Nick,

Tom, Daisy and Jordan on the other. All the other main characters, with their world-weary cynicism, superficiality and boredom even with their massive privileges, appear utterly disillusioned with the emptiness and shallowness of their own existence: unlike Dexter Green in 'Winter Dreams' whose dream had ended in despair Gatsby himself, despite Nick's doubts, seems to have died with the guiding dream of his life—earning again the love of the woman he had once lost but had never forgotten—intact.

Like many another great writer of fiction it is a hallmark of Fitzgerald's genius as a novelist that *The Great Gatsby* can be read and appreciated on any number of vastly different but congruent levels. It is arguably the greatest instance in literature of the Roaring Twenties and the Jazz Age, occupying a position in American fiction much like that of Evelyn Waugh's *Vile Bodies* in British literature. And yet, whatever its commentary on the American dream, on social class, on the corrosive effects of snobbery, of the arrogance and complacency of old money colliding with the new money of the vulgar parvenu and the soul-destroying getting and spending and waste of unearned money, the book is also at its core a tragic love story whose protagonists are members of the Lost Generation and are, to borrow the title of Fitzgerald's second novel, beautiful but damned. *Gatsby* is, amongst other readings, a tale of young love lost, re-found and quickly and violently lost again; a tale about the tragedy of remaining in thrall to the past and of endlessly trying to recapture and recreate it; the tragedy of desire unfulfilled and love unattained; the tragedy of a man who loved a goal—or, to others perhaps, an illusion—more than life itself and who, Nick reflects, "paid a high price for living too long with a single dream." Nevertheless Gatsby's emphatic utterance to Nick ("Can't repeat the past?" he cried incredulously. "Why of course you can!") indicates that he kept faith with life, with the woman he never ceased to love and with himself to the very end.

## III

Often a man of remarkable if not downright unsettling honesty Fitzgerald was frank about the novel's autobiographical roots. "The whole idea of Gatsby," he said, "is the unfairness of a poor young man not being able to marry a girl with money. This theme comes up again and again because I lived it." Clearly his other wound—that of the (only relatively) poor middle-class boy who couldn't marry the super-rich upper-class girl because of his lack of money and social standing—continued to rankle.

Reviews of Gatsby were mixed but those which were positive were extremely so. Fitzgerald himself was pleased with the widely appreciative opinion of the professional critics but was particularly gratified by the letters of praise he received from other writers whose work he admired, among them Willa Cather, Edith Wharton and T.S. Eliot, who told him that in his view it was the "first step American fiction has taken since Henry James." Since then it has come to be widely regarded not just as the greatest American novel of the period or even of the twentieth century but of all time. The publication of *The Great Gatsby* was in some ways the zenith of Scott's literary career and possibly of his private life. It "marked an advance in every way over Fitzgerald's previous work," wrote Matthew J. Bruccoli. "If he could develop so rapidly in the five years since *This Side of Paradise,* if he could write so brilliantly before he was thirty, his promise seemed boundless."[23]

But the second half of the 1920s would be decidedly different and in the eyes of most that promise would never be fulfilled. Cracks were beginning to appear in the façade of Scott and Zelda's marriage. Zelda increasingly came to feel a need to assert her own individuality, to cease to be a 'personality' who was merely an appendage to the famous writer. Throughout the latter half of the 1920s Zelda, who had had some ballet training as a young girl, decided to make herself into an accomplished dancer, a task that she pursued with a relentless, even punishing self-discipline.

As the decade came to a close friends were starting to notice certain oddities in Zelda's behaviour. The carefree Zelda had long been thought of as something of a live wire but now there seemed to be something different about her. It was a portentous sign of things to come for she experienced a severe mental breakdown — the first of many—in 1930. Her always excitable behaviour which had formerly been seen merely as high spirits or harmless eccentricity had become increasingly erratic: from this point on it was clear that she was seriously unbalanced and she had to be admitted to the Sheppard Pratt psychiatric hospital in Towson, a suburb of Baltimore. She was formally diagnosed as schizophrenic. The course of her illness was variable but Zelda was never entirely well again and for the rest of her days she had numerous relapses (including many suicide attempts) necessitating repeated spells in other hospitals: she and Scott never lived together as husband and wife again. For the last decade of Scott's life they saw each other increasingly infrequently and depended on a voluminous correspondence to stay in touch.

Things would never be the same again. If the 1920s had been something of a charmed decade for the Fitzgeralds in some respects—the first half especially—the 1930s would be decidedly otherwise. Almost immediately after *Gatsby* was published Scott had started writing a novel about a group of American expats living in the south of France. The book proved to have the longest, most troubled and complicated compositional history of all Scott's works: permanently dissatisfied with its course he wrote, rewrote, chopped, changed, added to, erased from and edited the manuscript for the best part of a decade with long periods of stasis not helped by his regular drinking binges. *Tender is the Night*—the title comes from Keats's 'Ode to a Nightingale'—, the last novel published in his lifetime, was finally completed in the fall of 1933 and published in April 1934, nine years after *Gatsby*. It sold respectably though unspectacularly and divided critics at the time although its stock has subsequently risen and it is now generally viewed as one of Fitzgerald's major works. That estimation would come later, after Fitzgerald's death: for now he continued to depend on the still successful sales of his shorter fiction but with a daughter in school, a seriously mentally ill wife and massive alcohol addiction money began to run short. Scott was labouring under ill health himself: in addition to his alcoholism in April 1935, after years of inactivity, X-rays revealed that his tuberculosis was again active and that he had sustained some lung damage though he continued to smoke heavily. Long-standing alcohol abuse disrupts healthy sleeping patterns so he was regularly taking powerful barbiturates such as Seconal, Nembutal and Barbitol to help him sleep at night—an

incredibly dangerous thing to do in combination with alcohol—
and to counter their intoxicating, hangover-like effects he took
Benzedrine to get him started in the morning.

Meanwhile Zelda was busy with projects of her own.
Following an attack of hysteria she was admitted to the Phipps
clinic at Baltimore's renowned Johns Hopkins hospital but in
spite of her illness she remained creative during her more able
periods, painting drawing and writing and in particular penning
a substantial semi-autobiographical novel called *Save me the Waltz*
which was published in October 1932. Reviews were almost
uniformly negative. "It is not only that her publishers have not
seen fit to curb an almost ludicrous lushness of writing," said the
*New York Times*, "but they have not given the book the elementary
services of a literate proofreader." The novel sold just 1,392 copies
for which she earned a mere $120.73 precisely. William McFee
of the *New York Sun* suggested that for all its egregious faults it
showed a glimmer of promise, writing: "In this book, with all its
crudity of conception, its ruthless purloinings of technical tricks
and its pathetic striving after philosophic profundity, there is
the promise of a new and vigorous personality in fiction." But
this was damning with faint praise and Zelda was crushed by
the hostile reviews her book had earned. A second planned novel
was never finished.

Scott himself was incensed. Matthew Bruccoli is probably correct to suggest that, other things aside, Scott was envious of the speed and the facility with which Zelda had finished her book when his own work on what would become *Tender is the Night*, now in its seventh year, had all but halted and the book often seemed to him to be unfinishable. More particularly Scott was angered by what he regarded as Zelda's raiding of their personal life together for material—the rankest hypocrisy from this most autobiographical of writers, one might well think.

Ginevra and Zelda—Scott's first and past love and wife in the present—did once meet in person. In 1933, during a period of relative stability for Zelda, she (but not Scott) went to Chicago to see that year's World Fair. Scott, perhaps rather naively, thought that it would be good for his wife to meet his old flame and he contacted Ginevra out of the blue, calling her long-distance to arrange a meeting. Zelda was aware that Ginevra had been her husband's first love but gamely agreed to the encounter. It started well—Zelda was initially gay and talkative—but she soon lapsed into uncommunicative silence and Ginevra had to lead the conversation more or less on her own for the remainder of what became an uncomfortable meeting.

Any improvement was temporary. Back in hospital Zelda experienced a severe religious mania: she attempted suicide several times. It was a dismal time for Scott also. Deeply in debt as ever, physically and mentally ill, his drinking out of control, Scott was interviewed for the *New York Post* on his fortieth birthday in September 1936. The interviewer did not scruple to tell the readership of Scott's shambolic inebriated state. When the paper appeared the subject was so mortified that he made an impulsive semi-serious suicide attempt of his own, swallowing an overdose of morphine which merely made him vomit. Possibly for the first time drinking was now interfering with his writing: whereas before he had been sufficiently disciplined to confine his alcoholic benders until after he had finished work, now he drank at the same time. The man who had once said "To me, narcotics are deadening to work" had undergone a 180-degree shift of opinion: now, he said, "Drink heightens feeling. When I drink, it heightens my emotions and I put it in a story . . . My stories written when sober are stupid . . . all reasoned out, not felt." Unsurprisingly, according to his definitive biographer Matthew J. Bruccoli, his art started to suffer:

> Since he was now writing to raise money for pressing debts, Fitzgerald was submitting what were really working drafts. The inevitable result was that his stories became harder to sell, forcing him to write more stories hastily . . . in 1935 his style was losing its distinction because he didn't have time to polish his prose. His plots had become loosely constructed and his characters were unconvincing. He was a sick, tired, depressed man of thirty-eight who thought he had lost the capacity to feel people intensely.

For the first time in his career he was producing what was really hack work.[24]

According to Scott Donaldson he was caught in the most impossible of situations: "He had to drink in order to write. He had to write in order to live. [But] He would not live long if he continued to drink."

Fitzgerald estimated that in the seventeen years between 1919 and 1936 he had earned $400,000—all of it spent. In 1936 he sold just one short story, the aptly titled 'Trouble,' for a significant amount of money—$2,000. Even the money he inherited after his mother's death left him with just $5,000 after his debts had been paid off. As penurious as ever he was forced to spend the last few years of the 1930s—and of his life—in Hollywood, driven there by dire financial straits to become a scriptwriter to make ends meet while continuing to work on his own books. In June 1937 he received an offer to write for MGM. It was a disagreeable state of affairs for all concerned: some thought that Fitzgerald was a washed-up and burnt-out old drunk who had not published anything worth reading in years, whereas Scott himself often saw movie work as trivial and degrading, at least initially, though he came to view it somewhat differently in time. "I hate the place like poison with a sincere hatred," he had written to his agent in January 1935: on another occasion he described it as a "hideous place . . . full of the human spirit at a new low of debasement." Be that as it may the thousand dollars a week for six months with an option for renewal at an even higher rate was an offer that Scott, with Zelda in hospital (she would be transferred to the Highland hospital in Asheville, North Carolina in April 1936) and Scottie in school and his usual debts piling up behind him once more, could not afford to pass up: of this amount he kept $400 per week for himself, the rest going on Zelda's medical bills, Scottie's school fees and his debts. And so in June 1937 he moved to Hollywood to become a scriptwriter, a job which saw him working very briefly and in an uncredited capacity on *Gone With the Wind* in 1939. By October 1937 he was writing: "I like the work which is . . . most often like fitting together a very interesting picture puzzle. I think I'm going to be good at it." (On the other hand, in the winter of 1939 he told Scottie: "I expect to dip in and out of the pictures for the rest of my natural life" even though "it is a business of telling stories fit for children and this is only interesting up to a point"). It says a great deal for the determination with which Fitzgerald pursued this latest phase of his career that by the end of 1938 he was almost debt-free. "It was an unlikely place," writes Scott Donaldson, "this city of gilt and make-believe, for a man in his forties to achieve maturity, but that is what he managed to accomplish during the three and a half years left to him."[25]

While Scott was in Hollywood the first and most painful ghost from his past reached out to him again in 1937. Scott and Ginevra met face to face one last time in October of that year: Ginevra was in California to see Buddy who was at a special school in Santa Barbara. Via a mutual friend in St. Paul called Josephine Ordway, Scott had heard about Ginevra's visit and the two made contact, suggesting that as they would be so relatively near to each other they should meet up. According to Scott's account below it was Ginevra who made contact with him but in a letter of the 12th of May 1948 to Arthur Mizener she said that Fitzgerald approached her first: James West speculates that perhaps he bent the truth for Scottie's sake. Ginevra also told Mizener that she was nervous about seeing Scott again after so many years: as with Charles Dickens and Maria Beadnell it had been two decades since they had last met face to face, twenty years in which their lives had shared some similarities but had also known a great many differences. Scott was simultaneously excited and also nervous and was caused considerable anguish by the prospect of seeing her. To Scottie he wrote on the 8th of October:

> I used to write endless letters throughout sophomore and junior years to Ginevra King of Chicago and Westover, who later featured in *This Side of Paradise*. Then I didn't see her for twenty-one years, though I telephoned her in 1933 to entertain your mother at the World's Fair, which she did. Yesterday I get [sic] a wire that she is in Santa Barbara and will I come down

there immediately. She was the first girl I ever loved and I have faithfully avoided seeing her up to this moment to keep the illusion perfect . . . I don't know whether I should go or not. It would be very, very strange. These great beauties are often something else at thirty-eight, but Ginevra had a great deal besides beauty.

We can only speculate that either one or the other or even both may possibly have entertained some hope, however faint, of rekindling some sort of relationship. By this stage Scott and Zelda's marriage was under serious strain: they saw each other rarely, communicating mostly by regular letters, whereas Ginevra's marriage to Bill Mitchell was already over.

In spite of his professed doubts to Scottie there cannot have been much likelihood that Scott would not meet Ginevra again. They did so on the 11th of October but the encounter—their last—was not exactly what either of them would have hoped for. To begin with Ginevra had invited Scott to a dinner party at a friend's house in Santa Barbara on the 9th but Scott declined so she travelled to Hollywood to see him two days later. Ginevra later gave an account of the meeting to Fitzgerald's biographer Arthur Mizener. It started out well enough: they met at the Beverly Wilshire Hotel where Ginevra was staying and had an enjoyably relaxed and carefree lunch, reminiscing about old times, at which Scott drank no alcohol: he told Ginevra (who was presumably aware of Scott's serious drink problem) that he had been dry for the past several months. However, fatally they went to the bar of the hotel, innocently enough to wait for one of Ginevra's friends who was due to meet her there. According to Ginevra it was only at this point that Scott started to drink quickly and heavily, ordering multiple doubles of gin. At some stage during their encounter Ginevra reputedly asked Scott if she really had been the model for one of his characters (possibly in *The Beautiful and Damned*, to which Scott is alleged to have asked, "Which bitch do you think you are?" More than one Fitzgerald scholar has cast doubt on the veracity of this comment while Ginevra's granddaughter pointed out that it is impossible to know what tone of voice Fitzgerald was using when he said it, if indeed he ever did. Professor James L.W. West has opined: "He might have said it playfully rather than savagely. That sounds more in character for him. He was not a cruel man." The flipside of this alleged comment is provided by Scott Donaldson's account that after Fitzgerald heard of Ginevra's divorce from Bill Mitchell in 1936 he sent her a copy of *The Beautiful and Damned* and asked her to guess which of the book's female characters was based on her: they were "all such bitches," she is supposed to have said, that she didn't feel like guessing that any of them were.[26] At any rate Ginevra later told Arthur Mizener that she was "heartsick" at seeing the pitiful state Scott had been reduced to by years of alcohol abuse and by his drinking while they were together this one last time. Apparently in the few days after their meeting there were several telephone calls between Scott and Ginevra but no further personal encounters. It was the last time they ever saw each other. The effect on Scott of this meeting and the dreadful error of judgement—if judgement is quite the word—that his drinking represented can be guessed. Mizener alleged that to the very end of his life the thought of Ginevra could still make Scott lachrymose, a statement supported by another of Scott's biographers. "Ginevra King was the love of his young life. The hurt of losing her never left him, and thinking about it invariably brought tears to his eyes . . . the wound would not heal, no matter how often he cauterized it."[27]

This final meeting between Scott and Ginevra provided the impetus, at least in part, for the last story he ever wrote with the female character modelled on Ginevra, 'Three Hours Between Planes' written in 1939 but not published (in *Esquire*) until July 1941 seven months after his death. The protagonist of the story is Donald Plant, a thirty-two year-old man and a widower for the past six years who stops off at a small airport while on a journey and realises that the town nearby is the home of a childhood sweetheart called Nancy Holmes last seen twenty years earlier when they were both just twelve years old. Donald impulsively decides to look her up.

With mounting excitement he looked through the phone book for her father who might be dead too, somewhere in these twenty years.

No. Judge Harmon Holmes—Hillside 3194.

A woman's amused voice answered his inquiry for Miss Nancy Holmes.

"Nancy is Mrs Walter Gifford now. Who is this?"

But Donald hung up without answering. He had found out what he wanted to know and had only three hours. He did not remember any Walter Gifford and there was another suspended moment while he scanned the phone book. She might have married out of town.

No. Walter Gifford—Hillside 1191. Blood flowed back into his fingertips.

"Hello?"

"Hello. Is Mrs Gifford there—this is an old friend of hers."

"This is Mrs Gifford."

He remembered, or thought he remembered, the funny magic in the voice.

"This is Donald Plant. I haven't seen you since I was twelve years old."

"Oh-h-h!" The note was utterly surprised, very polite, but he could distinguish in it neither joy nor certain recognition.

"—Donald!" added the voice. This time there was something more in it than struggling memory.

". . . when did you come back to town?" Then cordially, "Where *are* you?"

"I'm out at the airport—for just a few hours."

"Well, come up and see me."

"Sure you're not just going to bed."

"Heavens, no!" she exclaimed. "I was sitting here—having a highball by myself. Just tell your taxi man . . . "

## Donald goes to see Nancy:

As they walked inside, their voices jingled the words "all these years," and Donald felt a sinking in his stomach. This derived in part from a vision of their last meeting—when she rode past him on a bicycle, cutting him dead—and in part from fear lest they have nothing to say. It was like a college reunion—but there the failure to find the past was disguised by the hurried boisterous occasion. Aghast, he realized that this might be a long and empty hour. He plunged in desperately.

"You always were a lovely person. But I'm a little shocked to find you as beautiful as you are."

It worked. The immediate recognition of their changed state, the bold compliment, made them interesting strangers instead of fumbling childhood friends.

The meeting gets off to a positive start: Donald and Nancy reminisce about childhood pursuits—a sleigh ride, a picnic, a party. But Donald realises that he must seize the chance to steer the conversation into more personal and heartfelt territory:

"Nancy, whenever I talked to my wife about the past, I told her you were the girl I loved almost as much as I loved her. But I think I really loved you just as much. When we moved out of town I carried you like a cannon ball in my insides."

"Were you *that* much—stirred up?"

"My God, yes! I—" He suddenly realized that they were standing just two feet from each other, that he was talking as if he loved her in the present, that she was looking up at him with her lips half-parted and a clouded look in her eyes.

"Go on," she said, "I'm ashamed to say—I like it. I didn't know you were so upset then. I thought it was me who was upset."

"You!" he exclaimed. "Don't you remember throwing me over at the drugstore." He laughed. "You stuck out your tongue at me."

"I don't remember at all. It seemed to me you did the throwing over." Her hand fell lightly, almost consolingly on his arm.

Nancy goes upstairs to fetch a photo album and it is when they are sitting side by side leafing through the book that Donald realises that his long-buried feelings for Nancy are beginning to reawaken—and moreover that hers may be reviving as well:

Nancy moved him as a woman as she had moved him as a child. Half an hour had developed an emotion that he had not known since the death of his wife—that he had never hoped to know again . . .

"Oh, this is *such* fun," she said. "Such fun that you're so nice, that you remember me so—beautifully. Let me tell you—I wish I'd known it then! After you'd gone I hated you."

"What a pity," he said gently.

"But not now," she reassured him, and then impulsively, "Kiss and make up—"

". . . that isn't being a good wife," she said after a minute. "I really don't think I've kissed two men since I was married."

He was excited—but most of all confused. Had he kissed Nancy? or a memory? or this lovely trembly stranger who looked away from him quickly and turned a page of the book?

"Wait!" he said. "I don't think I could *see* a picture for a few seconds."

"We won't do it again. I don't feel so very calm myself."

Donald said one of those trivial things that cover so much ground.

"Wouldn't it be awful if we fell in love again?"

"Stop it!" She laughed, but very breathlessly. "It's all over. It was a moment. A moment I'll have to forget."

"Don't tell your husband."

"Why not? Usually I tell him everything."

"It'll hurt him. Don't ever tell a man such things."

"All right I won't."

But as they flick through images of the past that Donald realises with sick horror that Nancy doesn't actually remember him at all. In fact all along Nancy has mistakenly believe that he was somebody else entirely:

"Here's you," she cried. "Right away!"

He looked. It was a little boy in shorts standing on a pier with a sailboat in the background.

"I remember—" she laughed triumphantly, "—the very day it was taken. Kitty took it and I stole it from her."

For a moment Donald failed to recognize himself in the photo—then, bending closer—he failed utterly to recognize himself.

"That's not me," he said.

"Oh yes. It was at Frontenac—the summer we—we used to go to the cave."

"What cave? I was only three days in Frontenac." Again he strained his eyes at the slightly yellowed picture. "And that isn't me. That's Donald Bowers. We did look rather alike."

Now she was staring at him—leaning back, seeming to lift away from him.

"But you're Donald Bowers!" she exclaimed; her voice rose a little. "No, you're not. You're Donald *Plant*."

"I told you on the phone."

She was on her feet—her face faintly horrified.

"Plant! Bowers! I must be crazy. Or it was that drink? I was mixed up a little when I first saw you. Look here! What have I told you?"

He tried for a monkish calm as he turned a page of the book.

"Nothing at all," he said. Pictures that did not include him formed and re-formed before his eyes—Frontenac—a cave—Donald Bowers—"You threw *me* over!"

. . .

"Kiss me again, Nancy," he said, sinking to one knee beside her chair, putting his hand upon her shoulder. But Nancy strained away.

"You said you had to catch a plane."

"It's nothing. I can miss it. It's of no importance."

"Please go,' she said in a cool voice. 'And please try to imagine how I feel."

"But you act as if you don't remember me,' he cried, "—as if you don't remember Donald *Plant*!"

"I do. I remember you too . . . But it was all so long ago." Her voice grew hard again. "The taxi number is Crestwood 8484."

## Donald leaves the house crestfallen:

On his way to the airport Donald shook his head from side to side. He was completely himself now but he could not digest the experience. Only as the plane roared up into the dark sky and its passengers became a different entity from the corporate world below did he draw a parallel from the fact of its flight. For five blinding minutes he had lived like a madman in two worlds at once. He had been a boy of twelve and a man of thirty-two, indissolubly and helplessly commingled.

Donald had lost a good deal, too, in those hours between the planes—but since the second half of life is a long process of getting rid of things, that part of the experience probably didn't matter.

This of course is not a straightforward account of Scott's last meeting with Ginevra: we should look not for literal factual truth but the psychological truth behind the tale. Donald Plant, like Gatsby and Dexter Green and the man who created them, is a man for whom time has stood still and for whom the pain of the past can never be outrun, a man left baffled by "the hopeless impossibility of reconciling what different people remembered about the same event."

Given the state of his health Scott's rapacious drinking on this last meeting with Ginevra may seem quasi-suicidal. Nevertheless in spite of his physical and emotional condition there are certain indications that Scott retained some optimism and was looking forward to a happier future: the binge in the bar of the Beverly Wilshire Hotel seems to have been a one-off, probably intended—foolishly if understandably—to quell his nerves. In July 1937 he had met the British-born film columnist Sheilah Graham (1904-1988) who had divorced her husband just a month earlier and was already engaged to the Marquess of Donegal. Sheilah and Scott seem to have fallen in love with each other at first sight (Scott felt that she bore a striking resemblance to Zelda when young) and Sheilah's engagement was abruptly broken off: although Scott was still technically married to Zelda he and Sheilah became constant companions, entering upon what would turn out to be an all too brief but in its way fulfilling and supportive relationship. Sheilah offered Scott unstinting support in his battle to stay teetotal: despite several lapses it seemed that he might have turned a corner and at the last to have found a measure of domestic peace and contentment.[28]

Scott seemed finally, by the end of 1939, to have curbed his drinking once and for all. He was on the wagon and remained dry for what little time he had left to live but the worst damage had already been done. By this point he was not merely ailing but seriously ill: there are certain indications that he not only knew it but positively embraced it. Following a furious argument with Sheilah in October 1939 Scott wrote a typically contrite letter in which he said: "I want to die, Sheilah, and in my own way. I used to have my daughter and my poor lost Zelda. Now for over two years your image is everywhere. Let me remember you up to the end which is very close. You are the finest. You are something all by yourself. You are too much something for a tubercular neurotic who can only be jealous and mean and perverse." Sheilah took him back but could not persuade him to join Alcoholics Anonymous.

Though by now teetotal so many years of alcoholism had fatally undermined his constitution, as had decades of heavy smoking. "Did Fitzgerald's drinking kill him?" asks Scott Donaldson. "As a single cause, probably not. But liquor certainly undermined his health, just as it undermined his career and his relationships. And it was undoubtedly a contributing factor to the heart attack that struck him down in Sheilah Graham's ground-floor apartment."[28] Matthew J. Bruccoli is even more explicit that Fitzgerald's early death was hastened by alcoholic cardiomyopathy, a form of heart failure—weakening of the cardiac muscle resulting in less efficient pumping of blood—seen in chronic alcoholics. Men between the ages of thirty and fifty-five are especially at risk: in 1940 Fitzgerald was forty-four. Alcoholic cardiomyopathy is not inevitably fatal: today medications such as ACE inhibitors and beta blockers are commonly prescribed; diuretics can eliminate the swelling due to water retention. In severe cases pacemakers can be fitted to improve heart function. The one absolute is that for any hope of recovery consumption of alcohol must be stopped completely and this is something that Fitzgerald had apparently achieved, but sometimes, alas, just too much damage has already been done.

Supported and encouraged by Sheilah by late 1940 Scott had been sober for a year and was still working hard on what would turn out to be his final and unfinished posthumously published novel *The Love of the Last Tycoon* ("I am deep in the novel, living in it, and it makes me happy," he wrote to Zelda: "Two thousand words today and all good." And again just a week before his death, "The novel is about three-quarters through"). But in his final weeks he suffered two heart attacks or what were described to him rather innocuously as 'cardiac spasms.' After the first, which came out of the blue in a drugstore on Sunset Boulevard (where ironically he was buying cigarettes), he was ordered by his doctor to avoid any strenuous physical exertion though his appetite for writing—which he could still do in bed for a couple of hours every day with a board on his knees—was undiminished, so much so that his heart trouble was seen by him merely as a nuisance. "The novel progresses and I am angry that this little illness has slowed me up," he told Zelda: "I've had trouble with my heart before but never anything organic. This is not a major attack but seems to have come on gradually and luckily a cardiogram showed it up in time . . . I'm quite able to work, etc., if I do not overtire myself." Scott's apartment was reached by two flights of stairs whereas that of Sheilah just a block away was on the ground floor so Scott moved in with her. On the evening of the 20th of December 1940 Scott and Sheilah went out for dinner and then to the Pantages Theatre in Hollywood to attend the premiere of *This Thing Called Love*, a light comedy with Melvyn Douglas and Rosalind Russell. Afterwards, as the couple were leaving the theatre, Scott had a sudden dizzy spell and had difficulty in walking to the car. Visibly upset, a stone cold sober Scott woefully and anxiously remarked to Sheilah, "They'll think I'm drunk, won't they?"

The very next day, Saturday the 21st of December 1940, Scott slept late before drinking coffee in bed and getting up to get dressed. The night before he had refused medical help because he was due to see his doctor at home later that afternoon for a scheduled appointment with a portable electrocardiogram. In the afternoon he had been following a Princeton football game on the radio and then settled down in his armchair to read the Princeton alumni magazine, nibbling on a chocolate bar. Sheilah was curled up reading on a couch nearby. Suddenly Scott jumped out of the chair, gasped and seemed to clutch at the mantelpiece before crashing to the floor. After trying to force brandy through his clenched teeth a horrified and panic-stricken Sheilah ran to get the manager of the apartment building for help: when they returned Scott was already dead, having succumbed to a final massive and very sudden heart attack. He was just forty-four years old. According to fellow writer John O'Hara he had died "… of neglect in Hollywood, a prematurely old little man haunting bookstores unrecognized." Scottie was one of just thirty or so mourners to attend the funeral in Baltimore, Maryland though he was actually buried in Rockville, a suburb of Washington D.C. Zelda was still incarcerated in the Highland hospital and was too ill to attend her husband's funeral while Sheilah tactfully decided to stay away, grieving in private.

Zelda's own premature end was as tragic as much of her life had been. After Scott's death she continued to write and to paint, although her literary projects, principally another projected novel entitled *Caesar's Things*, came to nothing. She checked herself in and out of the Highland Hospital according to the vagaries of her illness, living with her mother when relatively well and readmitting herself when ill. Tragically she was back in the Highland when, on the night of the 10th of March 1948 a fire broke out in the hospital kitchen. It spread rapidly through the dumb-waiter shaft and soon the conflagration was general on every floor. Zelda had been scheduled for further electroconvulsive therapy at the time and had been locked in a room. Escape was impossible: she was one of the nine women who died in the fire. Her body was so badly burnt that she could be identified only by one of her slippers found beneath her and relatively untouched by the flames. She was forty-seven. Her remains were taken to Rockville to be buried alongside her husband.

Ginevra King's marriage to Bill Mitchell lasted for nineteen years and produced three children. She and Bill parted in 1937: Ginevra established a relationship with John T. Pirie Jr., another wealthy Chicagoan (he became the chairman of a prestigious department store) whom she married in 1939. Tragically in that same year Buddy, her disabled son, died. He had been taken to the Golden Gate International Exposition in San Francisco where he had caught a cold which developed into the pneumonia which proved fatal. Nevertheless Ginevra's second marriage was by all accounts an extremely happy one and lasted until she died in 1980, forty years after Scott, aged eighty-two.

Ginevra never publicly alluded to her brief and youthful romance with the Fitzgerald. Even by the time of his death Fitzgerald's literary reputation was in eclipse: when Zelda tried to sell her late husband's papers to Princeton for $3,750 the librarian offended her greatly by refusing to offer more than $1,000 for the detritus of a "second-rate Midwestern hack." The tide would turn eventually however: after a period of critical neglect the publication of the first biography in 1951, Arthur Mizener's *Far Side of Paradise*, reawakened public interest in Fitzgerald's writing (not coincidentally in that same year Princeton Library changed its mind about Fitzgerald's papers and accepted them) and by the 1970s his reputation as one of the very greatest of all American writers was restored. His posthumous celebrity became enormous, hence the famous 1974 movie version of *The Great Gatsby* with Robert Redford in the title role and Mia Farrow as Daisy Buchanan. Throughout it all Ginevra King Pirie, as she then was, said almost nothing, not wishing to be thought of as cashing in on her almost perfect hour with Fitzgerald sixty years earlier. Fitzgerald's biographers Arthur Mizener and Andrew Turnbull approached her and she consented to assist them but she proved to be evasive and contradictory and clearly desired to write off her relationship with Scott as a passing infatuation of no consequence. "He was one of the many beaux of her youth," writes Scott Donaldson of the official version of events that the aging Mrs Pirie wished to present to the world, "and when it came time she dropped him. In response to inquiries from biographers and others, she consistently referred to their romance in an offhand manner. She must have kissed Scott, but 'it wasn't exactly a big thing' in her life. She was sorry she hadn't kept any [of Scott's] letters, but . . . in 1947 she sent . . . two undergraduate pictures of Fitzgerald to biographer Arthur Mizener, and wiped the slate clean."[28] As we've seen in some detail her letters and diary of the time tell a very different story and we know only as much as we do about the affair because Ginevra's descendants—her daughter Ginevra Mitchell Hunter and two of her granddaughters, one also called Ginevra—rediscovered a large quantity of personal papers in April 2003, amongst them the numerous letters (amounting to 227 double-spaced pages in a black binder) from Ginevra to Scott and typed up by him and the diary covering the period of her romance with Scott, papers which they later donated to Princeton University library.[29,30] The letters had been found by Scottie Fitzgerald and given back to Ginevra ten years after her father's death. They "tell us a great deal about her," says Prof. James West:

> She emerges much more fully and favourably than before: we can now understand her attraction to Scott and his to her, and we can follow the progress of their romance and learn why it ended as it did. The romance, we now know, was much more than a shallow flirtation. Ginevra was entirely taken by Scott and he by her. She was drawn to him by his intelligence and charm, and she admired his talent with words. He was different from the other young men who pursued her; she was flattered by his attention and beguiled by his letters . . . Ginevra wrote to Scott as frequently as he did to her, and her letters reveal much about her personality. She was more complex and likeable than the characters Fitzgerald later based on her. She was perceptive about him: she knew that he was idealizing her and urged him in her letters not to do so, but of course he did. Ginevra was pleased by Scott's attention, but she was put off by his attempts to analyze her personality and by his persistent jealousy. These two factors, more than any others, caused their romance to end.[31]

In an article entitled 'One Hundred False Starts' that Scott had penned for publication in the *Saturday Evening Post* in March 1933 he had written something which, although he had been discussing the craft of writing and artistic inspiration, is couched in such tender and personal terms that it is hard not to think that of the "two or three great moving experiences" in his life his youthful romance with Ginevra King—the first love that he never forgot, the wound that never healed—may well have been in his mind:

> We have two or three great moving experiences in our lives— experiences so great and moving that it doesn't seem at the

time that anyone else has been so caught up and pounded and dazzled and astonished and beaten and broken and rescued and illuminated and rewarded and humbled in just that way ever before.

# Three:
# A Very Short Story

*If two people love each other, there can be no happy end to it.*
—Ernest Hemingway, *Death in the Afternoon*

Ernest Miller Hemingway was born in Oak Park, a leafy suburb of Chicago, on the 21st of July 1899, the second child of Clarence Hemingway, a doctor, and Grace Hall Hemingway, a musician who wrote light popular songs. Ernest's surroundings as he grew up were affluent and materially comfortable: he was spoilt by his mother though his father, a loving if stiff and rather distant man, was a strict disciplinarian.

Ernest graduated from high school in June 1917. Just two months earlier the United States of America's isolationist policy came to an end when it declared war on Germany on the 6th of April. America was involved in the so-called War to End All Wars at last and the country was swept, as European ones had been nearly three years earlier, by a wave of patriotic fervour. The seventeen-year-old Hemingway would not escape although at this point he was still below draft age and in any case showed little if any interest in military service despite the tub-thumping jingoism of President Teddy Roosevelt and his call for every adult male of whatever level of ability to do his bit for the war effort:

> Let him, if a man of fighting age, do his utmost to get into the fighting line—Red Cross work, YMCA work, driving ambulances and the like, excellent though it all is, should be left to men not of military age or unfit for military service, and to women; young men of vigorous bodies and sound hearts should be left free to do their proper work in the fighting line.

After spending the summer at Windermere, the Hemingway family's summer home on Walloon Lake in Michigan, the young Ernie decided to pursue his interest in journalism. His uncle Tyler lived in Kansas and was a good friend of Harry Haskell, then editor of the *Kansas City Star* which was widely regarded as one of the finest newspapers in the United States. Via uncle Tyler, Haskell arranged a position for Ernie and in October 1917 Ernest Hemingway, aged eighteen, moved to Kansas City to become a cub reporter. Like budding journalists the world over Ernie found himself at the bottom of the heap, initially writing obituaries but slowly working his way up the journalistic ladder to cover local crime stories.

At about the same time that young Ernie arrived in Kansas momentous events were occurring far away in Europe. The Austrian army had attacked the eastern front in Italy and the Italians had suffered a crushing defeat. Medical units helping the Italian army were overwhelmed and it became clear that there would soon be a severe shortage of ambulance drivers serving the front lines. The Red Cross began a recruitment drive, a call answered by Hemingway's friend and *Kansas City Star* colleague Theodore (Ted) Brumback. Ted had lost an eye in an earlier sporting accident and therefore was not eligible for service in the regular army but, eager to do his bit, he signed up to become a Red Cross driver and had already spent four months of 1917 on the front line in France. Hemingway's own eyesight had been defective from birth and he was rejected by the draft but following Ted's example he applied for a position as a Red Cross ambulance driver in December 1917 and was accepted. Hemingway resigned his position at the *Star* at the end of April 1918: after a brief vacation in Michigan he went to New York where he was commissioned as a second lieutenant and which he left on the *Chicago* in May with a group of prospective Red Cross drivers, arriving at Bordeaux two weeks later. Hemingway was on foreign soil for the first time in his young life. He and the rest of the group took the train to Paris where they stayed for a few days before taking a final train to Milan at which city's Garibaldi Station he arrived on the 7th of May. After reporting to the American Red Cross headquarters at 10 Via Manzoni they took another train to Vicenza where they boarded the ambulances which would take them to the ambulance unit at Schio.

Hemingway did not, contrary to popular belief, receive his wounds while driving an ambulance. After three weeks he volunteered to help run a Red Cross canteen for the Italian soldiers on the Piave front, a unit commanded by Captain James Gamble who soon became a close friend:

> As further assistance to the Italian military, the American Red Cross had established a network of canteens across the entire front. Each facility was under the direction of a Red Cross lieutenant . . . and the principal duties were to dispense coffee, chocolate (a particular favorite), jam and soup. There was space for the soldier to rest, and often musical entertainment was provided. A basic station would have guitars and mandolins, sometimes an accordion, and all of them had phonographs and records of popular music. One of them featured a motion picture projector . . . the fighting men could obtain refreshment, spread jam or sugar on their gray army bread, or wrote a letter home if they wished . . . The volunteers would also carry hot coffee and refreshments to the soldiers on the front line. A variation on the idea was the rolling canteen, a makeshift mobile trailer that could be moved up close to the lines. Hemingway was in charge of such a unit, Canteen No. 14, when he was wounded.[1]

In Hemingway's own words: ". . . what I am supposed to be doing is running a *posto di ricovero*. That is, I dispense chocolate and cigarettes to the wounded and the soldiers in the front line. Each aft and morning I load up a haversack and take my tin lid and gas mask and beat it up to the trenches."[2] These canteens were designed as places where the men could enjoy as much rest, recuperation and relaxation as their situation allowed but the danger of this should not be underestimated. "It was no secret that, along with the ambulance corps, the Red Cross branch that ran the most risks in Italy was the rolling canteen, or field kitchen, service . . . These *cucinas*, or 'American bars,' as they were called by the soldiers . . . were invariably located in the danger zone, close to the front-line trenches or at a strategic crossroads frequented by the troops."[3] Casualties from artillery bombardment and even Austrian snipers were high. Nonetheless Hemingway volunteered straight away, along with friends such as Bill Horne and Howell Jenkins. The danger was all part of the thrill: chafing at the bit Hemingway, with the cavalier but illusory immortality of youth, wanted to see some real action for himself. "There's nothing here but scenery and too damn much of that," he told his friend Ted Brumback. "I'm going to get out of this ambulance section and see if I can't find out where the war is." "Handing out smokes and chocolate bars was the best way to see the forward posts," he wryly told Henry Villard later, "only I didn't think the Austrians would oblige with a demonstration so soon."

Thus it was that on the 8th of July 1918, after a week at the front, *Sottotenente* Ernesto Hemingway, as he was known to the Italians, was seriously wounded on the west bank of the Piave. The exact details of what happened from this point on (and in fact for the rest of Hemingway's time in Italy, another six months) have always been contentious. Hemingway was known to embroider the details of his own life freely and this was particularly the case with his war service, employing at best creative embellishment and exaggeration and on at least one occasion resorting to outright fabrication. For instance, to a friend on the 22nd of June he said "I'm ranked a soto [sic] Tenente or Second Lieut. *in the Italian Army*"[4] and then, on the 11th of September, he wrote to his father: "Oh yes! I have been commissioned a 1st Lieutenant and now wear the two gold stripes on each of my sleeves. It was a surprise to me as I hadn't expected anything of the sort. So you can address my mail either 1st Lieut. or Tenente as *I hold the rank in both the ARC and Italian Army*."[5] After his return home in January 1919 he replied to a questionnaire for veterans reiterating that he had been a first lieutenant with the Italian army. This was blatantly untrue: he was a first lieutenant (only after promotion which came after his wounding) but with the ARC: he never served officially as a full member of the Italian army. While she was preparing her memoir *At the Hemingways* in the early 1960s the writer's sister Marcelline received a letter from Hemingway's friend and colleague Bill Horne in which he said: "Some people believe that Ernie ended the war as an officer in the Italian army; while you believe he did not. To the best of my knowledge, he did not. In my opinion that is one of those myths that grow up about colorful and famous people. When we arrived at . . . Schio . . . we were told that all of us ambulance drivers rated as honorary second lieutenants in the Italian army. How true that was I don't know." Quite apart from Horne's own uncertainty as to the veracity of such a claim the operative word here is 'honorary', though Horne went on to add: "If it comforts or pleases or gratifies any of those others who also love him to believe that he was an Italian officer—as well as a fine young American boy—then for gosh sake, let them believe it! Remember Lincoln's words—". . . beyond our poor power to add or detract"? What Ern was and what he did will live long years. What uniform he wore, or whose rolls bore his name those last few months signify nothing. He was, beyond those minor matters, a man. A fine man, who became an everlastingly great man. That ought to be enough for all and any of us." To compound the matter some biographers have been overly literal in treating Hemingway's war-inspired fiction as a more or less reliable guide to what really happened rather than as creative works of art inspired by, but certainly not limited to, actual events. The issue of Hemingway's brief wartime service is treated thoroughly in *Hemingway in Love and War: The Lost Diary of Agnes von Kurowsky* by Henry S. Villard and James Nagel: the bottom line, as Nagel puts it, is that "The conclusion is inescapable . . . [that] not only is Hemingway's fiction an unreliable guide to the truth but also that his pronouncements in public forums, letters and personal comments are suspect."

Nevertheless as far as can currently be ascertained the account probably nearest to the truth—backed up by the official report of Captain Gamble which we can surely depend upon as accurate—is as follows. Hemingway had volunteered to take chocolate, cigarettes and the like to the Italian soldiers and so on the afternoon of the previous day, the 7th of July, he had left the farmhouse where he was billeted and set off on his bicycle to ride for a mile or so through the village of Fossalta to the canteen by the Italian trenches. It was a dark night and Hemingway found the soldiers subdued. As ever in wartime, both at the front and at home, rumours had been circulating that a major offensive was imminent: Hemingway wanted to be as close to the thick of the action as possible and on the night of the 8th persuaded the Italian officers to let him go up to a forward listening post beside the Piave. Shortly before midnight Hemingway was talking with some of these servicemen when an Austrian projectile—a trench mortar, a five-gallon can full of explosives and shards of scrap metal that the Americans dubbed 'ash cans'—came over and exploded no more than a few feet away showering Hemingway and the other men with shrapnel. Only the fact that another soldier was standing between Hemingway and the explosion saved his life: that solider was killed instantly and others seriously wounded—one had both his legs blown off. Initially Hemingway was knocked flat on his back by the force of the blast and the impact of the shrapnel fragments: for a time he tried to breathe and could not. Despite his already noted unreliability on certain specific points of detail there is good reason to think that, for a change, in this case Hemingway's account of the wounding of Frederic Henry in *A Farewell to Arms* — his highly autobiographical 1929 novel which drew heavily on his wartime experiences both in combat and in his romance with Agnes von Kurowsky — is a relatively straightforward description of the writer's own near-death experience:

> Through the other noise I heard a cough, then came the chuh-chuh-chuh-chuh — then there was flash, as a blast-furnace door is swung open, and a roar that started white and went red and on and on in a rushing wind. I tried to breathe but my breath would not come and I felt myself rush bodily out of myself and out and out and out and all the time bodily in the wind. I went out swiftly, all of myself and I knew I was dead and that it had all been a mistake to think you just died. Then I floated, and instead of going on I felt myself slide back. I breathed and I was back. The ground was torn up and in front of my head there was a splintered beam of wood. In the jolt of my head I heard somebody crying. I thought somebody was screaming. I tried to move but I could not move. I heard the machine-guns and rifles firing across the river and all along the river. There was a great splashing and I saw the star-shells go up and heard the bombs, all this in a moment, and then I heard close to me someone saying, 'Mamma mia! Oh, mamma mia!' I pulled and twisted and got my legs loose finally and turned around and touched him. It was Passini and when I touched him he screamed. His legs were toward me and I saw in the dark and the light that they were both smashed above the knee. One leg was gone and the other was held by tendons and part of the trouser and the stump twitched and jerked as though it were not connected. He bit his arm and moaned, 'Oh, mamma mia, mamma mia,' then, 'Dio ti salvi, Maria. Dio ti salvi, Maria. Oh Jesus shoot me Christ shoot me, Mamma mia, mamma mia, oh purest lovely Mary shoot me. Stop it. Stop it. Stop it. Oh Jesus lovely Mary stop it. Oh oh oh oh,' then choking, 'Mamma mamma mia.' Then he was quiet, biting his arm, the stump of his leg twitching.

Though he did not yet realise it Hemingway had been wounded in both legs. In spite of his injuries even at this point he initially felt comparatively little pain and claimed that he managed to drag another badly wounded soldier a hundred and fifty yards through fierce machine gun fire to safety during which he was hit several times. Hemingway's injuries were horrendous: as well as 227 pieces of shrapnel in his legs (the pain of which, once it kicked in, was later described dismissively by him as being like the sting of wasps) he had machine gun bullets in his right foot and in his right knee (which can be verified by the evidence of X-ray photographs reproduced in Henry Villard and James Nagel's book). The official ARC report later described all but ten of his wounds as relatively superficial but those ten were sufficiently serious to threaten him with amputation for a time. Six weeks later he described the experience in a letter to his family:

> Shells aren't bad except direct hits; you just take chances on the fragments of the bursts. But when there is a direct hit, your pals get spattered all over you; spattered is literal.
>
> During the six days I was up in the front line trenches only fifty yards from the Austrians I got the 'rep' of having a charmed life. The 'rep' of having one doesn't mean much, but having one does. I hope I have one . . .
>
> Well, I can now hold up my hand and say that I've been shelled by high explosives, shrapnel and gas; shot at by trench mortars, snipers and machine guns, and, as an added attraction, an aeroplane machine-gunning the line. I've never had a hand grenade thrown at me, but a rifle grenade struck rather close. Maybe I'll get a hand grenade later . . .

The 227 wounds I got from the trench mortar didn't hurt a bit at the time, only my feet felt like I had rubber boots full of water on. Hot water. And my knee cap was acting queer. The machine gun bullet just felt like a sharp smack on my leg with an icy snowball. However it spilled me. But I got up again and got my wounded into the dugout. I kind of collapsed at the dugout.

The Italian I had with me bled all over my coat and my pants looked like somebody had made current jelly in them and punched holes to let the pulp out. Well, my captain who was a great pal of mine (it was his dugout) said, 'Poor Hem, he'll be R.I.P. soon.' Rest in peace, that is.

You see, they thought I was shot thru' my chest because of my bloody coat. But I made them take my coat and shirt off (I wasn't wearing any undershirt) and the old torso was intact. Then they said that I would probably live. That cheered me up any amount.

I told them in Italian that I wanted to see my legs, tho' I was afraid to look at them. So they took off my trousers and the old limbs were still there, but, gee, they were a mess. They couldn't figure out how I had walked a hundred and fifty yards with such a load, with both knees shot thru and my right shoe punctured in two big places; also over 200 flesh wounds.[6]

He was carried on a stretcher to the dressing station almost two miles away at Fornaci (". . . the stretcher bearer had to go over lots, as the road was having the entrails shelled out of it. Whenever a big one would come, whe-eee-eeee-whoo-oosh—boom, they would lay me down and get flat. My wounds were now hurting like 227 little devils driving nails into the raw") where he was given morphine and antitetanus injections and where a surgeon removed the larger pieces of shrapnel embedded in his flesh: the rest would have to wait. His injuries were so severe that amputation of one of his legs was seriously mooted for some time to come but fortunately rejected, though he would endure a fairly major operation a month later to remove the shreds of shrapnel and the bullets from his knee and foot. For his bravery Hemingway was promoted to first lieutenant (*Tenente*) and would eventually be awarded the War Cross of Merit and the Silver Medal of Valour. ("That's the highest military decoration Italy gave to living men," Bill Horne observed years later. "The fellows who get the Gold Valor were almost always dead").

It took two hours for an ambulance to arrive to transfer him to a field hospital in Treviso where he spent five days with the doctors anxiously watching for signs of infection which could have led to gangrene and amputation and/or almost certain death. No infection set in—the shrapnel seems to have been sterilized by the sheer heat of the explosion—so Hemingway, still on a stretcher, was taken by train to the base hospital in Milan, the Ospedale Croce Rossa Americana, in a large mansion at 4 Cesare Cantù[7] not far from the Red Cross headquarters in the Via Manzoni and close to the Duomo. Hemingway was transferred there along with three other wounded servicemen. The hospital had been open for little more than a month by the time that Hemingway arrived and excepting the fact that one had to be wounded or otherwise ill to be there in the first place, it offered a fair degree of pleasant rest and comfort. Henry Villard remembered:

The hospital proper on the top floor . . . consisted of sixteen bedrooms for as many patients . . . There were two toilets and several baths . . . [and] the kitchen was a source of justifiable pride . . . What came out of those spotless precincts three times a day never failed to remind American expatriates, at least those whose digestion allowed, of the meals that mother used to make . . . What made the small hospital premises an inordinately pleasant spot to spend an illness was the fact that half the rooms had balconies and the other half gave out onto a capacious terrace . . . which ran completely around two sides of the building. Under the striped awnings, which could be rolled up or down according to the temper of the sun, ambulatory or wheelchair patients were able to lounge at ease and have their meals brought to them: there were large wicker chairs, a chaise-lounge, green potted plants and, on the balustrade, decorative flower boxes. Within easy reach on a low table lay a selection of magazines and a portable, hand-cranked phonograph with all the current hits . . . From my contented viewpoint, the place seemed more like an exclusive rest home or country club than a war-begotten hospital for Americans serving in a foreign land. One thing was certain: no pampered patient ever complained about the accommodations, the food, or the service.[8]

There were eighteen nurses to look after the first four men and one of them would be the woman who, despite her brief appearance in his story, would change Hemingway's life for ever.

Agnes Hannah von Kurowsky was born in Germantown, Philadelphia on the 5th of January 1892. Her mother met her father Paul (German-born but of mixed German and Polish ancestry) while the latter was teaching languages at the Berlitz school in Washington D.C. The family moved back to Washington where Agnes's father died in 1910. After a first job as a librarian, in 1914, with the outbreak of the Great War in Europe, she decided that librarianship was too quiet a career for her and opted to train as a nurse. She attended a nurses training program at Bellevue Hospital's School of Nursing in New York city, graduating in July 1917, three months after America entered the war. She applied for service with the American Red Cross but because of her Germanic surname the processing of her application was delayed and it was not until June 1918—just five months before the end of the war—that she set sail for Europe on the SS *La Lorraine*. Her first posting happened to be in Milan (of the several ARC nurses who worked in the city four had been classmates of Agnes) and thus Agnes and Ernest came to meet.

Hemingway was in the room next door to another American volunteer Red Cross Ambulance driver, the previously mentioned Henry Serrano Villard (1900-1996) who had been hospitalised with jaundice and possibly malaria: Harry and 'Hem,' only a few months apart in age, became firm friends for the duration of their time in the hospital. In fact it is largely through Henry Villard's much later account of this time that we know as much as we do about the youthful romance between Ernie and Agnes. A native New Yorker, in the teeth of fierce opposition from his parents Villard threw over his studies at Princeton to volunteer as an ambulance driver with the American Red Cross. "It was a shortcut to the front, a passport to adventure in a romantic foreign land, the chance of a lifetime," he would recall. "I lost no time in seizing it." Thus far Villard's history of service was very much like that of Hemingway: he was also a second lieutenant in fact. Having driven ambulances at Bassano near Monte Grappa he had succumbed to illness and had been invalided to Milan, hence his presence next door to Hemingway. Hemingway's great friend Bill Horne, who had contracted malaria at San Pedro Novello, arrived at the hospital on the same day as Villard.

Contrary to earlier biographies and popular myth Hemingway had not earned the dubious distinction of being the very first American Red Cross soldier to be injured in the Great War, a mistake which Hemingway himself repeated in a letter to his family written on his birthday: "You see I'm the first American wounded in Italy" and was also mentioned in a passing comment in Agnes's personal diary. He wasn't: Lt. Edward Michael McKey was a New York-born portrait painter whose poor health had kept him out of the regular army: wanting to do his bit he had joined the Red Cross and had been killed by an Austrian shell on the 16th of June—coincidentally also at Fossalta di Piave—making him the first ARC man to be killed in the First World War. Even so, the circumstances of his wounding and especially the saving of the life of another man meant that although a noncombatant (Red Cross volunteers were not issued with weapons) he was considered to be something of a hero: whatever his subsequent embroideries and embellishments Hemingway's personal bravery cannot seriously be called into question. Henry Villard remembered that on occasion the nurses liked to show Hemingway off to visitors "as their prize specimen of a wounded hero." His injuries earned him the nickname 'Broken Doll' but he was a cheerful and upbeat patient who genuinely seemed to like and be liked by his fellow patients and the nursing staff generally, though there are conflicting reports that some of the nurses—Agnes's friend Elsie MacDonald in particular, at least for a short time—found him disagreeable: one nurse later recalled that in her opinion he was "impulsive, very rude, 'smarty,' and uncooperative." This was a rare exception: most staff and patients alike found him warm, likable and charismatic even at his tender age. The burly, heavily-bearded 'Papa' of Hemingway legend was decades in the future: at this point Hemingway, still in his late teens, was tall, slim, with thick chestnut hair and was considered very handsome with a square jaw, clear skin and a broad grin revealing bright, regular white teeth. Unsurprisingly the nurses were even more popular with their young charges and the beautiful Agnes seems to have been the most popular of all: it would seem that the men vied with each other to see who would be the first to have a date with her even though 'fraternisation' (a word always heavily laced with euphemism in such circumstances) between nurses and patients was forbidden. Henry Villard was welcomed into the hospital by Agnes herself and was clearly instantly taken with her:

> 'Why hello there! I guess we've been expecting you.' The fetching night nurse who answered my ring at the landing smiled cheerfully. 'Come right in. we have a room all ready for you.'
>
> I didn't have to be asked twice. It was the first feminine voice with an American accent I had heard since leaving the States and it belonged to a tall, slender, chestnut-haired girl with friendly blue-gray eyes, who seemed to combine brisk competence with exceptional charm. Though hardly at my best, I couldn't help responding to her encouraging welcome. What luck, I thought, to encounter such an attractive person . . . Her loose-fitting, ankle-length uniform, with belt and Red Cross arm band, was crisp and white; a starched white cap perched like a butterfly on the back of her head . . . [she was] cheerful, quick, sympathetic, with an almost mischievous sense of humour . . . tactful, fresh and pert and lovely in her long-skirted white uniform . . . she radiated zest and energy . . . Just before she switched off the light, I asked the name of this angelic creature who had admitted me into this spot of heaven. 'Agnes von Kurowsky,' she said, 'from Washington D.C.' As I drifted off, I kept thinking how sympathetic and lovely she was, doubly attractive so far from home. All right, she was a few years older than I, but then older girls are quite likely to appeal to young men who have lately turned eighteen.[9]

Villard admitted: "I myself came to have a real crush on Aggie, or Ag, as she was called by those who got to know her best, but then all the boys fell for Aggie to some degree. No wonder. In the close quarters of our top-floor ward, we were always conscious of her comely presence." Agnes was affectionately known as 'Von' to her friends—Hemingway was one of very few particularly close friends who would be allowed to call her Ag or Aggie—and was equally popular with all who knew her. She was extremely attractive and knew it: though she described herself as entirely innocent she was perfectly well aware of her effect on the opposite sex, patients included. In her diary on the 12th of August she wrote: "Mr Seeley—our oldest patient (not in yrs.) is inclined to be spoony, I fear. He was looking for shooting stars this evening—so I had to quietly but firmly leave. Enough said!" In past life she had had her share of suitors: in New York she had left behind a young doctor (known only as Dr. S. and still unidentified: in her diary Agnes nicknamed him 'Daddy') who apparently considered that they were engaged although Agnes herself appears to have thought decidedly otherwise on that score. Indeed her diary implies that she left the United States without even telling him; on the 16th of June, on board ship sailing for Europe, she wrote: "It's very hard to believe that I've gone at last—& that it's Sunday & Daddy will come back tonight & find me gone. I can't help saying 'It serves him right'—& that is wrong of me." Her attractiveness to the opposite sex and her willingness to play along with it up to a point scarcely changed either on her Atlantic crossing—she flirted with the soldiers on board ship—or in Italy: in fact almost as soon as she arrived at the Red Cross hospital she attracted the attentions of a Captain Enrico Serena, a wounded officer of the Alpini Corps who, though lame and blinded in one eye, Agnes described as "simply full of personality, and attractive in spite of his disfigurement . . . [he was] a fascinating person. He spoke English. I didn't have to worry about my Italian. He was very witty and good company." Captain Serena occupies a good number of entries in Agnes's diary throughout July and August. "Capt. S. asks me every day if he can call again," she wrote on the 15th of July, "& I say no—for various reasons. Such an ardent suitor I thought existed only in books. He's positively silly to my Amer. mind." A week later she said: ". . . this tempestuous Italian mode of wooing is certainly terrifying. He tells me how much he loves me, & when I say but I don't love you, it squelches him but a moment & then he begins again." Only seven days later though there were indications that she was changing her mind. "My Capt. grows even more ardent, & I am beginning to enjoy it, I believe." Whatever relationship Agnes and the Captain had was innocent—emotionally passionate on Serena's side, coolly amused but somewhat distant on hers—but innocent: they walked out together, met at the Galleria, ate ices, with Serena escorting her back to the hospital before lights out at ten o'clock.

Serena and Hemingway certainly met on several occasions and seem to have struck up a cordial friendship; on the 20th of July, the day before Hemingway's nineteenth birthday, Agnes confided to her diary: "The Capt. walked home with me again, & came in this time. He seemed delighted with our Hospital and took quite a fancy to Mr Hemingway." On the 2nd of August she noted: "The Capitano . . . came to call after I went upstairs on duty tonight— ostensibly to call on Mr Hemingway." According to Carlos Baker's biography Serena was in the habit of calling Hemingway 'Baby', thus making him the model for Rinaldi in *A Farewell to Arms*. Indeed it seems that Hemingway magnanimously try to match- make Serena and Agnes: "Oh, go out to dinner with the Captain, Ag" she records him as saying. Agnes relented on the 10th of August, unfortunately on the same day as Ernie's operation: she and Serena went that evening to a restaurant where Serena had wangled a private room, "much as I disliked the idea," as she told her diary afterwards. "However, I got home early and he seems to be more decent than I thought at first."

However at the end of August Captain Serena's mother fell ill and he was required to leave Milan urgently and to return home to see her. He left on the 26th: Agnes saw him off with some relief if her diary is any indication. "The old affair is over, thanks be!" she recorded. It was only at this point, with Serena out of the way, that Hemingway (who presumably had been biding his time) started to make a serious play for Agnes himself. He soon began writing notes and letters to her from his bed, sometimes every day, sometimes twice a day or even more, with them being taken downstairs for her to read by Agnes's fellow nurse and close friend Elsie MacDonald, a Scottish-born nurse trained in England known as Mac who would become the inspiration for Ferguson or 'Fergy' in *A Farewell to Arms*. Fifty-two of Agnes's letters to Hemingway survive: none of his to her do so—they seem to have been destroyed by a subsequent beau of hers in a fit of jealousy—and the romance with Agnes is notable for its absence from those letters Hemingway that wrote to his family back home. The fact that he is in love is mentioned just twice and Agnes is never once mentioned by name. One reference comes in a letter of the 29th of August 1918:

> Also Mom I'm in love again. Now don't get the wind up and start worrying about me getting married. For I'm not; as I told you once before. Raise my right hand and promise! So dont get up in the air and cable and write me. I'm not even going to get engaged! Loud cheers. So dont write any 'god bless you my children not for about three years.[10]

The other comes on the 11th of December, when Ernie tells his family that he has "just returned from a peach of a trip . . . Lieut. Hey and I went up to Treviso about 50 miles to see the girl. She is in a field Hospital there."[11] That is the sum total of Hemingway's disclosure of his romance with Agnes to his parents, though he was somewhat more candid with his siblings: in late November of 1918 he told his older sister Marcelline that he was in love with

Agnes (of whom he had already said "Ag is prettier than anybody you guys ever saw. Wait till you see her!") but asked her not to say a word to their parents, a promise which by all accounts she kept. "I'm not foolish and think I can get married now but when I do marry I know whom I'm going to marry," he said.[12]

Had it not been for the fact that his temporary home while in Milan was a Red Cross hospital for wounded American men, the picture painted from reading about these last five and a half months or so of 1918 could almost be seen as idyllic. It's true that to begin with at least there is no doubt that Hemingway was tormented by the very real fear of the amputation of one of his legs, a fear which did not fully evaporate until the surgery he underwent on the 10th of August. For the first month or so he was bed-bound: Henry Villard recalled that Hemingway was known to dig out the smaller and more accessible fragments of shrapnel from his own legs with a penknife, keeping the lumps of metal by his bedside. He certainly suffered considerable discomfort from his wounds at times and would continue to do so for many months more. Nevertheless as Villard made plain the surroundings were exceptionally comfortable, closer to a country club than the regimented wards of a hospital. The number of patients was sufficiently small (seven admissions in June 1918; another seven the following month including Hemingway; twenty-two in August; thirteen in September and twelve in October) that the nurses were never overburdened by their duties. Most patients were physically ill rather than injured—there were malaria and influenza epidemics that summer and jaundice was also common—; only three men were wounded in combat, Hemingway being one such. It was a fine summer and for the men hot, lazy days and sultry nights were spent passing the time as freely and languidly as their physical health and inclinations permitted, sitting or lying on their balconies or on the terrace. In early August Agnes swapped shifts and became a night nurse, coming on duty at eight o'clock in the evening. After she had finished her rounds she would make sure that all the other men were asleep and go to Ernie's room where the two of them would sit on the balcony outside his room and talk quietly in the warm Milanese night air:

> At first she was merely diverted by him—his constant stream of visitors, his unruly ways. The flashing smile, the dimples, and the romantic Latin colouring—all made him a dashing figure. Then she found out that he was not just another eager young contending for her favours. His magnetism went far beyond his physical presence. There was the tremendous vitality, the determination to be a free spirit, uninhibited by petty conventions. They were kindred souls, she discovered. During the long, quiet nights, when the hospital corridors were still and the sultry Italian air hung heavy over the balcony, she saw his gentle, serious side . . . Noticing that Ernest was a night owl too, she sat with him in his room, talking and listening.[13]

"When the August nights were especially hot," says Peter Griffin, "she moistened a towel for Ernest's forehead, wiped his neck and chest with cool water, and, to alleviate the itching beneath his bandages, scratched the soles of his feet."[14] Of necessity there was a high degree of physical intimacy between nurse and patient: as previously mentioned on the 10th of August Hemingway underwent a fairly major operation to have more of the shrapnel removed from his legs, after which his limbs were heavily bandaged once again and the wounded soldier was helpless and bed-bound for several weeks.

According to Red Cross regulations the keeping of personal diaries was not prohibited outright but frowned upon—quite usual in time of war—for fear that potentially sensitive information could fall into enemy hands. "All [Red Cross] Workers must thoroughly familiarize themselves with the censorship regulations of the American Expeditionary Forces. It principally prohibits mention in letters, post cards, diaries and all other written matter, the name of any place or locality in connection with any military organization . . . All communications to persons connected with the American Expeditionary Forces must be endorsed 'official' by the person designated in each department or bureau, and placed in the outgoing mailbasket unsealed." Yet Agnes kept just such a diary from June (when she was still in New York) to October

1918, from just before the beginning to about half way through her romance with Hemingway, after which point her letters tell the remainder of the story. Even here letters were scrupulously censored and Agnes broke the rules by sending and receiving letters outside the official channels. The Agnes that comes across in the diary in particular and is glimpsed from time to time in the recollections of those who knew her at the time was of a beautiful but often rather serious, mildly flirtatious but fairly prudish and conventional woman who enjoyed her nursing career and was keen to advance it but fought shy of developing any serious romantic relationships and often worried about becoming frivolous.

Hemingway makes his first appearance in Agnes's personal diary on Saturday the 20th of July 1918: "Mr. Hemingway . . . has the honor of being the 1st Amer. wounded in Italy. [As we have already seen this was not true]. He has shrapnel in his knees, besides a great many flesh wounds." The following day was Hemingway's nineteenth birthday; Agnes noted: "Mr Hemingway's birthday, so we all dressed up, & had Gelati [ices] on the balcony & played the Victrola. Then Mr Seely brought him in a large bottle of 5 star Cognac, and they did make merry." This is an indication that Hemingway was known to be a drinker even during his stay in the hospital, bribing a porter to smuggle in bottles of booze and to spirit away the empties. According to Henry Villard:

Early in our relationship, I noticed that the Hemingway stamina was being bolstered by a bottle of cognac, or some other spiritous liquor, hidden under his pillow (strictly against the rules, naturally), from which I would share a surreptitious nip on occasion. My own illness, unpleasant though it was, seemed trivial compared with the physical discomfort Ernie had to put up with. Who could blame him for 'fortifying the organic functions,' as one Cuban rum company used to advertise the purpose of its product, in order to keep up his morale, to still the shock of that terrifying moment of injury, and to speed his recovery? . . . Hem didn't hesitate to point with pride at what he liked to call his army of 'dead men,' empty bottles of brandy, vermouth, Cointreau . . . stashed away in the big oak armoire against an opportunity to have them smuggled out by the porter, who had brought them in for a small bribe in the first place . . . He had an unlimited capacity to swallow the contents of a bottle without betraying the fact that he had been drinking.[15]

Agnes herself, many years later, recalled that "he drank brandy all the time." This was officially frowned upon but the nurses turned a blind eye to his tippling as long as he didn't overdo it and appear obviously drunk, a rule that he appears to have kept to. This did not save him from "more than one violent run-in" with Miss DeLong, the hospital's stern supervisor (possibly one of which was fictionalised in chapter 22 of A Farewell to Arms). In fact at the end of the letter home to his parents that he wrote describing his wounding (quoted above) he scrawled a childish stick figure lying down with a speech bubble emanating from the mouth, the text of which read 'Gimme a drink!' Given that Hemingway had been raised in a rather puritanical household where indulgence in alcohol of almost any kind was frowned upon this was a gesture of maturity, a declaration of independence from — even rebellion against — his upbringing.

We know from the diary covering this time that at first Agnes was fairly dismissive of Hemingway's obviously burgeoning feelings for her, writing them off as a mere boyish infatuation of the kind she was used to from the other men and not to be taken seriously—yet. The age difference meant that by the 4th of August she was already calling him 'Kid' in her diary. On the 25th of that month she wrote: "Now Ernest Hemingway has a case on me, or thinks he has. He is a dear boy & so cute about it." The following day (the day that Captain Serena left Milan) she observed: "Ernest Hemingway is getting earnest. He was talking last night of what might be if he was 26-28. In some ways—at some times—I wish very much that he was. He is adorable & we are very congenial in every way. I'm getting so confused in my heart & mind I don't know how I'll end up. Still, I came over here for work and until the war is over I won't be able to do anything foolish, which is lucky for me. I used to pride myself on my sense. I wonder if I'm getting foolish or if I can blame the romantic country for it's [sic] effect on me." The next day: "All I know is 'Ernie' is far too fond of me, & speaks in such a desperate way every time I am cool, that I dare not dampen his ardor as long as he is here in the Hospital. Poor kid, I am sorry for him. Everybody seems to be down on him for some reason, and he gets raked over the coals right & left. Some of the heads have an idea he is very wild and he is—in some respects, but swears to me in a very honest way that he has always kept clean—& never been bad. I believe it—but the others—oh—no." In spite of this Agnes clearly has sufficient regard for Ernie to start hiding innocent things from him lest his jealousy be aroused—on the 30th of August she writes: "Mr Michels left this A.M. & I'm not ashamed to say I kissed him goodbye—though I didn't dare tell the Kid." On this same day Agnes told her diary that twenty days after his operation Hemingway was finally able to get around under his own steam, albeit with crutches and with his leg and foot still bandaged: "In the evening I escorted 'mia ammalato' on his first visit to the outside world in 2 months, which we both enjoyed hugely."

Agnes's prudent decision not to tell Ernie that she had given another patient an innocent kiss goodbye may have been due to the fact that Agnes and Ernie's relationship seemed already to be moving, however slowly and subtly, onto a different plane; on the last day of August she told her diary: "Tonight, my ½ night off, as a very special dispensation I was allowed to go to dinner with Mr Hemingway. We went to the Du Nord, as a nice quiet place where the food was good, & also had a bottle of Asti Spumante—which is getting to be my favorite beverage." Harry Villard noticed that of all the wounded soldiers vying for the attentions of the nurses and Agnes in particular Hemingway had won:

I didn't realize it then, but . . . for the first time in his life, Ernie was falling in love, and the object of his affections was none other than our glamorous night nurse, Agnes von Kurowsky. There was a tacit acceptance, a subtle understanding, by nurses and patients alike, of the special relationship that was developing between them. But possibly because he would have brooked no potential rivals, Ernie did not confide to me his amorous inclinations. We did not talk about Agnes except in general, noncommittal terms, and there was nothing in his demeanor, so far as I could tell, to call attention to the true state of his feelings. Not until later would I hear that he and Agnes had engaged in a running underground correspondence, exchanging notes and letters at a prodigious rate, usually with Mac as the trusted intermediary. But I was not privy to this little game and, during the relatively short time I was in the hospital, I remained unaware of its existence.[16]

For a spell Agnes's friend Elsie 'Mac' MacDonald seems to have taken against Hemingway, possibly after her berated her for leaving some of the Victrola records out in full sunlight on the terrace where they soon melted. On the 8th of September Agnes wrote in her diary: "Mac is not sleeping nights & it makes her so cranky daytimes it is terribly hard to get along with her. She picks on the poor Kid, whom she spoiled so at first, & as he says—'rides him all day.' I've lectured him so much about being polite to her that he doesn't dare answer her back the way he used to." Two days later: "The Kid was sick tonight . . . Mac says she hates him & doesn't care if he is sick." Whatever its cause this seems to have been a merely temporary spat as Ernie and Mac corresponded after the war and continued to do so almost for another two decades until the late 1930s.

By the 11<sup>th</sup> of September Agnes and Ernie's relationship seemed to be ascending to a still higher plane. Agnes gave him a ring, noting in her diary that she was "astonished to see how really pleased he was. It's strange to think how little an act will give a huge amt. of pleasure to someone." The ring is clearly visible in one photograph of Hemingway in uniform in particular: he is shown standing with his left hand on his hip almost as though ostentatiously showing off Agnes's gift.

He had every reason to flaunt it. Agnes von Kurowsky was Ernest Hemingway's first love: their romance was the first mature love affair of his adult life with all that that entails in terms not of only learning about another human being in the most intimate of ways but also learning about himself. In spite of his chiselled, square-jawed good looks, winning smile and glossy dark hair Hemingway's high school friends do not remember him as being a student who ever dated or ever showed much interest in girls or for that matter was a student in whom girls showed much interest. At the age of eighteen Agnes was the first woman with whom it can truly be said that he fell completely and utterly in love as a grown man. For that reason alone, irrespective of what would soon come to pass, she would have remained in his memory for the rest of his days. In contrast and taken at face value Agnes's writings, both those to Hemingway and those for her own eyes only, seem to suggest that Agnes (whose head-start in terms of years meant that she considered that she had loved before, more than once) underwent a remarkably speedy 360-degree change of heart in her attitude toward Hemingway and his feelings for her in the space of some six or seven months or so. In August she could tell her diary with a distinct note of patronising dismissiveness that he had a mere "crush" on her and was "too fond" of her: by September she had started to write repeated and tenderly romantic and passionate declarations of her love in her numerous letters to him; a short while later in early 1919 she would be giving him the brush-off in one of the most famous of all 'Dear John' letters in literary history.

But that was still in the future. As Hemingway's injuries healed he progressed from his bed to a wheelchair to crutches to a walking stick, which last he would retain for many months: as soon as he was more or less mobile once again he and Agnes walked out together, seeing the sights of Milan, taking in the Duomo, La Scala, the Galleria, going for open carriage rides, betting at the San Siro racetrack and eating out. The few surviving photographs of the pair together show an attractive couple very clearly deeply in love. "The heatwave continued into September and Agnes devoted herself to Ernest," writes Bernice Kert. "When she finished her routine duties, they sat on the balcony outside his room, whispering, caressing each other, watching the swallows on the roof. It was an atmosphere rich in sensuality — Ernest lying about in his pajamas, Agnes tenderly solicitous."[17] In spite of the physical intimacy which had existed between a nurse and her formerly bed-ridden patient there is absolutely no suggestion that Ernest and Agnes's romance was ever physically consummated, that it ever progressed past a few passionate kisses and tender embraces. Later on Hemingway liked to at least imply that they had slept together: Agnes stated the exact opposite. Hemingway's friend Eric 'Chink' Dorman-Smith told Hemingway's first biographer Carlos Baker in 1961 that "Hem said that it takes a trained nurse to make love to a man with one leg in a splint." This is of a piece with the scene in *A Farewell to Arms* where Frederic and Catherine make love for the first time in chapter 14, but seems to have been entirely fictional. Henry Villard's son Dmitri believes that Ernest and Agnes probably did sleep together, saying that "Agnes's letters are so passionate it's hard to believe there wasn't a [sexual] relationship between the two,"[18,19] whereas Villard senior himself did not believe Agnes and Ernie ever slept together. In Villard and James Nagel's book *Hemingway in Love and War* Nagel baldly states that Agnes went home still a virgin. It is true that some level of sexual contact between the two was suspected by others; on Saturday the 7th of September Agnes's diary records: "Lo'dy, Lo'dy, Goodness me—Mac found one of my yellow hairpins under Hemingway's pillow, & she and Mr Lewis will never let me forget it now. I think both Ernie & I got through it pretty well." The finding of one of Von's hairpin's beneath Hemingway's pillow clearly implied amorous behaviour of some sort between them but Villard later wryly observed: "While there can be no doubt that demonstrations of affection took place between Ernie and Agnes, in the circumscribed limits of the hospital things could not have gone very far. That a nurse's hairpin should find its way into a patient's bed does not mean that any part of her anatomy must follow." For all we know Hemingway merely found one of Von's hairpins and kept it under his pillow as a token or memento of the woman with whom he was so much in love. To Henry Villard, decades later Agnes herself said, "Let's get it straight—please. I wasn't *that* kind of girl." By now the truth is probably impossible to unravel though it seems to the present author that Nagel has the right of it and that Hemingway's implications of a sexual as opposed to an intensely passionate but chaste romantic affair were just another manifestation of his abundantly well attested tendency to embroider the truth—what *should* have happened, what he *wanted* to happen, rather than what actually *did* happen. It is quite possible that Agnes erected a barrier at this point for reasons of professionalism: she took her duties as a nurse very seriously indeed and Ernest was after all a patient in her care as well as a boyfriend of sorts. In the hospital he was a patient first and foremost: it was more than her job was worth for him to be anything else. The thrill of the forbidden doubtless added a frisson of excitement to their romance since fraternisation of this kind between nursing staff and patients was strictly prohibited by Red Cross regulations and Italian social mores alike. Nevertheless for a time the couple occasionally forgot themselves and were heedlessly open about their relationship, holding hands and looking lovingly at each other in front of the other men and nurses. "I knew he had the inside track," said Villard, "when I saw him holding her hand one day in a manner that did not suggest she was taking his pulse . . . I couldn't help noticing that he received an extra share of her attention, due partly to the special fondness that seemed to be developing between them . . . " Only relatively open, however: despite her cavalier approach to the stringent censorship regulations relating to diaries and letters Agnes usually made all efforts to conceal a romantic relationship with a patient knowing full well that had any such liaison been discovered she would have been summarily sacked and sent home. That Agnes's perhaps more than professional involvement with Hemingway had been noticed by the hospital supervisor in indicated by a note that Agnes made in her diary on the 3rd of September: ". . . as I was starting out at 5 to the Kodak shop with Mr Hemingway—Miss De Long told me I was not to go out with him again, which made me refuse to go, & got him all worried as he thought I was in Dutch."

The point about any sexual involvement between Ernie and Aggie (or rather the total absence of proof of the same) is important because at least one Hemingway biographer is on record as having solemnly informed the world, on the basis of absolutely no evidence whatsoever, that Ernie and Agnes really did sleep together as though this was an established fact proven beyond all and any reasonable doubt. In particular and most outrageously of all Kenneth S. Lynn's *Hemingway* (1987) tells the reader not only that they did have sex but even describes the position they enjoyed:

> For weeks their lovemaking routine was largely unvaried. As night fell, he would lie on his back in bed or recline in a chair on the balcony outside his room with his foot propped up on another chair. When he and Agnes embraced, the immobility of his leg presumably required that he stay beneath her. In years to come, there would be indications that he liked this posture—for reasons that would only gradually become clear.[20]

Another biographer who takes this tack is Peter Griffin, author of *Along With Youth*. Griffin cites certain passages in Agnes's letters as 'evidence' that she and Hemingway consummated their romance physically. "Personal interviews are essential to a biographer,'" says Griffin, "but you simply can't expect that Agnes Kurowsky when she was married to someone else would answer 'yes' when asked' 'Did you sleep with Ernest Hemingway?'"[21] Therefore for Lynn and Griffin 'no evidence' means 'cover-up' and 'no' means 'yes.' Needless to say this is complete and wholly unwarranted speculation from beginning to end. Regarding any sexual contact between Ernie and Agnes all the evidence is against it and none for it. In the words of James Nagel: "Lynn has no conclusive evidence for his assertions; rather, he speculates from rumor and from the fiction [i.e. *A Very Short Story* and *A Farewell to Arms* in particular], formulates a psychological thesis, and comes to regard his assumptions as fact." Griffin receives the same treatment:

> Agnes's diary, Villard's memoir, the recollections of his friends, and the social circumstances of the time suggest a rather different interpretation: that Ernest and Agnes were sexual innocents and their romance did not advance beyond the petting stage. Hemingway's high school friend Lewis Clarahan recalled that Ernest 'did no dating in high school at all. He just didn't. He had four sisters, so he was used to girls, but he just didn't care to date' . . . *There is absolutely nothing in her diary about the romance with Hemingway that supports an interpretation of sexual activity.*[22] [Present author's emphasis].

On the 24th of September Ernie and Agnes were parted for almost a week. Hemingway, walking but still limping heavily with his omnipresent cane, managed to get a ten-day pass which allowed him (along with another American patient called Johnny Miller, a fellow ambulance driver originally from Minnesota) to go north to Stresa on Lake Maggiore for convalescent leave. In her diary Agnes wrote: "I did not let Mr Miller & Mr H. go to Stresa in the rain. They left this PM—at 6. Ernie came downstairs to say goodbye to me, & Miss DeLong was close at hand, so it was rather formal until she went off & then I slipped into the elevator with him & we hand a more real farewell." (James Nagel states that "the elevator was one of the few places where two people could exchange an embrace without being observed"). This first visit imprinted upon him a deep and abiding love for the area: Stresa would become an important place for Hemingway since he returned to it again and again throughout the rest of his life. Ernie and Johnny were taken under the wing of the Conte Emanuele Greppi, an elderly diplomat who would be fictionalised (thinly) in *A Farewell to Arms* as Count Griffi. Hemingway spent his time playing billiards and drinking champagne with Greppi, rowing on Lake Maggiore and sightseeing, taking a trip to the top of the Mottarone; of the view from the 4,900-foot summit he said that it "beats paradise all to hell."

In spite of the stunning natural beauty and the calm atmosphere Hemingway missed Agnes so much that although he had ten days leave and although he had written constantly ("Today I had two letters from Ernie," Agnes told her diary on the

27th of September. "The nicest letters I ever got. Mac was dying for a look . . . but I only gave her bits of quotations as it would never do to let her in on them"), he cut short his holiday and returned to Milan to be with her. Their reunion was as passionate as might be expected (as far as it was able to be in the hospital) but Agnes broke bad news shortly afterwards. Another separation would part Ernie and Agnes, this time for much longer. She had volunteered to go to Florence—over a hundred and fifty miles away—to help nurse those who had succumbed to the Spanish influenza epidemic then rife across Europe, though some sources (Bernice Kert for instance) say that she went to Florence to nurse an ARC officer with typhoid: given that Agnes's Florence letters have several references to her patient (singular) the latter is more likely. According to her diary on the 15th of October she received last-minute notification that she was being transferred to Florence. Hemingway unsurprisingly did not take the news especially well:

> This AM at the breakfast table I was told I was to go to Florence by the noon train, so I had some tall hustling to do. Of course, Mac dashed in & woke up my Kid with the news I was leaving— he got up & dressed at 9AM an unprecedented performance, & then was so rude to Mac she nearly cried, & there was war in the air. I got after him but he was so broken up I hadn't the heart to say much.

Agnes left Milan carrying Ernest's photograph with her. While away she wrote to him at every possible opportunity, referring to him by a litany of rather gushing epithets such as: "The Light of My Existence," "My Dearest & Best," "Most Ernest of Ernies," "My hero" and the like. "Don't let me gain you only to lose you," she said in one such missive. "I love you Ernie . . . In spite of the sunshine, I am lost without you. I thought it was the dismal rain that made me miss you so." Hemingway was aware of her rather summary dismissal of the New York doctor ('Daddy') about whom she began to experience a degree of guilt after dreaming about him one night. Agnes was quite candid about all of this. "The dreadful thought came to me today," she wrote, "that maybe my punishment for this treatment of him would be to have you treat me in a like manner someday. I certainly need a dose of your presence, dear, to reassure and comfort me."

Back in Milan Ernest was understandably unhappy about their enforced separation but tried to keep up his spirits by keeping in touch with her by the only means available. 'Kid' and 'Mrs Kid' wrote to each other furiously, sometimes three or four times a day. He was determined to get better as soon as possible: he had always longed to get back to the front and to the fighting at the earliest opportunity, which turned out to be in late October, just three and a half months after he had been wounded. Though still limping badly and hobbling along with a walking stick he left the ARC hospital and returned to the front at Monte Grappa on the 24th of October. It turned out to be a short-lived return to active service: after just one day he came down with a severe attack of jaundice and in his weakened state this proved to be too much for his constitution so he was shipped straight back to Milan and the hospital.

"I just buried my face in my pillow and laughed for joy to think I am going to see you in Milan when I get back," Agnes wrote to him from Florence when she heard the news. "Dear Kid, hurry up and get well so I shant worry about you. Just imagine yourself kissed goodbye—by your own Mrs, Kid, Aggie." Hemingway had been extremely lucky: his bout of jaundice took him through the end of the war itself. The Italians captured Trieste and on the 3rd of November Italy and Austria signed an armistice: eight days later, at the eleventh hour of the eleventh day of the eleventh month of 1918, the war as a whole came to an end after four and a quarter years. On that same day Agnes came back to Milan from Florence but stayed with Hemingway for just a week before being sent to Treviso to look after more wounded American troops.

At some point not easy to specify in these summer and autumn months things began to sour for Agnes but not for Ernest. The process occurred with remarkable rapidity: as late as the 1st of December 1918 she was still expressing the wish that they could be married in Italy (although "since that is so foolish I must try and not think of it") and in fact she continued to speak of their romance and even their forthcoming marriage in exactly the same positive and hopeful terms as ever. Yet it is clear that Agnes's doubts about the future of their relationship were amassing rapidly. The seven-year age gap seems to have weighed far more heavily on Agnes than it ever did on Ernest: in their numerous letters to each other she called him 'Kid' and 'bambino' and other pointedly age-related terms of endearment while he replied in kind with 'Mrs Kid.' Agnes was twenty-six and eager to pursue a career in nursing: Ernest was just nineteen and had not yet finally decided on what future course his life might take. That Agnes was seven years older than him seemed to bother Ernest very much less than the fact that he was seven years younger bothered Agnes. Disparity in age clearly was not a deciding factor for Hemingway: in September 1920 he got married for the first time to Elizabeth Hadley Richardson who was eight years his senior, a greater age gap even than with Agnes—not coincidentally according to Bernice Kert, biographer of Hemingway's relationships with the women in his life. (Hemingway put Agnes's name on the list of those who were to be invited to the wedding though she does not seem ever to have received an invitation). There is the suspicion that already, even in the first flush of a romance which was passionate, heady and exciting for them both, Agnes suspected that it was a beautiful but doomed infatuation which could not possibly last and was looking for reasons—any reason—why the relationship could not be expected to work. At twenty-six Agnes considered that she was a mature woman who had seen something of the world whereas she thought that Ernest, for all that he was a wounded soldier, was a rather callow nineteen-year-old, his vocation as a writer by no means set in stone and rather aimless and unformed, a young man who had not yet found himself (which is surely a lot to demand of any nineteen-year-old).

On the 7th of December Ernest applied for a three-day pass: he had decided to make an unannounced visit to Treviso intending to surprise Agnes. He did indeed surprise her but perhaps not as pleasantly as he had hoped. Because of the 'flu epidemic then raging Hemingway decided not to take the day-long trip on the train: instead he hitched rides to Verona where he stayed overnight then carried on to Padua. At Tornacello he met up with a Lieutenant Hey (in love with one of Agnes's nursing colleagues, a Miss Smith) and it was Hey that drove them the last fifty miles to Treviso, arriving there on the 9th. The visit was a less than resounding success: still limping and leaning heavily on his walking stick Hemingway turned up wearing his medals and the short cape of an Italian officer (something he was not entitled to wear, though photographs exist of him wearing it) which caused some of the soldiers there to laugh at him and treat him as something of a figure of fun. "The men all laughed their heads off at him," Agnes recalled later. "They thought he was the biggest joke. He came in with his cane and all his medals and those American doughboys, they just roared."

The foursome—the two soldiers and two nurses—went to have a look from a safe distance at the Austrian trenches near Tremiglia, sallied across the pontoon bridge at Cremona and saw the ruins of houses at Negressa by moonlight. After just a few hours together Ernie took his leave of Agnes and he and Lieutenant Hey started back to Tornacello in the early hours of the morning. "By the time that he left Treviso," writes Peter Griffin, "Ernest had told Agnes he would return home immediately and work toward earning a steady two hundred dollars per month. When he did, they agreed, she would come home and marry him."[23]

Agnes was singing from the same hymn sheet—outwardly, at least. On the 13th of December she wrote to Hemingway that she had told her mother of her forthcoming marriage: "I wrote to my mother that I was planning to marry a man younger than I—& it wasn't the Doctor—so I expect she'll give me up in despair as a hopeless flirt. I'd hate to think I was fickle." As far as Ernie was concerned there was no indication that Agnes was having second thoughts; on the same day he wrote to Bill Smith:

> We went in the staff car up to TREVISO where the missus is in a Field Hospital. She had heard about my hitting the alcohol and did she lecture me? She did not.
>
> She said, 'Kid we're going to be partners. So if you are going to drink I am too. Just the same amount.' And she'd gotten some damn whiskey and poured some of the raw stuff out and she'd never had a drink of anything before except wine and I know what she thinks of booze. And William that brought me up shortly. Bill this is some girl and I thank God I got crucked so I met her. Damn it I really honestly can't see what the devil she can see in the brutal Stein [short for Hemingstein, i.e. a nickname for Hemingway that he and Agnes used] but by some very lucky astigmatism she loves me Bill. So I'm going to hit the States and start working for the Firm. Ag says we can have a wonderful time being poor together and having been poor alone for some years and always more or less happy I think it can be managed.
>
> So now all I have to do is hit the minimum living wage for two and lay up enough for six weeks or so up North and call on you for service as a best man. Why man I've only got about 50 more years to live and I don't want to waste any of them and every minute that I'm away from that Kid is wasted.[24]

If Agnes was sending out any mixed messages displaying her doubts about their relationship, intentional or otherwise, Hemingway did not see them; just a few days before Christmas she wrote to him saying: "I miss you more and more, and it makes me shiver to think of your going home without me. What if our hearts should change? . . . and we should lose this beautiful world of us [sic]." Since there was absolutely no sign that Hemingway felt any differently—far from it—was she in fact subtly advertising the fact that it was her own heart which had changed? They did not even spend Christmas together: little did either of them realise but, although they continued to correspond for several more weeks, they would never see each other again. The 9th of December 1918 was the last time they ever saw each other, not just in 1918 but in any year.

Or was it? In *Hemingway: A Life Without Consequences* James R. Mellow alleges (on the basis of confessedly circumstantial evidence) that Ernie and Agnes's last ever meeting may have been in Milan on the 31st of December 1918. This claim is made on the basis of "a careful reading of a letter to Hemingway which Agnes began on New Year's Eve 1918 and then continued on New Year's Day" which according to Mellow "reveals that she and Hemingway did, in fact, have a final rendezvous in Milan on December 31, just before Hemingway took ship for America." Mellow also suggests, also on the basis of some of the letters that Agnes wrote at this time as well as the Agnes-inspired fiction, that contrary to all prior biographical literature Ernie and Agnes spent some time together in Padua. Mellow regards these scenarios as "plausible" — how plausible it is must be for readers of Mellow's biography to decide for themselves.

On the 28th of November Hemingway had written to his family saying that Jim Gamble, his former commanding officer and now a close friend, had invited him to spend two months with him in Madeira and the Canaries. Ultimately nothing came of that plan but just a few weeks later Gamble asked Hemingway to spend Christmas with him at Taormina on the island of Sicily. This time Hemingway did so and spent the festive period of 1918 with Gamble in the villa that the latter had rented. Around this time Gamble made the remarkable offer to support Hemingway financially for a year if he remained in Italy. Hemingway was tempted and for a time gave the offer serious consideration. In his biography of Hemingway, Jeffrey Meyers intimates that Gamble was homosexually attracted to Hemingway, something that Agnes herself may possibly have suspected for many years later she said: "He would have accepted that invitation. I don't think that would have worked out. It wasn't the place for a young fellow."

Whether Gamble was romantically attracted to him or not Agnes continued to encourage Ernie to go back home to America. As well as her possible suspicions about Gamble's ulterior motives for wanting to keep him in Italy and to bankroll him for a year she had entertained some less than pleasant thoughts about Hemingway's seemingly aimless life and the chance that he might effectively become a drifter of some sort: for him to return home to pursue a career (in journalism, presumably) and to start to save money would be a demonstration of the seriousness of his intentions and an act of his faith in their future together. Many years later she would recall: "I sent him home. He hated me for that. I told him he'd never be anything but a bum if he sponged off someone else [i.e. Jim Gamble] . . . I think I felt more or less an obligation to look after him a little bit because I was older . . . He really would have gotten to be a bum. He had all the earmarks." To be fair if this sounds unduly harsh Agnes had a certain amount of evidence on which to base such as assessment; in a letter of the 11th of December he had told his family: "I'd like to stay over here and bum a while as I may not get another chance for a long while." Yet he also went on to say: "But I really feel as though I ought to get back and see you all a spell and then get to work . . . The climate and this country get you and the Lord ordained differently for me and I was made for to be one of those beastly writing chaps y'know. You know I was born to enjoy life but the Lord neglected to have me born with money—so I've got to make it and the sooner the better."

Having been granted an honourable discharge from the American Red Cross on the last day of 1918 Hemingway was shipped home on the SS *Giuseppi Verdi* out of Genoa arriving back in New York on the 21st of January 1919. He stayed in New York for a few days with Bill Horne and his girlfriend before taking the train to Chicago for an emotional reunion with his family.

His sister Marcelline recalled: "Ernest wasn't the same old friend and playmate I had known. Though much less than a year had passed since he had gone to Europe—and only a year and a half since we had graduated from high school together—a lifetime of new experiences, war, death, agony, new people, a new language and love had crowded into Ernest's life." While Agnes had given Ernie a ring theirs was never a formal and official engagement but more in the way of an 'understanding.' Hemingway fully expected that Agnes would come back to America and join him in due course and that as soon as he was settled into a regular job and had saved up enough money for them to start their married life together they would soon be wed.

She didn't and they weren't. After Hemingway's departure Agnes was transferred yet again to the hospital at Torre di Mosto on the 10th of January. "Goodness only knows when I'll get my letters mailed from out there, but I'll do my best," she told him. Postal problems aside a gradual but distinct change comes across in Von's letters to Ernest from this point on. Not only do they become less frequent but the tone changes: they become less hectically romantic and passionate, more distanced. (Even on the 1st of January 1919 she had told him: "This has been the most eventful year of my life . . . I've . . . grown very fond of my kid Ernie." "Very fond" is scarcely the stuff of great romance and grand passion). The reason, we now know, was that it was here that Agnes met and quickly fell in love with Lieutenant Domenico Caracciolo, an artillery officer in the Arditi and apparently the heir to a Neapolitan dukedom. Later Agnes would say that Caracciolo (who she called 'Nicky') was "very gentle, a gentle, nice soul—much more interesting to me than a nineteen-year-old Hemingway" which manages to be simultaneously rather dismissive of Hemingway and Caracciolo both. In the early stages Agnes felt sufficiently little for Caracciolo (or at least wanted to give that impression, both to Hemingway for obvious reasons and to the world at large in interviews decades later) that she even told Hemingway about him, remarking jokingly but no less patronisingly on his youth in much the same way that she had with Hemingway himself. "I have one devoted admirer here. Domenico—aged 14. [He was actually thirty]. He guides me on my pilgrimages to the sick folks around here, & then insists on going if he finds out I am to go. He also presents me with villainous looking Austrian sabres & guns & shells. How I'll ever get them home goodness only knows."

By spring it was looking as though Agnes's romance with Caracciolo was serious and moving into a higher gear, yet four and a half thousand miles away in Oak Park Ernie, blissfully unaware of all this, was still awaiting every letter from Italy, still trying to save money and still excitedly planning his future with his wife-to-be. Marcelline remembered:

> Morning after morning Ernie lay in his big, green-painted iron bed in his third-floor room. He rarely stayed in bed all day, but it seemed to help his aching legs if he was not up and walking for more than half a day. I can vividly remember the sight of his brown hair, dark against the white pillows. Usually he had his Red Cross knitted cover spread over him on top of his other bedclothes . . . with its gay green, red, black, yellow and white squares. He didn't like to be without this cover somewhere around. When we asked him why, he said it kept him from being so homesick for Italy.
>
> Ernie was remarkably uncomplaining about his suffering from the festered places in his skin. Tiny shrapnel bits kept working their way out of his legs and feet. He had visited Oak Park Hospital, where Daddy and his doctor colleagues examined Ernest carefully. Ernest didn't have to have any more actual operations, as I recall, but he needed constant medical care. He did go back to the hospital once, for treatment of an infection . . .
>
> Often Ernie was in real pain, but usually by the time he came downstairs he was quite cheerful. He wrote lots of letters to Italy, and he read for hours at a time in bed. He read everything around the house—all the books, all the magazines, even the A.M.A. *Journals* from Dad's office downstairs. Ernie also took out great numbers of books from the public library. Though Ernie rested most of the mornings when he first came home, by lunchtime he was usually dressed in his good-looking Red Cross uniform and his high, well-polished, brown cordovan boots. He was proud of these boots and shined them daily. After lunch with the family he would put on his overseas cap and, taking his cane, he would start out for a walk. Ernie tried looking up his old friends, but few of them were around town or free during the daytime as he was. Most of his pals now had jobs or had gone back to college after their demobilization. So Ernest began going to the high school in the afternoons; it was a place where he felt at home.[25]

Agnes was constantly on his mind. He had maybe fifty more years to live, he told a friend, and he wanted to spend them with Aggie.

Yet a different note had already entered Aggie's increasingly infrequent letters: a more mature and worldly-wise note perhaps but also a somewhat abstracted and distanced one. On the 1st of March she said:

> Dear Kid,
>
> I got a whole bushel of letters from you today, in fact haven't been able to read them all, yet. You shouldn't write so often. I can't begin to keep up with you, leading this busy life I do . . . I've learned to smoke. What do you know about that? Also I've learned a fascinating gambling game, 7½. Do you know it? I won 10 lire the other night. Oh, I'm going to the dogs rapidly, & getting more spoiled every day. I know one thing—I'm not at all the perfect being you think I am . . .
>
> I'm feeling very cattiva [wicked] tonight, so goodnight, Kid, & don't do anything rash, but have a good time.
>
> Afft [Affectionately]
> Aggie

Quite apart from the odd choice of words—"I'm not at all the perfect being you think I am"—that "Afft" coming as it did after weeks of signing herself off with 'Your own Kid,' 'Your Mrs Kid,' 'Your missus' and the like should have sounded warning bells to Hemingway. Just six days later Agnes decided that it was time to draw a line beneath the relationship she had had with Hemingway once and for all, penning arguably one of the most famous 'Dear John' letters in all literature, a missive by turns tender, patronising, conciliatory and apologetic, a letter which remained unknown to the world at large until after Agnes's death in 1984. Dated the 7th of March 1919 she wrote:

Ernie, dear boy,

   I am writing this late at night after a long think by myself, & I am afraid it is going to hurt you, but, I'm sure it won't harm you permanently.

For quite awhile before you left, I was trying to convince myself it was a real love-affair, because, we always seemed to disagree, & then arguments always wore me out so that I finally gave in to keep you from doing something desperate.

Now, after a couple of months away from you, I know that I am still very fond of you, but, it is more as a mother than as a sweetheart. It's alright to say I'm a Kid, but, I'm not, & I'm getting less & less so every day.

So, Kid (still Kid to me, & always will be) can you forgive me some day for unwittingly deceiving you? You know I'm not really bad, & don't mean to do wrong, & now I realize it was my fault in the beginning that you cared for me, & regret it from the bottom of my heart. But, I am now & always will be too old, & that's the truth, & I can't get away from the fact that you're just a boy—a kid.

I somehow feel that some day I'll have reason to be proud of you, but, dear boy, I can't wait for that day, & it was wrong to hurry a career.

I tried hard to make you understand a bit of what I was thinking on that trip from Padua to Milan, but, you acted like a spoiled child, & I couldn't keep on hurting you. Now, I only have the courage because I'm far away.

Then—& believe me when I say this is sudden for me, too—I expect to be married soon. And I hope & pray that after you thought things out, you'll be able to forgive me & start a wonderful career & show what a man you really are.

Ever admiringly & fondly,

Your friend,

Aggie

Marcelline Hemingway later recalled how her brother took the news. She remembered that he took the eagerly-awaited letter up to his room: instead of the hour-long silence which always indicated that he was crafting a reply, shortly afterwards she heard him vomiting violently in the second floor bathroom at the top of the stairs:

For days Ernie had been watching the mails. He was irritable and on edge with the waiting. Then the letter came. After he read it he went to bed and was actually ill. We didn't know what was the matter with Ernie at first. He did not respond to medical treatment, and he ran a temperature. Dad was worried about him. I went up to Ernie's room to see if I could be of any help to him. Ernie thrust the letter toward me.

'Read it,' he said from the depths of his grief. 'No, I'll tell you.' Then he turned to the wall. He was physically sick for several days but did not mention the letter again . . . I have thought many times since that day that the letter from Agnes may have been the most valuable one my brother ever received. Perhaps without that rankling memory, *A Farewell to Arms* might never have been written.[26]

Little by little Hemingway recovered after a fashion, or rather he assimilated such a grievous wound to the extent that anybody ever can. Some biographies imply that he replied to Agnes's rejection letter but the response, if any, is unknown because by Agnes's own much later admission Domenico Caracciolo had jealously destroyed all of Hemingway's letters to Agnes himself or demanded that Agnes destroy them. None are known to survive.

Hemingway unsurprisingly retreated into himself. "Literary history is full of jilted writers," says Scott Donaldson:

. . . suggesting that an early pang-at-the-heart may be salutary. Obviously, what matters is what one does with the hurt. Among the alternatives are sinking into the morass of sorrow, converting the pain to anger, adopting a stance of philosophical expertise, erecting barriers against future rejections, getting rid of the pain by writing about it, and above all proving the jilter wrong: *won't she be sorry, though?*

Hemingway went through all these reactions.[27]

Insofar as he ever discussed the matter with others Hemingway's tone was one of the studiedly artificial bravado of the man who had been deeply and bitterly hurt in the most painful way imaginable and grows a carapace of blithe indifference around himself to protect the proud flesh within. On the 18th of April 1919 he told Jim Gamble:

> There is a good deal of news which should be retailed [sic] to you, tho. First I am now a free man. All entangling alliances ceased about a month ago and I know now I am most damnably lucky— tho of course I couldn't see it at the time. Anyway everything is finished and the less said about it, as always with the unfair sex, the better. I did love the girl, though I know now that the paucity of Americans doubtless had a great deal to do with it. And now it's over and I'm glad, but I'm not sorry it happened because, Jim, I figure it does you good to love anyone. Through good fortune I escaped matrimony so why should I grumble? Not being philosophical though, it was a devil of a jolt because I'd given up everything for her most especially Taormina. And as soon as the Definite Object was removed queque kicks were implanted upon the w.k. [well kicked] ass for my ever leaving Italy. The first time you're jilted tho is supposed to be the hardest. At any rate I'm now free to do whatever I want. Go wherever I want and have all the time in the world to develop into some kind of writer. And I can fall in love with anyone I wish which is a great and priceless privilege.[28]

To another Red Cross friend he wrote: "I am a free man! That includes them all up to and including Agnes. My Gawd man you didn't think I was going to marry and settle down did you?"[29]

It was, needless to say, a pose from start to finish. There was also a possibly understandable but undeniably unattractive display of pettiness and bitterness in his reaction to the breakup: to Elsie MacDonald he wrote expressing the hope that when Agnes's ship bringing her home docked in New York she would trip on the dockside and knock out all her front teeth. We can safely write this off not as an expression of serious ill-will against Agnes but as the admittedly childish and spiteful outburst of a still very young and in many ways unformed man who had been grievously wounded and not just physically. On the same day that Hemingway received the letter of rejection from Agnes he wrote to his great friend Bill Horne what Horne later regarded as "the most heartbroken, heartrending letter" he had ever read:

> . . . having failed miserably at being facetious I'll tell you the sad truth which I have been suspecting for some time, since I've been back, and which culminated with a letter from Ag this morning.
>
> She doesn't love me, Bill. She takes it all back. A 'mistake.' One of those little mistakes, you know. Oh, Bill, I can't kid about it, and I can't be bitter because I'm just smashed by it. And the devil of it is that wouldn't have happened if I hadn't left Italy. For Christ's sakes, never leave your girl until you can marry her. I know you can't 'learn about wimmen from me' just as I can't learn from anyone else. But you, meaning the world in general, teach a girl—no, I won't put it that way—that is you make love to a girl and then she goes away. She needs somebody to make love to her. If the right person turns up, you're out of luck. That's the way it goes. You won't believe me, just as I wouldn't. but Bill, I've loved Ag. She's been my ideal, and Bill, I forgot all about religion and everything else because I had Ag to worship.
>
> Well, the crash of smashing ideals was never merry music to anyone's ears. But she doesn't love me now, Bill, and she is going to marry someone—name not given—who she has met since, marry him very soon, and she hopes that after I have forgiven her, I will start and have a wonderful career and everything . . . All I wanted was Ag. And happiness and now the bottom has dropped out of the whole world. And I'm writing this with a dry mouth and a lump in the old throat, and Bill I wish you were here to talk

to. The dear Kid. I hope he's [Agnes's Italian lover, i.e. Caracciolo] the best man in the world. Aw, Bill, I can't write about it because I do love her so damn much. And the perfectest hell of it is that money, which was the only thing that kept us from being married in Italy, is coming in at such an ungodly rate now. If I work full time I can average about seventy a week, and I'd already saved nearly three hundred. Come on out and we'll blow it. I don't want the damn stuff now.[30]

This is the raw flesh of Hemingway's still excruciatingly painful wound.

But in June Agnes out of the blue wrote to Ernest once again to say that her engagement was over. Her Italian lieutenant's high-born family (principally his mother it would seem) had decided that she was a title-hunter on the make—an entirely unjust slur—and had forbidden the marriage. The *Tenente* had been transferred away from Torre di Mosto (possibly as a result of the mother exerting her influence) and Agnes never heard from him again: a friend tried to find out what had happened and wrote to him but answer came there none. There is some evidence that Agnes and Caracciolo saw each other, accidentally and very briefly, one last time in Naples when Caracciolo and his mother crossed Agnes's path in a carriage: according to the account given decades later to Henry Villard "he had stood up and looked back and she would never forget the expression in his eyes." (Perhaps not surprisingly Agnes gave a different, completely contradictory account of this encounter: "He was with his mother I think," she is supposed to have said. "I pretended that I didn't see him." So did she never forget the devastated expression in her heartbroken lover's eyes, or did she coolly pretend not to see him?). Having jilted Hemingway she had in turn lost the subsequent romance with her Neapolitan lieutenant and she had gone back to New York "a sadder but wiser girl—feeling that I'd like to break something and preferably somebody, and [that] life really wasn't worth living" as she would say later. She would be coming home on the SS *Re d'Italia* as a single woman after all the following month—a detail included perhaps in the hope that even after all that had passed, Hemingway would forgive her and that they could put things behind them and carry on as before.

But Hemingway did not respond to Agnes's letter, evidently feeling that once the break had been made it had to be final. He did however discuss it in another letter to his friend Howie Jenkins:

> Had a very sad letter from Ag from Rome yesterday. She has fallen out with her Major [*sic*]. She is in a hell of a way mentally and says I should feel revenged for what she did to me. Poor damned kid. I'm sorry as hell for her. But there's nothing I can do. I loved her once and then she gypped me. And I don't blame her. But I set out to cauterize out her memory and I burnt it out with a course of booze and other women and now it's gone . . . [31]

Only the final three words—"now it's gone"—strike a jarringly false note here: in fact Hemingway pointedly added "but not gone entirely." It was not gone entirely: in some sense it would never be gone. Hemingway and Von's romance was, to borrow the title of one of his fictionalised accounts, a very short story in terms of the length of time that they actually spent together but in other respects for Hemingway the story never came to an end in his lifetime: the proud but bitterly hurt man who claimed that he had burnt her memory and his love for her out of himself kept Agnes's letters for the rest of his days. Three of them would be discovered amongst his effects after his death in 1961 by his widow Mary and returned to Agnes.

Agnes's pious hope in March 1919 that he would not be permanently damaged by her rejection of him seems to have been just that. That rejection, writes Bernice Kert in *The Hemingway Women*, became an emotional injury of enduring consequence, or as James Nagel puts it, the rejection "had hurt him severely, so deeply that he wrote about it all his life." One of the comparatively few things which seems to unite many of Hemingway's biographers is that the nineteen-year-old Ernie's rejection by Agnes scarred him for life and that in some sense he never truly got over the pain of it. The end of that particular affair may well have had a bearing on all of Hemingway's subsequent dealings with women. He was married four times: three of those marriages ended in divorce and Hemingway confessed to a friend not long before his suicide that he wanted to divorce Mary Walsh, his fourth and final wife, but could not afford to do so and did not want to endure the "hell" he thought she would put him through. All of his wives testified to his drunken, verbally and psychologically aggressive and manifestly unreasonable behaviour. Some of Hemingway's biographers claim that the young Hemingway was so devastated by Agnes's rejection that it established a template for the rest of his life: abandon a woman before she abandons you, which would certainly be in keeping with the man who famously wrote "if two people love each other, there can be no happy end to it." "To an impressionable young man," wrote Henry Villard, "who had never loved before, the shock of being rejected by the girl he believed was his must have been exceptionally severe and may well have conditioned his future attitude toward women." Jeffrey Meyers says much the same thing: "The trauma of her betrayal, for that is how he interpreted it, forced him into instinctive self-protection. For the rest of his life he guarded himself against betrayal and loneliness by conducting a liaison with a future wife during his current marriage; when he had ensured his own emotional security, he abandoned his wife before she could leave him." "He internalized the lesson she taught him," says Scott Donaldson, biographer of Hemingway's friendship-rivalry with Scott Fitzgerald:

... that those who love can be betrayed—and made sure that
he did not put himself at risk. Thus he had many friends and
in almost every case broke off with them, sometimes viciously,
before they could do so with him ... Throughout his life he was
reluctant to let anyone else get close enough to strike a blow to
the heart. To ward off the danger, he severed any human ties that
threatened to put him at risk. For Ernest Hemingway, even mortar
shells seemed less dangerous.[32]

Jeffrey Meyers goes further in making the bold but by no means
wholly implausible claim that Von's rejection "may have driven
Hemingway to strive for success as a writer"—in short that the
bitter gall of the end of their romance in some sense created
Hemingway the writer out of his need to hammer words into
shape in order to give form to his desperate pain. Scott Donaldson
agrees that Agnes's jilting "drove him toward achievement as
he sought to belie her charge of immaturity." As Hemingway
told Scott Fitzgerald in May 1934, "We are all bitched from the
start and you especially have to be hurt like hell before you can
write seriously." Hemingway had indeed been hurt in just such
a manner. One also has to wonder if the "course of booze" that
Hemingway prescribed for himself to drink Agnes's rejection
off his mind as a nineteen-year-old recently wounded soldier—
wounded in all senses of the word—might have set a course for
his later infamous alcoholism. Hemingway was certainly noted
for drinking large quantities of alcohol while in the Milan hospital
but it is at least possible that until Agnes's rejection he may have

remained a heavy drinker, even an alcohol abuser, without tipping over the edge into the florid and desperate alcoholism of later life. Whether this is the case or not Scott Donaldson says: "Agnes, unlike the Austrians, administered a hurt that not even time could make a healing of . . . it now seems clear that his jilting by Agnes von Kurowsky may have been the most lasting of the many hurts that fate was to deal Ernest Hemingway."[33] Jeffrey Meyers concurs: "The most influential woman in Hemingway's life, apart from his mother, was Agnes von Kurowsky. She first taught him, when he was young and vulnerable, to accept the care and protection of a woman . . . Agnes' unexpected rejection had a devastating effect on Hemingway. The emotional wound was as painful as the physical injury." James Nagel similarly agrees: "All his life Hemingway would write about his experiences in Italy, and always with a sense of loss and remorse for the woman who rejected him." In the hospital Hemingway, even after being seriously wounded, had acted and had been thought of as a happy and cheerful young man: along with his experience of war, of the worst that human beings can do to each other, it is a moot point as to whether the rejection by Agnes might have played a part in instilling what became Hemingway's ultimately tragic sense of life and a pessimistic view of a world where love can be met with rejection and where even the most happily fulfilled and reciprocated love must inevitably be ended by death. This is not to say that either personally or artistically was Hemingway a pessimist per se: if any label can be applied to his personal philosophy it must surely be stoicism—human beings suffer unjustly and randomly everywhere all the time and the best that we can do is to give meaning to such suffering by enduring it as best as we can for as long as we can. A French tag which became Hemingway's motto and model for his entire life (at least until the very end) which recurs again and again in his correspondence was *Dans la vie, il faut d'abord durer*—'In life, first one must endure.' But in the very depths of his stoicism he came close, very often, to an almost unbearably bleak pessimism where, as he would say in *A Farewell to Arms*, ". . . people bring so much courage to this world [that] the world has to kill them to break them, so of course it kills them. The world breaks everyone and afterward many are strong at the broken places. But those that will not break it kills. It kills the very good and the very gentle and the very brave impartially. If you are none of these you can be sure it will kill you too but there will be no special hurry." Another of Hemingway's biographers, Michael Reynolds, has written: "Agnes may not have thought theirs a serious affair, but Hemingway certainly did. She was the first mature woman who had loved him. Her rejection . . . was an emotional defeat . . . He was furious, hurt and much alone . . . It was not just a broken heart; it was a broken mirror. Agnes had believed in the young writer he created. Now, when he most needed her support, she deserted him. Hemingway never forgave her. Although their paths would not cross again, Agnes von Kurowsky was not forgotten."[34]

III

In late 1919 Hemingway took a job as a correspondent for the *Toronto Star Weekly*—even moving to Toronto for a time—, a position that he held for the next three years. All contact between Ernest and Agnes was not yet completely broken off, though. On the 3rd of September 1921 Hemingway married his first wife Hadley Richardson who was eight years his senior, a year older even than Agnes had been. Hadley had certain features that reminded Hemingway of Agnes, though she had a playfulness and gaiety that the more serious Agnes apparently lacked. In December 1921 the newlyweds moved to Paris where Ernest carried on with his job as correspondent for the *Toronto Star*. Life, for a time, was kind to Hemingway: he was living in one of the greatest cities in the world, mixing with an artistic milieu that included such luminaries as Gertrude Stein, Scott Fitzgerald and James Joyce, honing his craft as a wordsmith with his journalistic work, putting the finishing touches to his first book and he was a newly married man to boot. But Agnes was clearly still on his mind even then. Indeed, he and Agnes corresponded briefly more than a year after his marriage. Possibly in October of 1922 Hemingway wrote her a warm letter perhaps instigated by a sentimental journey that he and Hadley had made in June back to northern Italy and to many of his old haunts. Doubtless seeing many of the places which reminded him so strongly of Agnes and having the memories flood back inspired him to contact her again. In that communication, as well as telling Von of his marriage, he mentioned that his first book—*Three Stories and Ten Poems*—was about to be published and it is hard not to suspect that there was an element of 'see what you've missed?' Hemingway was able at least to offer conclusive concrete evidence that Agnes's fears that he would turn out to be an aimless idling drifter were unfounded: he was a married man (a year later his first child, Jack, would be born: Jack would go on to become the father of the actresses Margaux and Mariel Hemingway), an established journalist and soon to be a published writer of fiction. Agnes wrote an equally warm and friendly letter to Ernest forwarded from Paris to where he and Hadley were staying at Chamby in Switzerland at the time. There are some indications that even though he was an ostensibly happily married man Hemingway continued to entertain hopes that he and Agnes might still be together: he is said to have told the writer Lincoln Steffens (1866-1936) that he would leave Hadley if Agnes came back to him and that he would "give up everything for her." Agnes penned her reply from her home at 142 East 27th St. in New York just before Christmas:

December 22nd 1922

Dear Kid—
        Well, when your voice from the past reached me— after I recovered from the surprise, I was never more pleased over anything in my life. You know there has always been a little bitterness over the way our comradeship ended, especially since I got back & Mac [Elsie MacDonald] read me the very biting letter you wrote her about me . . . Anyhow, I always knew that it would turn out right in the end, & that you would realize it was the best way, and I'm positive you must believe, now that you have Hadley . . .

Agnes gave Hemingway a lengthy summary of her movements over the previous few years, including meeting up again with Dr S, 'Daddy' and her varied travels in the course of pursuing her career in nursing:

Oh, gosh, there's so much to tell you I can't tell where to start. The past 3 years have certainly been full of interest for me . . . In the first place—to dig up the ruins—I came back from Italy—a sadder and wiser girl—feeling that I'd like to break something & preferably somebody, & life wasn't really worth living. I was ruined for America, & when the poor Doc—much fatter—ambled around I was as nasty as possible, tho' he stuck fast until I sailed the 2nd time, when he promptly married, & he is now struggling along & has a young son.
    I worked in Miss Shaw's Tuberculosis Social Service Department for 6 months, & then went home for a visit, and came back to N.Y. just when things were beginning to stir up again in Europe—so I was slated for Russia & sailed in March 1920. I didn't dare tell my friends & relatives it was to be Russia, as they all had an idea it

was certain death as a suspected spy to venture over the borders of that poor land. But, darn it all, when I got to Paris, Russia was closed, especially for women workers, & I went to Bucharest with 2 other nurses to do some Baby Welfare work—as I was *not* a specialist in that line. I will never forget that trip on the Simplon Express—maybe you know it . . . I've slept on a bench in a station, ridden on an unlighted train, and, well you know how bad those countries can be. Italy during the war was luxury compared to what I've found since the war in Roumania.

I spent that summer in Bucharest—rather lonely as I lived & kept house with a devilish chief nurse—the other girls were scattered. She kept me because I learned Roumanian & spoke French & was therefore useful.

We turned over our Baby Work to Lady Paget's unit from the League of R.C. Soc. In Sept. & sailed from Constantsa on the Black Sea, via Constantiople & Athens—the Corinth Canal & finally— Naples. And there, I was surprised & relieved to find that I landed without any of the feelings that tormented me on previous visits— Naples being the home of a certain dashing young Artillery Officer [a reference to Domenico Caracciolo]. I had a wonderful time showing my pal & a Y.W.C.A girl about to all the spots I knew,—& hen on to Rome, Florence, Milano, Switzerland, & finally Paris in much straightened [*sic*] circumstances . . . After 4 months in Paris—Oct. to Feb— . . . I went back to Roumania for the Junior Red Cross, and by special request, & then I spent months in a little town in the Carpathians among peasants. We—my pal & I lived in a peasant cottage, whitewashed & simple, and really life was good, even if we did have a hard job. Then after a summer at a Tbc. Sanitarium in Constantsa—a wonderful experience—I asked for release & came back home Nov. 1921—after a vacation in Budapest—Vienna (a city of cities) and Prague.

In January I went on duty as a night supervisor at Bellevue & stuck it out for 9 long months, and then when a girl friend from Roumania arrived here with a scholarship . . . we took a tiny box of an apartment together, furnished it halfway, & now I am doing private nursing as a shortcut to wealth tho' certainly not fame.

Last month I had a very tempting offer from the Red Cross to go back to Europe—either to Warsaw—or Sofia, and—I turned it down.

Let it be said that never before have I turned a deaf ear to old Dame Opportunity when she suggested travel, but, I really began to fancy my little apartment, and couldn't rush right off and leave Christine Golitzi my Roumanian friend alone in a strange country. I've been there myself & I know.

But, sometimes I get lonesome, & then I kick myself for not going, & I dream of Paris—that dear old place, where I had so much time on my hands, and roamed about in so many funny places. If I could only stand just now—at early twilight—at the Place de la Concorde, and see the taxis spinning around those little corners, & the soft lights, & the Tuileries fountain—oh, my. I'm homesick for the smell of chestnuts on a grey, damp Fall day—for Pruniers, the Savoia (Noel Peters) and my pet little restaurant behind the Madelaine—Bernard's, where I ate crème chocolate every night. Maybe I'd better stop, or the paper will get soft & blurry out of sympathy for my sorrows.

Agnes ended her letter with a declaration of pride in Hemingway's achievements and entertained the hope that they could remain friends and continue to correspond:

It is so nice to feel I have an old friend back because we were good friends once, weren't we? And how sorry I am I didn't meet & know your wife. Were you in Paris when I was there a year ago this Nov.? Is there any chance of knowing when your book will be out? How proud I will be, some day in the not-very-distant future to say 'Oh yes, Ernest Hemingway—Used to know him quite well during the war.' I've always known you would stand out some day—from the background, and it's always a pleasure to have one's judgment confirmed.

May I hope for an occasional line from you? Friends are great things to have, and I appreciate them more every year—but oh, there's a woeful waste of them—and some disappear as fast as you collect new ones.

I'm not reminiscing on Milano, Padova, etc.—on purpose, because I really must stop, but, it's been great—'priceless' to have this long talk with you—tho' I haven't said any of the things I meant to when I began.

With my best wishes to you & Hadley—if I may speak of her so—and a string grasp of the hand—as they say in Roumania.

Your old buddy—
Von
(oh excuse me, it's Ag).

It was not to be. Curiously, in spite of the fact that Hemingway had made the first approach, he ignored Agnes's sincere and touching expressions of goodwill and overtures of friendship. He did not write back to her and the two never had any contact ever again. The olive branch that she had extended to him was rejected. We do not know why. Perhaps he saw something in Agnes's letter that compelled him not to take matters any further: perhaps he meant to but never got around to it and then felt that he had left it too late: perhaps Hemingway took a malevolent pleasure in revenge, in curtly rejecting the one who had rejected him. We will probably never know for sure. What we do know is that unless James R. Mellow is right in suggesting that they really did meet in Milan on the last day of 1918, Ernest Hemingway and Agnes von Kurowksy never met again in person after that day in Treviso on the 9th of December 1918 and they never wrote to each other or had any further direct contact after this brief exchange of letters at the end of 1922. Many years later Agnes observed: "I was surprised to hear from him, but I wrote saying I was pleased to have an old friend back, and how proud I'd be one day to say I once knew him well. [But] I never heard from him again."

For all that, we know that she continued to occupy his mind for a very long time after their brief Italian romance ended if indeed at some level she ever left it. Hemingway affected to be a man who looked always to the future and disavowed harking back to the past. "Chasing yesterdays is a bum show," he wrote in 1922 following a return visit to Fossalta during a trip to Italy. To his friend Bill Horne the following year he said: "We can't ever go back to old things or try and get the 'old kick' out of something or find things the way we remembered them. We have them as we remember them and they are fine and wonderful and we have to go and have other things because the old things are nowhere except in our minds now." This is what Hemingway *said*, but what he said was completely belied and contradicted by the fact so much of his fiction is nakedly autobiographical. He was never able to leave the past—his own past—alone, least of all his wartime activities and the romance with Agnes von Kurowsky which were obviously experiences that he needed to work through in his own time in the only way that he knew how. Throughout his career Hemingway was seemingly unable to prevent himself from drawing upon his own real-life experience of the war years and transmuting it for artistic purposes. Jake Barnes, the hero of Hemingway's second novel *The Sun Also Rises* (1927) for example—considered by many to be his finest—, is a young American expat journalist living in Paris who received an unidentified war wound in the genitals which has rendered him impotent. There are the short stories, probably most famously *A

*Very Short Story* among them, which touch upon his war years and most notably of all there is *A Farewell to Arms*. But this was not merely a military matter: for Hemingway the war years were intimately and indissolubly bound up with the initially beautiful, passionate and tender then bitter, excruciatingly painful and humiliating romance with Aggie.


III

One of the first fruits of Hemingway's several attempts to make sense of his loss (and also one of the most explicitly autobiographical) comes in the form of the appropriately named *A Very Short Story* first published in the collection *In Our Time* in 1925. The title is straightforwardly accurate: the vignette runs to just 633 words, taking Hemingway's proverbially laconic and stripped-down prose to perhaps its ultimate conclusion. In the story the unnamed narrator is a young American soldier in Italy who has been wounded in combat, hospitalised and who falls in love with the nurse (named Luz) who cares for him. Luz is quite clearly modelled on Agnes von Kurowsky: indeed in the original draft of the story and upon its first publication in 1925's *In Our Time* the nurse was named Ag—the nickname that only the young Ernie and a few other particularly close friends had been allowed to use—and the story was set in Milan and Torre di Mosto. But in July 1938, while preparing *The Fifth Column and the First Forty-Nine Stories* for publication, Hemingway instructed Maxwell Perkins, his editor at Scribners (and that of Scott Fitzgerald as well), to change the real-life specifics. Milan and Torre di Mosto were replaced by Padua and Pordenone respectively and most importantly of all Ag was changed in favour of Luz. "It should stay as Luz in the book. Ag is libelous. Short for Agnes," he wrote.[33]

*A Very Short Story* is in some ways a potted history, compressed into slightly over six hundred words, of some of the salient features of Hemingway's romance with Ag and the sights and sounds of his time in Italy. "They wanted to get married, but there was not enough time for the banns, and neither of them had birth certificates. They felt as though they were married, but they wanted everyone to know about it, and to make it so they could not lose it." And then: "After the armistice they agreed he should go home to get a job so they might be married. Luz would not come home until he had a good job and could come to New York to meet her. It was understood he would not drink, and he did not want to see his friends or anyone in the States. Only to get a job and be married. On the train from Padua to Milan they quarreled about her not being willing to come home at once. When they had to say good-bye, in the station at Milan, they kissed goodbye, but were not finished with the quarrel. He felt sick about saying good-bye like that."

Agnes's betrayal—as he perceived it—with Caracciolo is also woven into the tale. "Living in the muddy, rainy town in the winter, the major of the battalion made love to Luz, and she had never known Italians before, and finally wrote to the States that theirs had only been a boy and girl affair." (If Luz and the soldier's romance had been only a 'boy and girl affair' the implication is clear: she has jilted a boy—a 'Kid'—in preference for a man). "She was sorry, and she knew he would probably not be able to understand, but might some day forgive her, and be grateful to her, and she expected, absolutely unexpectedly, to be married in the spring. She loved him as always, but she realized now it was only a boy and girl love. She hoped he would have a great career, and believed in him absolutely. She knew it was for the best." This is, as we have seen, about as directly autobiographical a summary of Agnes's 'Dear John' letter of March 1919 and her feelings toward Hemingway as could possibly be. However after the tenderness of much of the vignette the last line of the tale, with its sudden descent into bathos, seems like a calculated joke: "The major did not marry her in the spring, or any other time. Luz never got an answer to the letter to Chicago about it. A short time after he contracted gonorrhea from a sales girl in a loop department store while riding in a taxicab through Lincoln Park." This last detail, at least, seems to be pure fiction.

Then there are other short stories such as 'A Way You'll Never Be', 'In Another Country' and 'Now I Lay Me' which have quite explicit parallels to Hemingway's real-life experiences in Italy. The short story 'The Snows of Kilimanjaro,' first published in *Esquire* in 1936 and regarded by many as his finest effort in the genre, is not war-related but it contains a passage which is at least strongly suggestive that it harks back to the romance with Agnes. A writer named Harry—taken by many to stand for Hemingway himself—is on safari in Africa with his wife Helen when a thorn puncture on his leg becomes so infected that gangrene sets in and soon it is clear that, far from help, the infection will prove to be fatal. As he lies dying with the vultures roosting in the trees nearby his mind ranges back across what he sees as a wasted and dissolute life and amongst other areas comes to rest upon his love life and a certain individual in particular:

> He had whored the whole time and then, when that was over, and he had failed to kill his loneliness, but only made it worse, he had written her, the first one, the one who left him, a letter telling her how he had never been able to kill it . . . How when he thought he saw her outside the Regence one time it made him go all faint and sick inside, and that he would follow a woman that looked like her in some way, along the Boulevard, afraid to see it was not she, afraid to lose the feeling it gave him. How every one he had slept with had only made him miss her more. How what she had done could never matter since he could never cure himself of

> loving her. He wrote this letter at the Club, cold sober, and mailed
> it to New York asking her to write him at the office in Paris. That
> seemed safe. And that night missing her so much it made him feel
> hollow sick inside . . .

Is this yet another not especially heavily disguised harking-back to his feelings for Agnes? We cannot know for sure but it is easy to make the connection. There are certainly very sound, credible reasons for doing so.

Even a full decade after the affair Hemingway was brooding on his very short story with Agnes yet again. In March 1928 he started to sketch out what at first seemed to him might be another short story based on his experiences in the last six months of 1918. "He had been trying for years to make fictional use of his war experiences of 1918," wrote Hemingway's first biographer Carlos Baker. "He wanted to tell a story of love and war, using as an epigraph the cynical lines from Marlowe: ' . . . but that was in another country,/ and besides the wench is dead.' The other country could only be Italia, and the girl Agnes von Kurowsky. She was neither a 'wench' nor was she dead. But the story ached to be told. The whole affair now lay ten years in the past, suffused with an aureate glow which none of the intervening visits to Italy had succeeded in expunging."[34] Unexpectedly the short story grew and grew in the telling: over the next few months it became a novel, one widely regarded as his masterpiece (or at least one of his masterpieces along with 1940's *For Whom the Bell Tolls* and *The Old Man and the Sea* of 1952). It was published in September 1929 and he gave it a title which comes from a lyric poem by the Elizabethan dramatist and poet George Peele—*A Farewell to Arms*. Despite Hemingway's avowal that "None of the characters in this book is a living person" it is quite evident that the work is autobiographical no less than *A Very Short Story*.

The novel relates, in first person narrative, the tale of Frederic Henry, a young American serving as a Lieutenant in the Ambulance Corps—clearly Hemingway himself in many respects once again. Agnes becomes Catherine Barkley, a British VAD nurse still grieving for the loss of her fiancé in the Battle of the Somme in July 1916. Even in a writer as autobiographical as Hemingway so often was one can take the parallels too far, as Michael Reynolds is the first to state emphatically. "To read any of Hemingway's fiction as biography is always dangerous," he warns, "but to read *A Farewell to Arms* in this manner is to misread the book."[35] There is nothing like a one-to-one correspondence between the real Agnes von Kurowsky and the fictional Catherine Barkley. Agnes had short dark hair, Catherine long blonde hair; Catherine has a sexual relationship with Frederic Henry and dies in childbirth while there is no evidence whatever that Agnes and Ernest ever consummated their relationship; Hemingway was ultimately spurned by Agnes whereas Frederic and Catherine's relationship only ends in her death in childbirth at the end of the novel and so forth. In actual fact Catherine is a composite figure made up out of some of the most important women in Hemingway's life to date, Agnes (of course), his first wife Hadley and second wife Pauline Pfeiffer among them, calling to mind Scott Fitzgerald's creation of composite female characters in his own stories. Hemingway's concern as an artist was to create a work of fiction rather than fictionalised autobiography. "Hemingway has not made it easy to understand what really happened to him in the war," writes James Nagel:

> What dominates the imaginations of most people is the story of Frederic Henry and Catherine Barkley, caught in war and desperately in love, who escape to Switzerland to await the birth of their child, only to have Catherine and the baby die in hospital. It is a crushing and moving tragedy, one that lives in the mind of anyone who has read *A Farewell to Arms*, but it is not, of course, what actually happened.[36]

Be that as it may there can be absolutely no question that the novel truly is intensely autobiographical in certain specifics — Henry's experiences of combat and of being wounded, for instance — and especially that the Catherine Barkley of the novel is very largely drawn from life and from Agnes in particular. Agnes herself certainly took it that way. "Without Agnes there would have been no Catherine," writes James Nagel. "In no other work did Hemingway describe his heroine in terms of such passionate tenderness; so many of his women appear tough and cynical in comparison. There is not one iota of cynicism in the story of Catherine; the tale had its wellspring in something wholly unfeigned by the writer. And the fact that Ernie had in his possession three of her letters until the day of his death shows that he had not forgotten."[37]

At the book's opening Lieutenant Frederic Henry is an American Red Cross volunteer ambulance driver serving alongside the Italian army. Henry is taken to a British hospital to meet Miss Barkley by his friend, the surgeon Captain Rinaldi who considers himself to be in love with her:

> Miss Barkley was in the garden. Another nurse was with her. We saw their white uniform through the trees and walked toward them. Rinaldi saluted. I saluted too but more moderately.
>   'How do you do?' Miss Barkley said. 'You're not an Italian, are you?'
>   'Oh, no.'
>   Rinaldi was talking with the other nurse. They were laughing.
>   'What an odd thing—to be in the Italian army.'
>   'It's not really the army. It's only the ambulance.'
>   'It's very odd though. Why did you do it?'
>   'I don't know,' I said. 'There isn't always an explanation for everything.'
>   'Oh, isn't there? I was brought up to think there was.'
>   'That's awfully nice.'
>   '*Do* we have to go on and talk this way?'
>   'No,' I said.
>   'That's a relief. Isn't it?'
>   'What is the stick?' I asked. Miss Barkley was quite tall. She wore what seemed to me to be a nurse's uniform, was blonde and had a tawny skin and grey eyes. I thought she was very beautiful. She

was carrying a thin rattan stick like a toy riding-crop, bound in leather.

'It belonged to a boy who was killed last year.'

'I'm awfully sorry.'

'He was a very nice boy. He was going to marry me and he was killed on the Somme.'

. . .

'Had you been engaged long?'

'Eight years. We grew up together.'

'And why didn't you marry?'

'I don't know,' she said. 'I was a fool not to. I could have given him that anyway. But I thought it would be bad for him.'

'I see.'

'Have you ever loved anyone?'

'No,' I said.

Frederic and Catherine meet a few more times and, not at all unusually in time of war, a relationship quickly blossoms between them:

She looked at me. 'And do you love me?'

'Yes.'

'You did say you loved me, didn't you?'

'Yes,' I lied. 'I love you.' I had not said it before.

Yet in spite of Frederic's assertion that he had lied in telling Catherine that he loved her, following his wounding (described earlier) and his removal to the hospital in Milan he realises that he really is passionately in love with her after all. On the first occasion that Catherine comes to see him Frederic suddenly realises that in spite of himself he has fallen head over heels in love with her:

She came in the room and over to the bed.

'Hello, darling,' she said. She looked fresh and young and very beautiful. I thought I had never seen anyone so beautiful.

'Hello,' I said. When I saw her I was in love with her. Everything turned over inside of me. She looked towards the door, saw there was no one, then she sat on the side of the bed and leaned over and kissed me. I pulled her down and kissed her and felt her heart beating.

'You sweet,' I said. 'Weren't you wonderful to come here?'

'It wasn't very hard. It may be hard to stay.'

'You've got to stay,' I said. 'Oh, you're wonderful.' I was crazy about her. I could not believe she was really there and held her tight to me.

. . .

She went out. God knows I had not wanted to fall in love with her. I had not wanted to fall in love with anyone. But God knows I had and I lay on the bed in the room of the hospital in Milan and all sorts of things went through my head . . .

Catherine immediately becomes consumed by the impetuous and impulsive self-denial and self-abnegation of passionate love:

"I'll say just what you wish, and I'll do what you wish and then you will never want any other girls, will you?' She looked at me very happily. 'I'll do what you want and say what you want and then I'll be a great success, won't I? . . . I want what you want. There isn't any me any more. Just what you want."

Frederic and Catherine manage to find the time and privacy to sleep together: shortly afterwards Catherine breaks the news that she is pregnant with his child. Henry is diagnosed with jaundice but Miss Van Campen, the tyrannical supervisor of the hospital, discovers a cupboard full of empty bottles in Henry's room and accuses him of drinking heavily and bringing jaundice upon himself in order to evade active service: she has his leave revoked and Henry returns to his unit at the front. At the battle of

Caporetto Austro-Hungarian forces break through the Italian line and the Italians retreat. Henry and his team of ambulance drivers decide to break away from the column of evacuating troops and take smaller back roads. The following day they are apprehended and taken away by the so-called 'battle police', the rear guard of the retreating Italian army who are interrogating, trying and summarily executing those, even commanding officers, believed to be guilty of the 'treachery' which led to the Italian defeat. After hearing one such unfortunate being shot after a kangaroo court Henry makes a break for freedom by jumping into a river. He escapes and makes his way back to Milan by train but learns that Catherine has gone to Stresa, where he follows her and they are emotionally reunited. As he will be viewed as a deserter and in imminent danger of being arrested he and Catherine borrow a rowing boat and under cover of darkness row all night across Lake Maggiore and into Switzerland and safety. They settle down happily in Montreux, agreeing to put the war behind them and to live out the rest of their lives together in peace. Spring comes and the time for the birth of their baby draws near so they move to Lausanne. Catherine goes into a painful, frightening and difficult labour and a Caesarian section is performed, but the baby is stillborn (gruesomely described as looking like "a freshly-skinned rabbit") and Catherine herself is now mortally ill:

It seems she had one haemorrhage after another. They couldn't stop it. I went into the room and stayed with Catherine until she died. She was unconscious all the time, and it did not take her very long to die.

*A Farewell to Arms*, as with Scott Fitzgerald's *The Great Gatsby*, can be read on any number of levels. It is for one thing one of the world's great anti-war novels, on a par with other Great War classics such as Eric Maria Remarque's *All Quiet on the Western Front*, Henri Barbusse's *Le Feu* and Frederic Manning's *Her Privates We*. But also just like *Gatsby* by many it has been viewed (especially in its various cinematic versions, particularly in the 1932 adaptation starring Helen Hayes and Gary Cooper which Hemingway himself hated: "I did not intend a happy ending," he complained bitterly) as a tragic love story. After the experiments of 'A Very Short Story' and other pieces he poured into the novel not only much of what he felt about men at war but the scarcely less wounding effect on his psyche that losing Agnes had left behind. "*A Farewell to Arms*," says James Nagel, "is related, in effect, by a man who feels he has nothing left in the world, nothing but the memories of the most painful and meaningful episode of his life."[38]

## IV

The remainder of the story of Hemingway's life is well known and is beyond the scope of the present work. Such was the power of Hemingway's mythopoeia that much of it has become the stuff of modern legend (not to mention the raw material for umpteen biographies amounting almost to a cottage industry). Young Ernie of course became 'Papa' Hemingway: the legendary writer, exponent of the inimitable (but much copied for all that) terse Hemingway style; winner of the Pulitzer Prize for Fiction in 1953 and the Nobel prize for literature the following year; the phenomenal boozer and latterly desperate alcoholic; big game hunter; deep sea fisherman; bullfight *aficionado*; international traveller; journalist; war correspondent; adventurer; daredevil. In his last years Hemingway became increasingly physically and mentally infirm: decades of alcoholism, innumerable accidents of varying degrees of seriousness, illness and general physical abuse left him frail in body and latterly in mind. He became not only more and more deeply depressed but, toward the end, delusory, suffering paranoid spells where he felt that the FBI were keeping tabs on him. Repeated and well-intentioned sessions of electroconvulsive therapy at the Mayo clinic seriously affected his memory which struck at the absolute core of Hemingway's sense of self as a man and as a writer: his way with words. When he loaded his favourite .12 gauge Boss shotgun and placed both barrels against his head in the tiny, sunlit, five-foot-by-seven-foot foyer of his last home in Ketchum, Idaho at about half past seven in the morning of Sunday the 2nd of July 1961 it was the last desperate, but arguably inevitable, decisive act of the sad shell of the man that Hemingway had become.

Agnes von Kurowsky had a very long and in her own way adventurous and well-travelled life. She continued to nurse, for many years with the Red Cross, and married twice. Her first marriage (at the ripe age of thirty-seven) was to Howard Preston Garner (known as 'Pete') in the Haitian capital Port-au-Prince in November 1928 while she was stationed with the Red Cross, though this seems to have been considered by her a mistake since she obtained a quick divorce in Reno, Nevada in 1931 after her assignment in Haiti came to an end the previous year. Moving back to New York she got married for the second time to William Stanfield Jr., a hotel manager and widower with three children, in 1934. Whether Hemingway knew about either of these marriages is unknown. During the Second World War Agnes worked at the Fifth Avenue blood bank in New York city while her husband served in the US navy. After Bill came home with the end of the war the couple relocated first to Virginia Beach and then in 1951 to Key West at the very southernmost tip of Florida, less than a hundred miles from Cuba, where the warm climate suited an aging couple and where Agnes resumed her first career as a librarian. By an amazing coincidence Agnes and Bill had moved into a house within a mile or so of one of Hemingway's former homes: he and his second wife Pauline had lived at 907 Whitehead Street in Key West throughout most of the 1930s—the first true home of his own that he had ever possessed—though he had moved on long before Agnes and her second husband arrived. "I never saw Ernest Hemingway after he left Italy," she told Henry Villard. "When we went over to Cuba a few times from here [i.e. Key West] I was told he drank so heavily that I did not feel like looking him up. Since I have met his wife, Mary, I am rather sorry now that I didn't see him again."[39] After her husband's suicide Mary Walsh Hemingway went to Key West to collect some of Hemingway's effects which he had kept at his favourite bar, the subsequently famous Sloppy Joe's: Mary met Bill and Agnes Stanfield cordially several times. Mary donated a set of her late husband's books to the library while Agnes gave Mary some photographs from her time in Milan.

The story of Agnes's wartime diary and how it came to be known to the world decades later is interesting in itself. Henry Villard lost touch with both Ernie and Agnes after the First World War but in 1962, a year after the legendary writer's suicide, Villard (then living in Switzerland) was contacted by Professor Carlos Baker (1909-1987) who was preparing research materials for what would become one of the best-regarded scholarly biographies of Hemingway when finally published in 1969. Baker passed on Agnes's current address to Villard and the two corresponded again after an incredible fifty-three years. Thereafter the two stayed in regular contact until Agnes's death in 1984, after which her widowed husband passed on to Villard many of her private papers including her wartime letters and diary. In 1989 Villard collaborated with Dr. James Nagel on the book *Hemingway in Love and War: The Lost Diary of Agnes von Kurowsky* which contained Villard's own lengthy testimony of that time along with extensive extracts from these and other documents of both Agnes and Hemingway, finally revealing Agnes's diary and surviving letters (her 'Dear John' letter to Hemingway included) to the world at large.

Like Ginevra King with Scott Fitzgerald, in old age Agnes sought to minimise or even conceal the true nature of her brief but passionate relationship with a nineteen-year-old Ernest Hemingway. In various interviews that she gave in old age Agnes gave wildly contradictory accounts of her feelings for him all those decades before:

> Ernest had been very serious about wanting to marry her, no doubt about that; he had done his best to persuade her. She, on the other hand, had 'liked' him without being 'in love' with him; she had found him 'interesting' but he was 'impulsive, hasty, not to say impetuous.' 'He didn't really know what he wanted.' He 'hadn't thought out anything clearly.' In short, he was just too young and

immature for a girl seven years older, as she was, to fall truly in love with him. She had been afraid that he was going to turn into an aimless wanderer after the war, an expatriate, without roots, as he had shown signs of doing. She had put him off, advising him, perhaps in the manner of an older sister, to return to America after hostilities ended. He had departed in January 1919, and when she ultimately broke with him that spring she had simply 'put him out of' her mind. Admittedly, they had had what she chose to call a 'flirtation,' but the relationship, she said firmly, had never gone beyond that.[40]

Just like Ginevra and Scott, years after her involvement with Hemingway, Agnes seemed to want to downplay the seriousness of her involvement with the young writer-to-be, claiming that while she certainly liked him she had never been truly in love with him and that it was merely a passing infatuation of no very great consequence. She disliked the fact that she was considered to be the model for Catherine Barkley in *A Farewell to Arms* (widely so after the mid-1970s) and particularly the implication that if Frederic and Catherine had slept together in the book then their real-life counterparts must have done so too. For Agnes, Catherine was "an arrant fantasy," she told Henry Villard. "Ernest never conceived the story while he was in the hospital," she continued, where he was "completely spoiled." "He was much too busy enjoying the attention of friends and well-wishers to think about the plot of a novel; he invented the myth years later—built out of his frustration in love. The liaison was all made up out of whole cloth." To Bernice Kert, author of *The Hemingway Women*, she "conceded that she may have unduly encouraged her smitten young patient." "I think I felt—more or less—an obligation to look after him a bit. I don't think I was ever crazy mad about him," she said, "[although] he was a very attractive person. He had wit and you could enjoy his company . . . I think Hemingway and I were very innocent at the time—very innocent—both of us . . . I was looking for adventure . . . and I was very fickle."[41] (She also said that her brief romance with Domenico Caracciolo in Torre di Mosto was similarly meaningless. "I was fascinated by him but never expected to marry him," she would claim—yet in her 'Dear John' letter of March 1919 she had averred: ". . . believe me when I say this is sudden for me, too—I expect to be married soon"). All of this was said, needless to say, with the benefit of hindsight many years after the fact and smacks of revisionism (or, as James R. Mellow wryly puts it "How malleable the personal past can be"). Agnes's letters of the time are replete with declarations of passionate love. On the 7th of October 1918 she wrote: "I guess every girl likes to have some man tell her . . . he can't do without her. Anyway, I am but human, and when you say these things I love it and can't help but believe you so don't be afraid I'll get tired of you. I haven't really started to worry yet over your forgetting to love me as you do now." And again: "Old dear, consider yourself severely hugged . . . I think every day of how nice it would be to feel your arms around me again. I am so proud of you and the fact that you love me, that I want to blurt it all out . . . If this hits you about Xmas time, just make believe you're getting a gift from me (as you will some day) . . . let me tell you I love you." (Could this 'gift' be an oblique reference to the eventuality that they would sleep together after marriage—the gift of her virginity? Several of Hemingway's biographers have understandably interpreted it as such). Bill Horne, a friend of Hemingway's who visited him in the hospital and saw Hemingway and Von together at close quarters, remembered that "they fell in love—very very much . . . She truly loved Ernie, I'm sure."

　　All the evidence says that she did indeed but in old age she sought to downplay or even deny this:

> Agnes . . . granted interviews to Hemingway biographers Carlos Baker (in the sixties), Michael Reynolds (in the seventies), and Bernice Kert (in the eighties). In each interview, Miss Kurowsky [sic] characterised her relationship with Hemingway as 'condescending'. To Baker, she was the 'older sister'; to Reynolds, the tolerant and indulgent nurse; to Kert, the woman of the world, delightfully afflicted by the charming adolescent. And each biographer took her at her word.
>
> Unquestionably, personal interviews are essential to a biographer. But the sixty-year-old memories of a woman both Hemingway and Bill Horne described as superficial—memories in which she always ascends to a role superior to her young admirer (she never admits lover) where Hemingway becomes . . . enthralled by Miss Kurowsky—should not be accepted unquestioningly.[42]

Agnes von Kurowsky and Ginevra King are very far from the only people in the world to have sought to rewrite their own youthful romantic history but here everything tells us that however briefly or however long the most intense era of their romance may have lasted Agnes did indeed love Ernest while they were together in Milan during those last five and a half months or so of 1918. One can only speculate about the reasons why Agnes and Ginevra sought to edit the truth about their young lives: understandable loyalty to current spouses perhaps or embarrassment that a major part of their emotional lives had been aired in public. In both cases however not just eyewitness testimony but hard documentary evidence—Ginevra's letters; Agnes's letters and diary—tell a very different tale. "The terms of endearment with which her letters abound," observed Villard, "stand out in sharp contradiction to her effort later in life to minimize the relationship and dismiss it as a mere flirtation":

> It has always been assumed that the relationship was more fervent on his part than on hers, that while she reciprocated his sentiments it was by no means clear that she had fallen in love to the same headlong extent as he had. Indeed, without the corroboration provided by the diary and letters, it might be difficult to gauge the degree to which she had singled out Ernie from the other patients in Milan for her special attention. The letters, however, give ample evidence of her concern and devotion. Compared with the diary's relative restraint in chronicling her daily doings at the hospital, the letters pour out a veritable torrent of loving solicitude.[42]

That Agnes von Kurowsky was the first and most painful love in the life of a young Ernest Hemingway did not become known to the world at large until 1961 when Hemingway's younger brother Leicester published *Ernest Hemingway, My Brother*. Even then most biographies did not pay particular attention to this fact until considerably later: not until the publication of Michael S. Reynolds's *Hemingway's First War: The Making of 'A Farewell to Arms'* in 1976 was there any relatively lengthy mention of Agnes as the great writer's first love and most painful memory. Even then few if any people identified Agnes von Kurowsky as she had been during the Great War with Mrs Agnes Stanfield. Agnes lived a quiet, highly private life and maintained a very low profile. Years later, when she had re-established contact with Henry Villard as detailed above, she observed: "I've kept quiet about all our war experiences, and so far, nobody has recognized my picture in Les Hemingway's book. Of course, folks down here never heard my maiden name anyhow." She also reiterated to Villard that she had been displeased to have been nominated as the main model and inspiration for Catherine Barkley in *A Farewell to Arms*. "One thing was clear: Agnes thoroughly resented being taken for 'the alter ego of the complaisant Catherine Barkley' and thus indirectly the mistress of the man who wrote the book . . . So strongly did she object to the insinuation that she and Ernest were lovers in the fullest sense of the word, that she and her husband had decided to move away from Key West, where the tourist guide at Hemingway's former home, turned into a museum in 1962, persisted in referring to her as ''Hemingway's girl'.'' Of the writer's suicide, she said: "It was a messy way to die but what he did was understandable, considering that his mind was impaired, that his powers as a man and a writer were failing. The whole world knew that he had been undergoing psychiatric treatment."

Despite some physical frailty and a failing memory toward the very end Agnes's second happy marriage lasted until her peaceful passing in Gulfport, Florida on the 25th of November 1984 at the age of ninety-two. As the former US ambassador to Libya, Senegal and Mauritania her old friend Henry Villard used his influence to make sure that she was buried in the Soldier's Home National Cemetery in Washington D.C. Upon his own death some years later Bill Stanfield joined her.

In spite of James R. Mellow's inferences, there is no conclusive evidence that after the 9th of December 1919 Ernest Hemingway and Agnes von Kurowsky ever saw each other again. Unlike the case of Scott Fitzgerald and Ginevra King there is no evidence that Hemingway deliberately sought to find out about the course of Agnes's later life or accidentally stumbled across any such information. Or vice versa, although as we have seen Agnes regretted not catching up with Ernie during his time in Cuba, put off as she was by his then notorious alcoholism. Hemingway himself of course had become a legend in his own lifetime, an international celebrity, possibly the most famous writer in the world at the time, whose exploits were impossible for the ordinarily informed person to miss. There is some evidence that Ginevra King, not regarded by those around her as a great reader, kept up with Scott Fitzgerald's literary career to a certain extent and even read several of his books: there is no concomitant evidence that Agnes ever did so with Hemingway.

Yet there is one small but interesting snippet relating to the story of Ernest and Agnes's relationship decades after their last contact. In August 1960 it was reported that Hemingway, at that time in Malaga in his beloved Spain, had been taken ill while watching a bullfight: a heart attack was suspected. In the event it turned out that this was merely an entirely unfounded rumour of unknown origin: Hemingway had not suffered a heart attack at all and eventually sent a telegram to his alarmed fourth and last wife, Mary Walsh, refuting the rumours. But before the denial had circulated Mary had anxiously telephoned all their friends to break what was still thought to be bad news. One such friend was a lady by the name of Betty Bruce who worked at the library in Key West. Betty made a remark about Hemingway's alleged illness in the presence of another librarian—a tall, upright, still attractive woman in her late sixties. The other woman's name was Agnes Stanfield and she asked if it was true that 'Ernie' had had a heart attack. A surprised Betty remarked that anybody who referred to the great Ernest Hemingway, the Nobel laureate and the most famous writer in the world, as 'Ernie' must know him extremely well. Agnes replied that she had indeed known him very well indeed all those decades ago during the First World War: it then turned out that by an amazing coincidence Agnes and her husband lived less than a mile from the house on Whitehead Street that Hemingway and his second wife Pauline Pfeiffer had occupied years previously, though they had never been near neighbours at the same time. Agnes told Betty that she still had some wonderful photographs of the two of them as young lovers in Italy in the closing months of the Great War and she would be glad to give them to Betty who might wish to pass them on to Hemingway for old times' sake. Betty assumed that he would be interested and broached the issue with him: Hemingway suggested instead that she send them to Scribners, his publisher. Betty was embarrassed and tried to find a tactful way out of the situation with Agnes: when she hesitantly tried to talk her way through the issue Agnes laughed and understood immediately why he had rebuffed her. He had still never forgiven her for jilting him and breaking his heart when he was just nineteen, over forty years previously.

Nevertheless, whether she was forgiven or not, that Hemingway retained some feelings for Agnes, however vestigial they may have been, is indicated by the fact that he kept her letters to him to the day he died, three of which his widow Mary found amongst his private papers after his suicide and subsequently gave back to Agnes. "Imagine keeping them so long!" Agnes observed in mock surprise. Yet she knew full well why he had done so.

She had never been forgotten.

Star friendship.—We were friends and have become estranged. But this was right, and we do not want to conceal and obscure it from ourselves as if we had reason to feel ashamed. We are two ships each of which has its goal and course; our paths may cross and we may celebrate a feast together, as we did—and then the good ships rested so quietly in one harbour and one sunshine that it may have looked as if they had reached their goal and as if they had one goal. But then the almighty force of our tasks drove us apart again into different seas and sunny zones, and perhaps we shall never see one another again,—perhaps we shall meet again but fail to recognize each other: our exposure to different seas and suns has changed us! That we have to become estranged is the law above us: by the same token we should also become more venerable for each other! And thus the memory of our former friendship should become more sacred! There is probably a tremendous but invisible stellar orbit in which our very different ways and goals may be included as small parts of this path,—let us rise up to this thought! But our life is too short and our power of vision too small for us to be more than friends in the sense of this sublime possibility.—Let us then believe in our star friendship even if we should be compelled to be earth enemies.

—Friedrich Nietzsche,
*The Gay Science*, 279.

sic erit; haeserunt tenues in corde sagittae,
et possessa ferus pectora versat Amor.
Cedimus, an subitum luctando accendimus ignem?
cedamus! leve fit, quod bene fertur, onus . . .
a, nimium volui—tantum patiatur amari;
audierit nostras tot Cytherea preces!
accipe, per longos tibi qui deserviat annos;
accipe, qui pura norit amare fide!

—Ovid, Amores.

The past is never dead. It's not even past.

—William Faulkner,<br>Requiem for a Nun

# Notes

Introduction:

1. http://www.fitzgerald.narod.ru/bio/donaldson-hemvsfitz.html
2. http://www.psychologytoday.com/blog/sticky-bonds/200906/teenagers-in-love
3. Tallis, Frank: *Love Sick* (London, Arrow, 2005).
4. http://berkeley.edu/news/media/releases/2001/02/07_love.html
5. http://www.guardian.co.uk/lifeandstyle/2009/jan/18/relationships-love
6. http://www.dailymail.co.uk/femail/article-1121103/Why-SHOULD-forget-love-The-memories-ruin-future-relationships.html
7. *ibid.*
8. Book X, l. 272


Chapter One: Enough Love to Drown In

1. Ackroyd, Peter: *Dickens* (London, Sinclair-Stevenson, 1990).
2. *ibid.*
3. Kaplan, Fred: *Dickens: A Biography* (Baltimore, Johns Hopkins University Press, 1988).
4. *ibid.*
5. *ibid.*
6. *ibid.*
7. CD to Thomas Powell, 2nd August 1845
8. Nicoll, William Robertson: *Dickens' Own Story: Sidelights on his Life and Personality*, London, Chapman & Hall, 1923.
9. Ackroyd, *op. cit.*
10. Baker, George Pierce: *Charles Dickens and Maria Beadnell ('Dora'): Private Correspondence between Charles Dickens and Mrs Henry Winter (nee Maria Beadnell), the Original of Dora Spenlow in* David Copperfield *and Flora Finching in* Little Dorrit (St Louis, private publication for William K. Bixby, 1908).
11. Slater, Michael: *Charles Dickens: A Life Defined by Writing* (London, Yale University Press, 2009).
12. Forster, John: *The Life of Charles Dickens* (London, Cecil Palmer, 2 vols., 1872 & 1874).
13. Slater, Michael: *Dickens and Women* (London, J.M. Dent & Sons, 1983).
14. Tomalin, Claire: *The Invisible Woman: The Story of Nelly Ternan and Charles Dickens* (London, Penguin, 1990).
15. Adrian, Arthur A.: *Georgina Hogarth and the Dickens Circle* (London, OUP, 1957).
16. Slater, 2009.

17. Ackroyd, *op. cit.*
18. Baker, *op. cit.*
19. Grahame Smith, 'The Life and Times of Charles Dickens' in the *Cambridge Companion to Charles Dickens* (ed. John O. Jordan; Cambridge, Cambridge University Press, 2001).
20. Baker, *op. cit.*
21. Baker, *ibid.*
22. Slater, 1983.
23. *ibid.*
24. Adrian, *op. cit.*


Chapter Two: Living Too Long With a Single Dream

1. Bruccoli, Matthew J.: *Some Sort of Epic Grandeur: The Life of F. Scott Fitzgerald* (London, Hodder & Stoughton, 1981).
2. http://www.fitzgerald.narod.ru/bio/donaldson-hemvsfitz.html
3. West, James, L.W. III: *The Perfect Hour: The Romance of F. Scott Fitzgerald and Ginevra King, His First Love* (New York, Random House, 2005).
4. *ibid.*
5. FSF to Frances Turnbull, 9th November 1938.
6. Bruccoli, *op. cit.*
7. Donaldson, Scott: *Fool for Love: F. Scott Fitzgerald* (New York, Congdon & Weed, 1983).
8. West, *op. cit.*
9. FSF to Anne Ober, 4th March 1938.
10. http://www.princeton.edu/pr/news/03/q3/0905-fitzgerald.htm
11. West, *op. cit.*
12. *ibid.*
13. FSF to Mollie McQuillan Fitzgerald, 14th November 1917.
14. http://www.princeton.edu/~paw/archive_new/PAW03-04/04-1105/feature1.html
15. Bruccoli, *op. cit.*
16. http://fitzgerald.narod.ru/bio/graham-threalscott35.html
17. West, *op. cit.*
18. West, *op. cit.*
19. *ibid.*
20. *ibid.*
21. *ibid.*
22. http://fitzgerald.narod.ru/critics-eng/mizener-20s.html
23. Bruccoli, *op. cit.*
24. *ibid.*
25. Donaldson, *op. cit.*
26. http://www.fitzgerald.narod.ru/bio/donaldson-hemvsfitz.html
27. Donaldson, *op. cit.*

28. http://fitzgerald.narod.ru/bio/graham-threalscott35.html
29. http://query.nytimes.com/gst/fullpage.html?res=9C06E0D8163BF93BA35
    75AC0A9659C8B63&pagewanted=1
30. http://www.princeton.edu/pr/news/03/q3/0905-fitzgerald.htm
31. West, *op. cit.*


Chapter Three: A Very Short Story

1.  Villard, Henry S. & Nagel, James: *Hemingway in Love and War: The Lost Diary of Agnes von Kurowsky* (New York, Hyperion, 1989).
2.  EH to Ruth Morrison, 22nd June 1918.
3.  Villard/Nagel, *op. cit.*
4.  EH to Ruth Morrison, *ibid.*
5.  EH to Dr C.E Hemingway, 11th September 1918.
6.  EH to his family, 18th August 1918, quoted in Hemingway, Marcelline: *At the Hemingways: A Family Portrait* (Boston, Little, Brown, 1962).
7.  To date almost all Hemingway biographies have consistently placed the American Red Cross hospital in Milan at 10 Via Manzoni. (Peter Griffin's *Along With Youth: Hemingway, The Early Years* is a rare exception, placing it at 3 Via Bacheto). However Henry Villard's account in *Hemingway in Love and War* makes it clear that it was merely the *headquarters* of the ARC at the Manzoni address: the ARC *hospital* itself seems to have been nearby at 4 Via Cesare Cantù. This is also supported by references in Agnes von Kurowsky's personal diary first published in the aforementioned book in 1989 and thus not available to biographers prior to that date. For example, on Monday the 15th of July 1918 Agnes wrote: 'I am getting ready tonight to move to 4 Cesare Cantù tomorrow.'
8.  Villard/Nagel, *op. cit.*
9.  *ibid.*
10. EH to Grace Hall Hemingway, 29th August 1918.
11. EH to his family, 11th December 1918.
12. Hemingway, Marcelline: *op. cit.*
13. Kert, Bernice: *The Hemingway Women* (New York, Norton, 1983).
14. Griffin, Peter: *Along With Youth: Hemingway, The Early Years* (Oxford, OUP, 1985).
15. Villard/Nagel, *op. cit.*
16. *ibid.*
17. Kert, *op. cit.*
18. http://www.nytimes.com/books/99/07/04/specials/hemingway-diliberto.html
19. http://www.nytimes.com/1997/01/26/movies/a-hemingway-story-and-just-as-fictional.html
20. Lynn, Kenneth S.: *Hemingway* (New York, Simon & Schuster, 1987).
21. Griffin, *op. cit.*

22. Villard/Nagel, *op. cit.*
23. Griffin, *op. cit.*
24. EH to William B. Smith Jr., 13th December 1918.
25. Hemingway, Marcelline, *op. cit.*
26. *ibid.*
27. http://www.vqronline.org/articles/1989/autumn/donaldson-jilting-ernest-hemingway/
28. EH to James Gamble, 18th April 1919.
29. EH to Lawrence T. Barnett, 30th April 1919.
30. EH to William Horne, 30th March 1919.
31. EH to Howell G. Jenkins, 16th June 1919.
32. http://www.vqronline.org/articles/1989/autumn/donaldson-jilting-ernest-hemingway/
33. *ibid.*
34. Reynolds, Michael S.: *The Young Hemingway* (Oxford, Blackwell, 1986).
35. EH to Maxwell Perkins, 12th July 1938.
36. Baker, Carlos: *Ernest Hemingway: A Life Story* (New York, Charles Scribner's Sons, 1969).
37. Reynolds, Michael S.: *Hemingway's First War: The Making of 'A Farewell to Arms'* (New York, Blackwell, 1987).
38. Villard/Nagel, *op. cit.*
39. *ibid.*
40. *ibid.*
41. *ibid.*
42. *ibid.*
43. Kert, *op. cit.*
44. Griffin, *op. cit.*
45. Villard/Nagel, *op. cit.*

# Bibliography

Ackroyd, Peter: *Dickens* (London, Sinclair-Stevenson, 1990).

Adrian, Arthur A.: *Georgina Hogarth and the Dickens Circle* (London, OUP, 1957).

Baker, Carlos: *Ernest Hemingway: A Life Story* (New York, Charles Scribner's Sons, 1969).

Baker, George Pierce: *Charles Dickens and Maria Beadnell ('Dora'): Private Correspondence between Charles Dickens and Mrs Henry Winter (nee Maria Beadnell), the Original of Dora Spenlow in* David Copperfield *and Flora Finching in* Little Dorrit (Saint Louis, private publication for William K. Bixby, 1908).

Barks, Cathy W. & Bryer, Jackson R. (eds.): *Dear Scott, Dearest Zelda: The Love Letters of F. Scott & Zelda Fitzgerald* (London, Bloomsbury, 2002).

Bruccoli, Matthew J.: *Some Sort of Epic Grandeur: The Life of F. Scott Fitzgerald* (London, Hodder & Stoughton, 1981).

Donaldson, Scott: *Fool for Love: F. Scott Fitzgerald* (New York, Congdon & Weed, 1983).

Forster, John: *The Life of Charles Dickens* (London, Cecil Palmer, 2 vols., 1872 & 1874).

Griffin, Peter: *Along With Youth: Hemingway, The Early Years* (Oxford, OUP, 1985).

Hemingway, Ernest (ed. Carlos Baker): *Selected Letters 1917-1961* (London, Granada, 1981).

Hemingway, Marcelline: *At the Hemingways: A Family Portrait* (Boston, Little, Brown, 1962).

Jordan, John O. (ed.): *The Cambridge Companion to Charles Dickens* (Cambridge, Cambridge University Press, 2001).

Kaplan, Fred: *Dickens: A Biography* (Baltimore, Johns Hopkins University Press, 1988).

Kert, Bernice: *The Hemingway Women* (New York, Norton, 1983).

Lynn, Kenneth S.: *Hemingway* (New York, Simon & Schuster, 1987).

Mellow, James R.: *Hemingway: A Life Without Consequences* (London, Hodder & Stoughton, 1993).

Meyers, Jeffrey: *Hemingway: A Biography* (London, Macmillan, 1986).

Milford, Nancy: *Zelda: A Biography* (New York, Harper & Row, 1970).

Nicoll, William Robertson: *Dickens's Own Story: Sidelights on his Life and Personality* (London, Chapman & Hall, 1923).

Preston, Caroline: *Gatsby's Girl* (New York, Houghton Mifflin, 2006).

Reynolds, Michael: *Hemingway's First War: The Making of 'A Farewell to Arms'* (New York, Blackwell, 1987).

Reynolds, Michael: *The Young Hemingway* (Oxford, Blackwell, 1986).

Slater, Michael: *Charles Dickens: A Life Defined by Writing* (London, Yale University Press, 2009).

Slater, Michael: *Dickens and Women* (London, J.M. Dent & Sons, 1983).

Villard, Henry S. & Nagel, James: *Hemingway in Love and War: The Lost Diary of Agnes von Kurowsky* (New York, Hyperion, 1989).

West, James, L.W. III: *The Perfect Hour: The Romance of F. Scott Fitzgerald and Ginevra King, His First Love* (New York, Random House, 2005).

Lightning Source UK Ltd.
Milton Keynes UK
UKOW050216180911

178849UK00001B/55/P